around her.

...and how much I'm going to miss you and your voice."

"My voice?"

Josie told Caleb about the warm milk and how his voice made her feel, especially when she was afraid.

"You can always drink a glass of warm milk with chocolate in it when I'm not around." He was trying to be flippant, but his heart felt heavy.

"It won't be the same." Josie looked at him and slowly kissed the corner of his mouth. "Kiss me, Caleb."

He couldn't resist. He took her lips with a fiery hunger fuelled by a year of glances, touches and yearnings. For a brief moment he ignored the warning in his head and tasted her tongue, her lips, her mouth, and let himself feel everything that he shouldn't. He couldn't do this to her, to himself, to Eric. Once her memory returned, she would regret this lapse.

Josie belonged to someone else.

Available in September 2007 from Mills & Boon® Superromance

A Man of Duty

LINDA WARREN

MILLS & BOON®

Pure reading pleasure

*First published in Great Britain 2007
by Harlequin Mills & Boon Limited,
Eton House, 18-24 Paradise Road, Richmond, Surrey TW9 1SR*

© Linda Warren 2006
(Original title: *Son of Texas*)

ISBN: 978 0 263 85798 6

38-0907

*Harlequin Mills & Boon policy is to use papers that are
natural, renewable and recyclable products and made from
wood grown in sustainable forests. The logging and
manufacturing processes conform to the legal environmental
regulations of the country of origin.*

*Printed and bound in Spain
by Litografía Rosés S.A., Barcelona*

Dear Reader,

Thank you for the many letters asking about Caleb McCain and Belle Doe from *Forgotten Son*. I'm happy to tell you that this is their story.

Many of you wrote asking who Belle Doe is. I have to tell you a secret. Her character just sort of evolved in *Forgotten Son*, and at the time I had no idea who she was or who had shot her. When I was faced with writing her story, I had a blank page. I knew I wanted her to be from south Texas. Other than that, Belle Doe really was Belle Doe – as mysterious to me as she was to you.

People often ask me where I get my ideas for stories. In this case, the process was simple yet very complex. I had to unravel the mystery of Belle Doe – the mystery I had created. I was halfway through the book and I still had no idea who had shot Belle. Her story kept changing as the characters took over. Luckily, I have a very understanding editor.

I had fun travelling to south Texas and solving this mystery. So come along and see what happens.

Happy reading,

Linda Warren

PS It's such a pleasure to hear from readers. You can e-mail me at Lw1508@aol.com or write to me at PO Box 5182, Bryan, TX 77805, USA or visit my website at www.lindawarren.net or www. superauthors.com. Your letters will be answered.

To Pamela Litton, Christi Hendricks and Naomi Giroux – the ladies who sat at my kitchen table many nights munching popcorn and critiquing my first manuscript. Thanks for helping make a dream come true. This is book number fifteen. Look what you started.

ACKNOWLEDGEMENTS

One of the very good things about being an author is that I get to meet a lot of nice, friendly people who share their lives with me. One of those people is Becky Wood, RN. Thank you so much for your support and for allowing me to share *Chula* with readers.

Another person is Viola Barker – thanks for sharing your interesting life, especially your home remedies. It's been a pleasure getting to know you.

Any errors in this book are strictly mine.

CHAPTER ONE

WHO AM I?

What's my name?

The sharp probing questions jabbed at Belle Doe with the power of a professional boxer, but her mind fended them off like a pro as it did every day. Her memory was blank as a newborn's, yet she wasn't a baby waiting for a mind to develop. She was a grown woman struggling to remember her life.

Who am I? Why can't I remember? Her therapist, Dr. Karen Oliver, said not to force herself, but at times she felt so frustrated and confused. Her memory loomed in front of her like a wall she couldn't get through or over. Dr. Oliver said this was normal, a protective instinct for post-traumatic stress-disorder victims who'd survived horrific events. Eventually she would become stronger and allow the memories of her past to break through.

But when?

Sitting in the window seat at the home of Ms.

Gertrude Parker, Belle slowly counted to ten to ease her frustration. She looked out at the beautiful spring day. A clear blue sky beckoned and suddenly a red robin landed on a hibiscus bush outside the window. The sight calmed her even more. She took note of lilies blooming, the lush live oaks, the brilliant new green of the St. Augustine grass that Wendell, the gardener, tended.

It had been over a year, that was as close as the authorities could figure the timeline, since she'd been rescued from a cult in the Texas Hill Country. Over a year since the doctors had found the bullet in her head. She had no name, no memory. She'd spent four months in the hospital and she'd now been with Ms. Gertie for almost eight. The authorities were unsure how long she'd been in Austin before the cult had found her. The cult members had found her walking the streets of Austin and had taken her in, named her Jezebel, made her a slave and beat her regularly. She was saved from that nightmare by a Texas Ranger, and another ranger helped her to face her fears and live again. *Her Texas Ranger.* That's how she thought of Caleb McCain.

The FBI, the Texas Rangers, doctors and therapists tried to piece together what had happened to her. Seeing that she cringed when anyone called her Jezebel, Caleb insisted they rename her Belle and had the hospital records changed to Belle Doe. That was the first time she became aware of him. He cared. The others were doing a job, but Caleb actually cared about her. He was the first person she'd come to trust after her nightmare ended, and he'd been there for her ever since.

As she slowly began to recover from the physical violence, she was faced with being moved from the hospital to a mental institution until her memory returned. The doctors didn't have a choice and had to abide by hospital rules. With no memory she knew the institution would be as bad as the cult—only in a different way.

Caleb spoke with the doctors and they agreed it would be best for Belle to live outside the hospital and establish the necessary framework for a normal, healthy lifestyle so she could function in the present. This would, hopefully, facilitate her memory's return. But they didn't have the resources to find someone to take her in. It was Caleb who went the extra mile.

He'd found her a job as a companion to Ms. Gertrude Parker, a widow who hadn't remarried after the love of her life died in WWII. Living with Ms. Gertie had been a blessing. She was truly an angel in disguise and she and Belle had formed a bond that would never be broken. Dr. Oliver had said that the relationships Belle formed now would build a strong foundation of trust and deep roots, which would help strengthen an inner connection within herself. But the doctor also warned that once her memory returned, those foundations wouldn't be as strong. Her old life, the person she used to be, would take precedence.

Belle lived cautiously, taking each day as it came, and was grateful for the kind people who now filled her world. Gertie was a wealthy eccentric of undeterminate age, but Belle guessed she was somewhere in her eighties. The woman had wrecked four cars in one year; her lawyer deemed it unsafe for her to drive. Ms. Gertie had resisted her loss of independence, firing chauffeur after chauffeur. Gertie was a cousin of Caleb's stepfather and when Caleb heard about the problem, he thought Belle would be a perfect companion and helper.

And Belle desperately needed a home. Caleb had arranged for her to get a driver's license and Gertie hired her at their first meeting. Now she had a home and she'd found a measure of peace in Ms. Gertie's colorful world.

Gertrude's Victorian home had been in her family for years. It was equipped with a pool and tennis courts, and filled with priceless antiques and artworks. She lived in the big house with two cats, Prissy and Prudy, and a Jack Russell terrier named Harry. Belle was sure she'd never lived in such opulence before. Despite the comforts of her present life, everything felt foreign to her, and she lived with this unsettled feeling every day.

She ran her hands through her long dark hair, then reached for the colorful band and tied it into a ponytail, then looped it again to make a knot so it wouldn't bounce around. The action was natural, as if she'd done it many times before. This was an implicit memory, behavioral knowledge without conscious recall, as Dr. Oliver called it, just as Belle knew how to read and write but she couldn't remember how she'd learned those skills.

From what she'd learned about her condition, parts of her memory should have returned by now. After a year, there was less chance of it returning at all. She feared she'd be in this limbo forever.

Sighing, she glanced at her watch—just after twelve. Gertie was resting as she did every day unless she had an appointment. This was the time Belle used to practice the exercises the doctors had taught her to help regain her memory.

Taking a deep breath, she asked out loud, "What's my name?"

There was no answer, just a numbness of her mind and her spirit.

The sky darkened to almost black and Belle watched a thunderstorm roll in, chasing away the spring day. Crazy Texas weather. She didn't know much, but she knew about the unpredictable weather in Texas, another implicit memory. Thunder echoed loudly and lightning zigzagged across the sky. Wendell, who'd been fertilizing the yard, hurried to the garages just as the skies opened up.

The rain made a drumming noise against the windows and lightning zipped across the grass with dangerous flashes of lights and spine-tingling sounds. Belle knew she should move, but something was happening in her mind. She could feel it.

In her sessions with Dr. Oliver she'd learned a current event or experience could trigger long-forgotten memories. Sounds, smells or other stimuli such as the weather had the capabilities of sparking her mind. And the memories could return bit by bit or all at once or not at all.

Thunder rumbled through her as continual flashes of the lightning streaked the sky. She shivered, watching the storm and waiting for a miracle. Rain poured down the windows in trails and she was mesmerized by the movement. She could almost feel it reaching into her—washing away. *Washing away.* She grabbed her head as it began to throb. Thunder blasted like a gun and memories, beautiful forgotten memories, floated to the surface.

"Tell Daddy your name." The words were clear almost as if her mother was standing beside her.

"I scared. Don't like rain. It's too noisy."

"There's nothing to be afraid of. Mommy and Daddy are right here. Tell Daddy your name."

"Don't know."

"Yes, you do. We practiced all day. Tell Daddy your name."

"My name is Joscelyn Marie." She said it proudly and loudly.

"Yes. Yes, it is. Now what's your last name?"

"Beckett. My name is Joscelyn Marie Beckett."

Her mother clapped. "Isn't that wonderful for a two-year-old?"

Belle could feel her father's arms as he held her and she could smell Old Spice, his favorite cologne. "My girl is getting big. What does Daddy call you?"

"Josie Marie. Josie Marie. Josie Marie."

The storm ended and so did the memories. "No. No. No," she cried. "Please let me remember more. Please." But the blankness returned and all she was left with was a name. *A name!* After all this time, she knew her name.

Josie Marie Beckett.

She jumped from the window seat, eager to call Caleb. She should call Dr. Oliver, but she had to tell Caleb first. Hurrying toward the phone, she stopped in her tracks. Ms. Gertie came into the sunroom with a large hat on her head. That wasn't unusual as Gertie was known for her hats. But in the midst of the bright flowers and feathers on the hat was a small birdcage with a live yellow canary inside. Prissy and Prudy trailed behind her, looking at the hat as if it might be their dinner.

"What do you think, Belle, darlin'?"

Gertie, a tall, big-boned woman, moved with an inherent grace. Her white hair was coiled neatly at her nape and she wore a purple suit to match the purple in the hat. As always there were pearls around her neck. But Belle kept looking at the little bird.

"Ms. Gertie, there's a live bird on your head." Pointing this out seemed unnecessary, but she didn't know what else to say.

"Of course, darlin'. We're going to auction off this hat at the charity ball. They just delivered it and I think it's a wonderful idea. A definite attention grabber."

She'd been so wrapped up in her thoughts that she hadn't even heard the doorbell. *Josie Marie*. She had a name.

"Wendell has a cage for the canary and before we go to the ball tomorrow night, Wendell will put him in the hat-cage again. The highest bidder will get the cage, the hat and all the food the little thing will need for a year." Ms. Gertie made a face. "I just hate the thought of a bird pooping on my head. But I'll do anything for charity—at least once."

"Whose idea was this?" Belle asked, trying to keep her thoughts on the conversation.

"Mine, of course. No one else is that brilliant."

"Of course not," Belle agreed. One of the things she loved about living with Gertie was that she laughed a lot. And she needed that.

Prissy reared up on Gertie's skirt, her eyes on the bird. Prudy, fearing Prissy might get the prize, joined her.

"Look at this." Gertie sighed. "You'd think they were never fed. Get down, you spoiled cats."

Prissy and Prudy crept to a corner, their feelings hurt.

"Oh, my babies. I didn't mean it." Gertie tried to soothe the cats. "You'll get a special treat tonight."

Harry raced into the room, barking at the hat. Just then the doorbell rang.

Gertie straightened the hat and her suit as if she knew who was at the door. Martha, the housekeeper, showed Caleb into the sunroom. Dressed in dark slacks, a white shirt and cowboy boots with his Texas Ranger badge proudly displayed over his left pocket, he smiled a welcome. Belle's heart rate kicked up a notch as it always did when she saw him.

He was without his gun and white hat. He usually left those in the car when he was visiting. Tall and lanky, he had soft dark eyes and dark hair. He had to be the most handsome, kindest and caring man she'd ever met. Of course, she remembered nothing of other men she'd known. She suddenly wondered if there were many.

Shaking the thought away, she wondered instead what Caleb was doing here. His office was in a town outside of Austin, but he stopped by sometimes when he was in the city. Maybe this was one of those days. Or maybe he sensed that she needed him. In a way they had an uncanny connection.

"Caleb," Gertie said. "Have a seat. I've been expecting you."

She sagged at the revelation of Gertie's words. Gertie had called him.

Caleb just stared at the hat on Gertie's head. "Ms. Gertie, there's a bird on your head," he said in his deep voice that wrapped around Belle like warm sunshine.

"Yes, Caleb, there is. Tomorrow evening this hat and bird will be auctioned off at a charity ball and Belle and I need an escort. Are you free?"

"Yes, ma'am. It would be a pleasure."

"Good. Be here at six and a limo will pick us up. Now I have to see if I can get this thing off my head. Martha," she called, walking gingerly from the room, her animals following her.

CALEB LOOKED AT BELLE, her long black hair pulled back, her eyes as dark as the mysteries in her head. An olive complexion stretched over high cheekbones and he thought, as he had since the first day he saw her, that she was the most beautiful, striking woman he'd ever seen.

"Hi," he said, unable to keep the warmth out of his voice. "How are you?"

"Fine. There's never a dull moment around here."

"Is she really auctioning off that hat-bird contraption?"

"You know Ms. Gertie."

"Oh, yeah." He watched her face. She seemed excited and he sensed it had nothing to do with Gertie. At times he could almost read her expressions—he knew her that well. The first time he saw her in the hospital she was curled into a fetal position and refused to look at him. His heart broke at what had happened to her and he just wanted to help. The doctor warned him about getting emotionally attached because Belle's emotions were very fragile, but from the first moment he looked into her dark eyes he was trapped, captivated.

"I was going to call you." Her words came out in a rush.

"Oh." That was unusual. He was the one who did all the calling.

"Yes." Her hands clasped her cheeks. "I remembered something."

"Oh." He took a seat on the wicker sofa, moving a green-and-white-flowered throw pillow out of the way. She'd been discovering little things—she loved chocolate and old movies, she knew how to work a computer and she liked the outdoors and exercise. She jogged five miles every morning. Every piece of information was building her personality and telling her who she was. But they didn't have the full picture yet.

"I remembered my name," she said in excitement. "I remembered my name!"

"What!" He was at a loss for words. This was big. This could help to place her back with her family.

"Yes. I was sitting in the window seat when the storm blew through. With the thunder and lightning, my head started to throb and I remembered something from when I was two years old. I could feel my mom's and dad's presence, their warmth and their love. I was saying my name to my dad."

"What is it?" His voice was hoarse.

"Joscelyn Marie Beckett. Everyone calls me Josie."

"Josie Marie Beckett." He said the name slowly, trying it out, the feel and the taste of it.

"Yes. Yes." She clapped her hands. "That's my name. I know it is."

He'd never seen her eyes so bright or her cheeks so flushed and he knew they were on the verge of finding her true identity, her family. He was happy about that. She'd been in limbo long enough, but a part of him was sad. This would be her first step away from him and he had to let her go. It was time.

He knew this day was coming and he should be prepared, but he wasn't. Still, he'd do what he had to. As a Texas Ranger he could do no less. He'd taken an oath to protect the people of Texas, and as a son of Texas he'd never break that oath.

"I'll run a background check right away. I should have more information on Joscelyn Beckett soon." He got to his feet.

"You'll call as soon as you find out something." A shadow crossed her face.

"Yes." He paused at her expression. "What is it?"

She closed her eyes for a second. "I feel as if I've been in this deep, dark hole and I've suddenly glimpsed a sliver of light. But I'm afraid of the brightness and what it will reveal. Will it burn me? Will it scar me further? Maybe it's safer to bury myself in the hole where I can't be hurt again. After all, someone tried to kill me."

Walking to her, he looked into her troubled eyes. He was there when they brought her in with scars on her back from being beaten repeatedly. And he was there when the tests revealed a bullet in her head. After some investigation they determined that the people in the cult hadn't shot her.

Someone else had. He was with her through all those long weeks in the hospital when he didn't think she'd ever make it back from the abuse she'd suffered. He was there to prepare her to testify against the cult members, but when the cult leader died, the others took a plea bargain. He was relieved that she wouldn't have to go through a trial, but she'd been ready to do whatever was necessary to keep them behind bars. Belle Doe wasn't a quitter. She was a fighter, a survivor—that's why she was still alive.

"You survived because you have more strength than anyone I've ever met. Whatever we find out about your life, you'll be able to handle. There's no doubt in my mind. The fear is just a part of it. You wouldn't be human if you weren't afraid of the unknown. We all are."

Her eyes glistened. "I don't think you're afraid of anything."

Losing you. He'd been afraid of that for a long time now, and it was happening. He'd handle it just as she would—with courage.

"Ah, Belle. Don't put me on a pedestal."

There was silence for a moment.

"Give Dr. Oliver a call. She'll be able to reassure you," he finally said.

She nodded, her eyes catching his. "I'll never

be able to thank you for everything you've done for me."

"Just be happy—that's what I want for you." He meant every word, even if that happiness wasn't with him. "I better get going so I can make it happen."

"Caleb." She stopped him.

He turned to look at her and wished he hadn't. Her sad eyes, her sweet face twisted his gut.

"I'm sorry you got recruited for another escort job."

He grinned. "Oh. I'm looking forward to this. I want to see the fool who buys that hat." He was being flippant, but it would be the last time that he'd go anywhere with Belle on his arm. She would soon become Josie—a completely different person.

She grinned back. "It should be fun."

"It will be. We'll dance the night away—probably the last time that I'll be able to call you Belle."

A pregnant pause followed his words; and emotions they'd been denying simmered close to the surface.

"You can always call me Belle. Right now Josie doesn't seem quite right."

"But it will." They both knew that and they both were feeling that pang of change.

"Maybe." Her eyes held his. "You'll call as soon as you find out something?"

"Yes, and try not to worry." He turned and walked out before his strength gave way.

Outside he took a long breath. *Josie Marie Beckett. Who are you? Do you have a husband, a lover waiting for you?* Those two questions were uppermost in his mind and he hated himself for that selfish reaction. He got in his car and headed for his office to find out the truth about Belle, putting his emotions aside and concentrating on her and her future.

He just wished he could get rid of the knot in his stomach, a knot that told him he was about to lose everything he'd ever wanted. But he would deal with it like a man—the man she wanted him to be. If he preached to himself long enough and hard enough, he might be able to pull it off.

BELLE IMMEDIATELY CALLED Dr. Oliver and told her about the memory. As Caleb had said, Dr. Oliver reassured her and Belle felt better knowing that finally her memory was returning. She held her name in her heart like a sacred pledge, so afraid it was going to slip away like the rest of her memories. Although she had told Caleb, and he'd make sure her future would now unfold.

She would face the light and the fears inside her. It was long overdue. Someone had put a bullet in her head and left her on the streets of Austin to die.

LINDA WARREN 23

Who had caused her all this misery? And who had hated her that much? No matter how hard it would be, Caleb would help her find the truth. It was time to stop being afraid and embrace her life—whatever it had been.

She knew she was a good person and made friends easily. Caroline Coltrane, the wife of Eli, the ranger who'd rescued her, was a very good friend, and her sister, Grace, was, too. They met for lunch every now and then and Belle enjoyed their company and their friendship. She wondered what type of friends she had in her old life. Belle was beginning to drive herself crazy with all the wondering, so she went in search of Ms. Gertie. After all, she did have a job. Some days that was hard to remember because Ms. Gertie tended to pamper her. But she wasn't an invalid and she'd made that plain from the start.

She found Gertie in the pool, floating and relaxing. Harry paddled around entertaining her. Prissy and Prudy lay on the tiled floor watching, but not daring to get in the water. The pool and the hot tub were enclosed, so Gertie swam daily year-round.

"Do you need me to do anything, Ms. Gertie?" she asked.

Instead of responding, she answered with a question. "Did you have a nice visit with Caleb?"

"Yes." She sat in a pool chair and Prissy jumped

onto her lap. She stroked the cat for a moment, listening to her purr. "I wasn't aware you'd called him to be our escort for tomorrow night."

"If I'd told you, you would have said not to bother him. But it's unseemly for a woman to attend functions without a male escort." She paused, splashing water on Harry. "And I've seen the way you look at him."

Belle shifted uncomfortably. "Ms. Gertie, you know I can't get involved with anyone. I don't know who I am and that would be so unfair to Caleb."

"Oh, Belle, darlin'. That doesn't keep the heart from getting involved."

She knew that all too well. But now that she knew her name, her feelings would change. *Wouldn't they?* That's what she'd learned in her sessions. Though her feelings for Caleb seemed strong now, once her memory fully returned those emotions would lose their strength. Her feelings for Caleb were based on her fears and insecurities. He was her security blanket.

In her mind, she recognized the logic of that. In her heart she wasn't so sure. Caleb, with his kind and gentle ways, was a part of her. She knew his smile, that crooked grin and the way his brows knitted together when he was deep in thought. But most of all she knew his voice—that deep soothing tone that had brought her so much comfort. And his touch. For so long she jumped if anyone touched her.

Slowly and surely Caleb's gentle touch had shown her that not all people were bad. Caleb was good to the core and she couldn't imagine loving anyone the way she loved him. But that was her private secret. She had no right to love Caleb or to give him hope that one day there could be a future for them. Until she regained her memory, she had no future.

But now she had a name. In a few hours Caleb might be able to tell her where she was from, if she had a family, a husband. The thought ran through her with anticipation and dread. Once she found that out, Caleb would become a part of her past and she wasn't ready to let go—not of Caleb.

She was smart enough to realize that everything Dr. Oliver had cautioned her about was true. Her attachment to Caleb was hindering her memory recall. She had to let go and allow herself to remember. She wasn't in love with Caleb, she only thought she was. How many times would she have to say that to herself before she believed it?

"Belle, grab Harry. He's getting tired." Ms. Gertie's voice penetrated her thoughts and she jumped up, Prissy growling at the interruption of her sleep. Belle grabbed a towel and gathered Harry into her arms, drying him thoroughly.

When she put him down, she knew exactly what he was going to do. He shook his whole body, splattering her with remnants of water.

"Harry," she scolded, but laughed at his anguished expression. She picked him up and rubbed him again until he was panting with delight.

"I better get out. I have a dozen phone calls to make."

"Is there anything I can do?" Belle asked again.

"Yes. Make sure Martha has that canary locked in the dining room. I don't want the girls having a feast of him tonight."

"The girls never leave your bed." Gertie called the cats her girls and she treated them as such, too.

"Oh, but temptation is sometimes too great." Gertie stepped out and wrapped a towel around herself. "Think about that, Belle. Sometimes it's good to give in to temptation."

"Ms. Gertie." She was shocked.

"I'm not talking about the girls. I'm talking about Caleb."

"Ms. Gertie!" She was even more shocked.

"I'm going to change, then I'll be in my study." She walked off, not saying another word, the animals marching behind her.

Belle went to check on the canary, trying to ignore the message behind Gertie's words. She knew how Belle felt about Caleb. Everybody probably did, but Caleb. And she never wanted him to know. It would only complicate things.

CALEB SPENT THE AFTERNOON searching for every piece of information he could on Joscelyn Marie Beckett. Before long, he knew a lot about her. She was born in Corpus Christi, Texas to Brett and Marie Beckett. She attended school in Corpus and went on to Texas A&M at Corpus and eventually became a police officer. A police officer! That threw him and angered him. How could a police officer disappear without anyone knowing? But it would explain her strength and courage.

He forced himself to continue. Later, she was on the police force in Beckett, Texas. Caleb had heard of the town, but looked it up on the map to get the exact location. South Texas—between Corpus Christi and Laredo.

None of this was making sense. She was a police officer and no one had reported her missing. And no one had answered the ads asking for information about her that were plastered in all the big newspapers. Why?

A little more checking and he discovered she'd never been married. That was a relief for now, but Belle had a whole life out there that didn't include him. He shoved the thought aside. Her parents were dead, killed in an auto accident and she had a grandfather who lived in Beckett. Even Caleb had heard of Boone Beckett and the Silver Spur Ranch. Cattle and oil wells made Boone a formidable figure in Texas, especially when it came to politics. His backing could almost guarantee a win.

So why hadn't a man like Beckett searched for his granddaughter? There were so many unanswered questions and he knew the only way to find the answers was to go to Beckett, Texas.

First, he had to talk to Belle. It wasn't going to be easy to explain that her parents were dead. Or that her grandfather hadn't cared enough to report her missing.

He grabbed his hat, knowing he had to be honest with her, but he wasn't looking forward to the conversation.

CHAPTER TWO

BEFORE CALEB DID ANYTHING, he called Dr. Oliver and she asked him to come to her office. He was glad to do so. He didn't want to do anything to impede the return of Belle's memory.

"Howdy, ma'am." Caleb placed copies of the information he learned about Belle on Dr. Oliver's mahogany desk. Removing his hat, he took a seat across from her. The room was done in soothing pastels, and calming water sounds played softly in the background.

"Ranger McCain, I'm glad you took the time to come by and bring the information," Dr. Oliver replied. Somewhere in her fifties, Dr. Oliver's hair was short and completely gray and she spoke as softly as the sounds wafting from the intercom.

"We've been waiting for this and I wanted you to have all the details."

"Thank you. Remembering her name is very good, but it is only the start."

"So how much information should I give her?"

Dr. Oliver flipped through the papers. "Tell her the basics. Ask questions and let her fill in the blanks. No pressure. If she asks a question, answer as little as you can. Let her strive for the complete picture."

"Okay."

Dr. Oliver continued to read through the papers. "A police officer? Never would have guessed that, but she's very independent and strong, so that fits." She looked up, her eyes thoughtful. "And no one reported her missing. That's a puzzle. When you feed her this information, do it slowly."

His eyes narrowed. "Do you think it's wise to tell her any of this?"

Dr. Oliver looked at him over the rim of her glasses. "Ranger McCain, we're not keeping secrets from her, but with a little coaxing I'm hoping she'll remember it on her own."

"I see." He leaned forward. "Do you think going back to Beckett would be good for her?"

Dr. Oliver folded her hands. "In my opinion, it would be very good for Belle to be around familiar sights and sounds. That might be the stimulus she needs for a full recovery. There is no such thing as a quick fix when it comes to healing from trauma, but Belle has made remarkable strides. She's established a healthy lifestyle and she functions very well. She's strong enough to cope with integrating the present and memories of the traumas with her other memories, as they reveal themselves."

Caleb ran his thumb along the rim of his white Stetson. "I hear a 'but' in your voice."

"I'm going to be straightforward."

"Please do."

"We've talked about this before."

He knew what was coming—Belle's attachment to him.

"Belle's emotional state is very fragile. She trusts and leans on you, and in the beginning that was very good because she'd lost all trust in people. From the fragments she recalled while in the hospital, we've ascertained there is a man in her life. Once her whole memory returns she won't need to lean on you. She'll become a fully functioning person again with an old life and a new life. If she's torn about hurting you, it will make things very difficult for her. And I know you want the transition to go smoothly and for Belle to recover without any guilty feelings over misleading you."

He stood and held his hat in his hand. "I'd be lying if I said I didn't care for Belle, but everything I do I do with her best interest in mind."

Dr. Oliver stood also. "I know. That's why I haven't asked you to back away from her. You've been good for Belle and you're probably the reason she's recovered so well. But the day is coming when she won't need you. Don't make her feel guilty about that. It could compromise her full recovery."

"I would never do anything to compromise her recovery." He placed his hat on his head. "Any advice on what to expect?"

"She'll continue to have headaches, some severe, confusion and some dizziness. Just be patient and let everything happen naturally. Bits and pieces of her life may come back gradually, like this morning, or she could be flooded with memories all at once. Other times, she may not be aware she's remembering. The information will just come out in something she says. I have an appointment with Belle in the morning and we'll thoroughly go over the details, but she's read so much and studied PTSD that she's well aware of what's happening. She's become so strong, a pale comparison to the shell of a woman I first saw in the hospital. I have no doubt she'll overcome all of this."

He lifted an eyebrow. "I hear another 'but.'"

"Memory loss related to traumatic experiences may serve as a protective function. If Belle feels a strong secure attachment in the present she may never allow herself to remember."

He swallowed. "So make it clear that we are only friends?"

Dr. Oliver nodded. "Yes. That would help her tremendously. She may not realize it now, but she will later."

How will he feel later? Hurt and alone. But he'd known that from the start and he wouldn't change anything he'd done for Belle.

As if sensing his thoughts, Dr. Oliver added, "I know you care deeply for Belle and she was lucky to have someone so unselfish and caring on her side. She has basically overcome the physical abuse of the cult—painful flashbacks and dreams are normal and Belle knows that. But once she becomes aware of the reason why she was shot she has to be able to cope. And I believe she can."

"Me, too. Thanks for being so honest."

"Belle's future is in her hands." She scribbled a number on the back of a business card. "That's my cell. Call if you feel you need me, but Belle trusts you and you're probably the best person to reveal tidbits about her past."

Caleb tipped his hat and walked out, wondering exactly what the future held—for Belle. And him.

WHEN HE REACHED the Parker house, Belle was waiting for him. He followed her into the living room. Gertie was upstairs.

She turned to him. "Did you find my family?"

He removed his hat and sat on the sofa, trying to find the right words. "Sort of."

She frowned. "What does that mean?"

He patted the spot beside him. "Sit, and let's take this slow."

"Okay." She did as he asked.

Her dark hair hung down her back and her eyes were bright. How could he tell her? How could he douse that light from her eyes? He had no choice. Taking a long breath, he said, "Your parents' names are Brett and Marie Beckett."

Her frown deepened and he waited. Her hands framed her face, her eyes heavy with memories. "Yes. My parents." Suddenly tears filled her eyes. "They're dead. I remember the awful car accident. I remember. Oh, no! Oh, no!" She wrapped her arms around her waist and rocked to and fro, her hair obscuring her face.

Caleb's stomach churned with a sick feeling, but he didn't interfere as she dealt with her parents' deaths all over again. He wanted to touch or hold her, but he knew it was best not to. So he just gave her time.

Slowly she wiped away tears with the back of her hand. "They were too young to have their lives cut tragically short. And they were so much in love."

"Did you live with them?" Dr. Oliver wanted him to ask questions, so that's how he started.

Her brow wrinkled in thought and she touched her forehead. "No. I had my own apartment. Daddy didn't like it, but Mama said I was grown up and since I was a..." Her voice halted as another memory surfaced.

Her eyes grew big. "I was a police officer. Oh, my God! I was a police officer!"

"Yes," he acknowledged. "In Corpus, then in Beckett, Texas."

Her eyes became even bigger. "It's my name. Beckett. Beckett." She repeated the name, testing it, running it through her brain. "My grandfather lives there." She frowned. "I worked there?"

"Can you remember?"

Her frown became fierce. "Why would I work in Beckett? My parents didn't even live there. Oh, wait." She held her head in a vice as memories tortured her. "After my parents died, I went there at my grandfather's invitation. His name is Boone Beckett."

"Yes," Caleb confirmed. "Can you remember anything else?"

She jumped to her feet. "No, and I don't want to."

He stood facing her. She was barefoot and she barely came to his shoulder. "I know this is painful, but it's what you wanted—to know the truth about yourself."

"Yes." She looked him in the eye. "Did my grandfather report me missing?"

This was the hard part. He shook his head. "No. No one has reported you missing."

"That doesn't make sense."

"All I have are facts, no concrete answers. To find those you have to go back to Beckett."

Fear flashed in her eyes and he was quick to tell her, "I'll go with you."

"You will?"

"Yes. I'll stay with you until your full memory returns."

"Thank you. I'd like that." She shrugged. "I'm not sure I could do it alone."

"You don't have to."

"When can we go?" she asked, her voice anxious.

"How about the morning after the charity ball? That will give you time to get your thoughts together, talk to Dr. Oliver and explain to Gertie."

"Yes." She tucked her hair behind her ear. "I'll hate to leave her. She's been so good to me."

"She'll understand. We all want you to regain your memory."

"Yes," she replied in a melancholy voice.

He restrained himself from touching her wet cheek. "Try not to think about it too much. We have the ball tomorrow night and then we'll find the answers you need."

Her face softened. "I'm sorry you got roped into that."

"Aw, shucks, ma'am. I'd never have any fun if I didn't squire Ms. Gertie around town."

She smiled. "Thanks."

"You're welcome. Now get some rest."

"Caleb."

"Yes?"

She licked her dry lips. "How old am I?"

"Thirty."

"Oh. Yes, that feels right." She swallowed then asked, "Am I married?"

He saw the worry in her eyes and didn't think it would hurt to tell her. "No."

She heaved a sigh of relief. "Thank you."

"Talk to you later," he called on his way out the door, feeling the same way she did.

THE NEXT MORNING Belle spent an hour with Dr. Oliver and felt good about the visit.

"I'm so glad it's finally happening," Belle said, curled up on the peach sofa.

"Yes," Dr. Oliver agreed, pushing her glasses up the bridge of her nose. "Do you have any questions?"

She shrugged. "No. Not really. I believe we've covered everything about a hundred times."

Dr. Oliver smiled. "You've been one of those

patients who desires to know everything and you've researched PTSD thoroughly. Just be patient and let your memory unfold. You may not even be aware of it at times, and at others you may be flooded with events and scenes. Dreams and flashbacks are normal. So are the headaches, but once your recall is complete they will be less frequent, then may disappear completely."

Belle uncurled her legs. "Caleb is going with me to Beckett."

Dr. Oliver paused in writing notes in a file. "I know."

"I'm surprised you didn't object to that," she said with an impish grin.

"You've been confused many times with my cautionary words about Caleb." Dr. Oliver looked directly at her. "When your memory is complete, you'll understand them. They are for your own peace of mind. And that's what I want for you— for you to be at peace with your past and your present, not torn between the two. Less trauma is what you need now." She returned to her notes. "You trust Ranger McCain and so do I. I'm relieved that he will be with you."

"He's a wonderful man." The words slipped out before she could stop them.

Dr. Oliver looked up. "And there's probably a wonderful man waiting for you."

"Mmm." She chewed on her lip, wondering about the man she'd mentioned in the hospital. He wasn't her husband. So he had to be a boyfriend. Yet, she couldn't bring up his face. All she could see was Caleb. She wouldn't tell Dr. Oliver that. She would handle her feelings in her own way because she knew them for what they were. That was the main thing.

THAT NIGHT BELLE had a restless sleep, tossing and turning as parts of her life flashed through her mind like a frenetic video. She was a little girl running to meet her father when he came home from work, then she was older and her mother was teaching her to cook and how to set the table. They were on a family trip to Six Flags Over Texas, laughing and having a good time. Then school and showing her parents her report card— all A's and she was proud. Her parents were even prouder. Friends, Cathy and Gilda, stayed over and tried on makeup and they did each other's hair. They talked about boys, dating and the prom. Graduation and smiles then college. Texas A&M at Corpus was close so her parents were thrilled with her choice. She had to make a decision about a career and it was easy. She'd go into law enforcement like her father.

Finally the video stopped and she fell into a

deep sleep. She woke up refreshed as some of the fogginess had left her. She had a happy childhood and she'd remembered so many things that her head hurt from the reel running in her mind. Her memory was returning just as Dr. Oliver had said. Now she had to wait and the rest would fall into place. Soon she'd know the face of the person who'd shot her.

She quickly dressed in shorts and a tank top, making sure her back was covered. She had deep welts there from the beatings she'd received at the hands of the cult. The racist leader said she was evil because her skin and eyes denoted her lineage was from a group not acceptable to their faith. She had to be beaten to drive out the demons and this had gone on for months.

Now her life was within her grasp. She just had to keep remembering.

She hit the front door running, taking her usual route through the affluent neighborhood. It was barely six so everything was peaceful and quiet on this April morning. Birds chirped and she could hear an occasional plane or car, but otherwise she was alone. She kept her mind blank as she jogged down the sidewalk in front of the large two-story homes and manicured lawns. The fragrance of blooming flowers wafted to her nostrils and she sucked in the scent, but didn't pause to admire the view. She needed the exercise more than the scenery or the elusive memories that were surfacing faster than she could take them in.

An hour later she jogged back through the door breathing heavily and walked through the house to the pool area, where she quickly changed. She dived in and swam until she was completely exhausted, then she crawled out, grabbed a towel and collapsed into a lounge chair. The sky roof was open and the early-morning sun poured in. She felt at ease and at peace for that moment. Prudy hopped onto her lap and Belle knew Ms. Gertie was awake. Strange, but she still thought of herself as Belle. She wondered how long that would last. How long before she made the journey back to who she used to be and accepted it totally?

"Morning, Belle, darlin'." Ms. Gertie, in a blue flowing silk robe, took a lounge chair next to hers.

"Morning, Ms. Gertie." Belle knew she had to tell Gertie she'd remembered her name.

"I told Martha we'd have breakfast out here. It's such a beautiful day."

"Yes, it is. I ran this morning and the yards are looking so nice and there's a scent in the air that's indescribable."

"It's spring, darlin', and there's pheromones in the air. Turns a head to thinking about love."

Belle stroked Prudy, smiling. "Ms. Gertie, you're a natural born matchmaker."

"Mmm. Too bad I didn't do too good with myself. Living alone is not much fun, but without Harry, there's not much fun, either."

Harry, hearing his name barked loudly. Gertie had named her dog after her husband. She said it brought her comfort.

Gertie reached down and picked up Harry, cuddling him. "So, Belle, my darlin', don't let real love slip by."

Maybe if Ms. Gertie knew her memory was returning she'd stop her matchmaking with Caleb. "I have to tell you something."

Martha laid a tray of bran muffins, fruit, coffee and juice on a small table between them. "Thanks, Martha," Gertie said, reaching for a cup of coffee. "Now, darlin', what do you have to tell me?"

Belle reached for a glass of juice. "I remembered my name."

Gertie's head jerked toward her. "Oh, that's marvelous."

"Yes," Belle agreed. "And Caleb found out a lot of other information, too."

"So what is your name?"

"Joscelyn Marie Beckett, but everyone calls me Josie."

"Beckett?" Gertie's fine eyebrows crinkled in

thought. "Any relation to the Becketts of South Texas?"

"Boone Beckett is my grandfather."

"Oh, my goodness. I think I need something stronger than coffee."

"Do you know him?"

"Darlin', everybody in Texas knows Boone, the old scoundrel, reprobate, womanizer without a scruple to his name."

"Sounds as if you know him very well."

"I've run into him over the years at political fund-raisers and political events. Never saw eye to eye on much of anything. It's hard to believe that someone as sweet as you could be his grand-daughter. Evidently you don't have much of your grandfather in you."

"My memories of him are vague, but Caleb and I are leaving for Beckett in the morning to find answers."

"Oh, darlin'. I don't like the thought of you leaving me, and I like the thought of you getting hurt even less."

"I'll be fine, Ms. Gertie, but I hate deserting you on such short notice."

"Don't give it another thought. You just get your life back, and if that life doesn't appeal to you, you always have a home here."

"Ms. Gertie, you're truly an angel."

"Oh, darlin', don't look too closely or you'll find the horns." She rose, Harry comfortable in her arms. "I'll get dressed and meet you in the study. We have a lot to get done before the ball."

"Yes, ma'am. I'm right behind you."

In her room, she called Caroline to let her know what had happened.

"Oh, Belle, that's marvelous," Caroline said. "But I'll miss you."

Caroline had been a true friend when she'd needed one and Belle would never forget that. "I'll miss you, too, our talks, our lunches. Both you and Grace. Please tell her for me." Grace was Caroline's sister and they were very close. They both had made Belle feel not so alone and she was grateful for that.

"Sure," Caroline agreed. "I'm glad Caleb is going with you. I won't worry so much. He'll take very good care of you."

"Yes, he always does that." Belle bit her lip, realizing not for the first time how kind people had been to her since her ordeal.

"Mmm."

Belle didn't miss the hint in Caroline's soft voice—that there was more than friendship between Belle and Caleb.

"Promise you'll call and visit Eli and me often."

"I will." Belle would be forever indebted to Eli,

who'd rescued his future wife, Caroline, and Belle from the cult.

"Be happy, Belle, that's what Eli and I want for you."

"Thanks, Caroline, and thanks for being a good friend." Tears welled in her eyes.

"This isn't goodbye forever," Caroline said. "I won't let it be."

"Me, neither." She'd never forget her friends in Austin.

"Bye, Belle."

Belle. Belle. Belle. But she wasn't Belle. She was Josie Marie Beckett.

She hung up the phone, feeling sad. In Austin she had friends, people who cared about her. What awaited her in Beckett, Texas?

CALEB STARTED HIS DAY by calling Jeremiah Tucker, a friend and fellow ranger, to see if he'd cover for Caleb while he was away. Tuck was affable and hardworking and he readily agreed, wishing Caleb all the best in placing Belle back with her family.

Then he headed for Waco to tell his parents in person. Andrew Wellman was his stepfather, but he was Caleb's father in every way that counted. Joe McCain, his biological father, never claimed Caleb or acknowledged his existence. Joe was an angry, controlling, jealous man and he'd put Caleb's mother, Althea, through hell. The only place he'd let her go alone was to church and there she found the courage to get out of a rotten marriage.

Jake and Beau, Caleb's older brothers, were supposed to go with her, but Jake, the oldest, refused to go and stayed with his father. Jake believed all the lies his father had told him about his mother—that the baby she was carrying was the bastard son of Andrew Wellman. Althea grieved for her oldest son, and Caleb grew up with her heartache. But five years ago Althea and Jake had finally found each other again and Caleb had found his brother. They were now a family.

Joe McCain had fathered four sons, but he hadn't been a father to any of them, not even Jake, the one son he acknowledged. The oldest, Eli, was a son by another woman and Joe never claimed him, either. But Eli found his own kind of peace in the arms of Caroline—a woman who loved him just the way he was.

All the McCain men had scars and Caleb knew his ran deep. Andrew gave him everything he needed, but he could never explain why his father didn't want him. He had a good life with good parents, but at the oddest times he would think about his biological father and wonder if he'd ever have any good feelings about the man.

He drove around to the garages of the two-story colonial house he'd grown up in, and entered through the breakfast area. Andrew and his mother were sitting at the table, eating. His petite mother had salt-and-pepper hair and brown eyes like all her sons. Andrew was thin and tall with a thatch of gray hair. They both smiled as he walked in.

"Caleb." Althea ran to hug him. "What a pleasant surprise."

Andrew gave him a bear hug. "Good to have you home, son. If you have a while, we can get in a round of golf."

"Andrew, give him a chance to take a breath," Althea scolded. "Have a seat and I'll fix you some breakfast."

Andrew winked at him. "She just wants to cook for someone other than me."

His mother loved to cook. She always had and her children were the center of her world. And now that she had Jake and his family back, she was happier than Caleb had ever seen her.

"We're having waffles and bacon, but I can fix you anything you like."

"That's fine, Mom." Caleb removed his hat and took a seat.

Andrew sat beside him. "You look a little down, son. Something wrong?"

Andrew knew him so well and their bond was

close, as close as blood, and Caleb loved the compassionate, kind man. A lot of people who didn't know Caleb wasn't Andrew's biological son said Caleb took after him. Caleb considered that a compliment. Andrew had been the best role model, and everything that he'd learned he'd gotten from him.

"I'm fine, Dad," he replied. He'd always called him Dad because he was the only father he'd ever known. It had taken Beau a while, but he called Andrew Dad, too.

Althea placed coffee, maple syrup and a plate of waffles and bacon in front of him. He dived in, realizing he was hungry. His parents watched him as they would a two-year-old—with love and affection.

Caleb laid his fork down. "I just came by to tell you that I'll be gone for a few days."

Andrew took a sip of coffee. "Oh. An important case?"

"Belle has remembered her name and I'm taking her back to her family."

"Oh, dear, that's wonderful," Althea exclaimed, then her face grew somber. "Are you okay with this?"

"Of course. Her memory is returning and that's what I've wanted—for her to find her way back from all the pain."

Althea covered his hand on the table. "Caleb, my son. I know how you feel about her. Maybe it would be best if someone else escorted her home."

"Mom." He patted her hand. "I'm not a kid. I'm the one who has to do this. I have to know that she's happy."

"I'm just worried about you."

"Thea," Andrew intervened. "Caleb is a grown man and we'll support him in whatever he chooses to do."

"Of course, dear." Althea took Caleb's plate to the sink, her expression saying more than words. She was worried about her son.

"What's her name?" Andrew asked.

"Josie Marie Beckett."

Andrew lifted an eyebrow. "Any relation to Boone Beckett?"

"He's her grandfather."

"Now isn't that something."

"Do you know him, dear?" Althea asked, returning to the table.

"Met him a few times in the nineties when I was helping Gertie with some fund-raisers. He's quite a character, opinionated and mule-headed, but he comes from oil money so people put up with him."

"Oh, dear, he doesn't sound like Belle at all. Does she remember anything about their relationship?"

"No. But bits and pieces are coming back to her

and the doctor feels that being in Beckett will help to restore all her memory."

"Be careful, son."

"I will, Mom, and don't worry."

"Oh, please." Althea gave an aggravated sigh. "The older my sons get, the more I worry."

"Anybody home?" Beau shouted a moment before he walked in with a black-and-white puppy in his arms. "Hey, Caleb."

"Morning, Beau."

Beau was the second son of Althea and Joe McCain. He was a family man to the core and he kept them all bound together with continual lunches and gatherings. Beau had the biggest heart of anyone Caleb had ever known. He got that from his mother—always caring for others.

"What have you got there?" Althea asked, kissing Beau's cheek.

"An orphan. Do you know anyone who needs a puppy?"

Caleb laughed. "Don't tell me. Another one of Macy's rescues."

Macy was Beau's neighbor and had been most of his life. She lived down the street when they were kids and now she lived in the condo next to Beau. Macy was an animal lover and she rescued more animals than the animal shelter. She and Beau had been friends all their lives, but neither was willing to take their relationship to the next step. Caleb didn't think they ever would.

"Yes." Beau stroked the small dog. "He has some scars on his stomach. Someone did a number on him. Since Macy works nights at the hospital, I've had him two nights in a row. Macy can't seem to find a home for him so I'm lending a hand."

"I've lost track of the number of dogs and cats Macy has conned you into taking. You're such a sweet man."

"Yeah, Mom. That's me." A slight flush stained Beau's cheeks and Caleb saw his pain. Caleb wondered if they were both destined for broken hearts.

Althea took the dog from Beau. "Poor little thing," she cooed.

Andrew joined her. "Look at those big brown eyes, Thea."

At that moment, the puppy licked Althea's face. "Oh, Andrew, he's so cute."

While they were cooing over the dog, Beau went to get a cup of coffee and Caleb followed. "You planned that brilliantly, didn't you?"

Beau took a swallow of coffee. "Thought it might work."

"Beau," Althea said. "We'll keep him."

"Yeah," Andrew added. "We'll buy him a dog-house and put it in the backyard."

"Backyard?" Althea seemed offended. "We'll put it on the patio or in the garage."

"Yes, dear," Andrew replied. "There's a box in the garage and we can make him a bed until then."

The two disappeared out the door.

Caleb leaned against the cabinet and told Beau the news about Belle.

"Wow. That's great." Beau paused, watching Caleb. "Isn't it?"

"Yes. I knew this day was coming."

Beau patted his shoulder. "Love is hell."

Caleb shook his head. "What do you know about love? You spend all your time with a woman you won't even ask out."

Beau grimaced. "Don't start about Macy. We're just friends."

"Oh, Beau." Caleb sighed. "For such a brilliant lawyer, you can sometimes be very dense."

They heard a squeal of delight from the garage and they knew who it was—Katie, Jake's four-year-old daughter. Althea kept her while Elise worked as an English professor at the university. Their son, Ben, was already in school.

Katie walked slowly into the breakfast room, carrying the dog. Jake was behind her. "Look, Uncle Beau and Uncle Caleb, this is Bandy. Grandpa called him that cause he's got a white Band-Aid over his eye."

Caleb swung her up in his arms, kissing her cheek, and shaking Jake's hand. "Morning, brother."

"Morning. Didn't know we were having a family meeting."

All the brothers were tall with brown hair and eyes, but Jake and Caleb took after their father with lean, lanky frames. Beau had more meat on his bones, as Althea put it.

Katie got down to play with the puppy and Caleb told Jake about Belle. "That's good news. I hope it turns out well for her—and you."

Caleb caught that note of concern in his voice. "I'm fine really, so you, Beau, Mom and Dad can stop worrying about me."

Jake punched his shoulder playfully. "That's what families are for, little bro."

"Yeah," Caleb smiled in his easygoing way, realizing he was getting a bit sensitive.

"Wait a minute." Beau saw the extra plate in the sink. "Caleb, did you have waffles this morning?"

"Sure did. The best Mom ever made."

Althea walked in, hearing the conversation. "Sit down, boys, and I'll make a fresh batch."

Caleb kissed his mom. "I've got to run and I've already had waffles. Guess I'm the favorite."

Guffaws followed that.

"Now, boys," Althea said, but she was smiling.

Caleb hugged his dad. "Son…"

"I know, Dad." Caleb hugged him tighter. "I'll be careful."

"I'll let everyone know when I get back." He gave Katie a quick hug and a kiss and walked out. Jake and Beau followed him.

They embraced before Caleb got in his car. "If you need anything, just call us," Jake said.

"Even if it's in the middle of the night," Beau added.

"I will, and thanks."

"Have you talked to Eli?" Jake asked.

"I spoke to Tuck, but I'll call Eli when I get to my office. Being a newlywed, I didn't want to intrude on his morning."

Caleb drove away knowing whatever happened he had the love and support of his family. And he had a feeling he was going to need it.

CHAPTER THREE

WHEN CALEB REACHED his office, Eli, his half brother, was waiting for him. Tuck was Eli's foster brother and had told him the news. Because he'd been the one who'd rescued Belle, at times he felt responsible for her life.

"How is she?" Eli asked, a note of worry in his voice.

Eli was a big muscular man and the only son who had Joe McCain's blue eyes.

"She's scared." There was no reason to lie.

"She's been scared for a long time."

"Yeah. But this is different." He sank into his chair. "I think I'm a little scared, too." That wasn't easy for him to admit.

Eli watched him. "Let me take her back. End the relationship now and spare yourself the pain."

Caleb slowly removed his hat. "Would you have let me help Caroline?"

"Hell, no."

"My answer is the same."

Eli nodded. "Then I'll go with you. Between the two of us, we can protect her and make sure no one gets the chance to hurt her again."

Caleb lifted an eyebrow. "What about Caroline?"

"She'll understand."

She probably would, Caleb thought. They both cared and worried about Belle. But something held him back.

He laid his hat on his desk, running his finger over the rim of the Stetson. "I have to do this alone. I have to do it for her—and for me."

Eli nodded, understanding as Caleb knew he would. "Just nail the bastard who put her through hell."

"I intend to."

"And Caleb…"

"What?" Caleb saw the concern in Eli's eyes and knew exactly what the concern was about. "I'll be fine, Eli."

"But it won't be easy."

"No." It wasn't going to be easy to return Belle to another life—a life without him in it—and Eli understood that. Even though they'd only known each other a short time, their bond was close—as brothers should be.

They talked a bit more then Eli left for his office. Caleb took care of things that needed his immediate attention before the trip, then he headed home, packed his clothes and dressed for the ball.

BELLE WAS IN A RUSH all day and didn't have time to dwell on a lot of painful thoughts. Gertie had a hundred things for her to do and she was glad to soak in a hot tub before she dressed for the evening. She stared at the black gown with a V-neck and long sleeves. Sequins decorated the bodice and glistened like tiny stars. The pencil-slim skirt had a slit up the side, showing off her leg and ankles. The dress was expensive and she'd balked at the extravagance when she'd first started working for Gertie. But Gertie insisted it was part of the job. Belle had to dress the part, so she acquiesced. But she was sure she'd never worn clothes like this before. They didn't feel familiar.

She braided her hair, entwining a sparkly ribbon through it, and coiled it into a knot at the back of her head, curling several loose tendrils around her face. She'd done her hair like this before. When she was small, her mother had done Josie's hair the same way. Many times. Marie would brush Josie's hair until it shone, then she would braid it to keep it out of her eyes. As Josie grew older Marie would interweave a colorful ribbon to match Josie's clothes. For the prom, Marie had done Josie's hair just as it was now.

Belle's cheeks felt warm from the memory of her wonderful mother. She was remembering more now and her heart hammered so fast she had to take a deep breath.

Later she would relive the memories until they were permanent, never to be forgotten or destroyed again. But now she had to concentrate on the evening.

She slipped on sandaled heels and buckled the strap across the ankle. Standing, she felt light-headed from the height. Good grief, how was she supposed to walk in these things? Wearing heels this high obviously wasn't a part of her daily life. After a few trips around her bedroom, she went to help Gertie.

CALEB WAS AT GERTIE'S on time and when he saw Belle, his heart stopped. She was more than beautiful. She was radiant, and Caleb felt privileged to have her on his arm.

The night was melancholy. Caleb and Belle were both aware that tomorrow their lives would change. Caleb put it out of his mind and enjoyed the evening. The ball was in full swing and Caleb held her close as they danced the slow tunes and laughed as they cut up during the fast ones. They didn't talk much. They didn't need to.

They circled the dance floor to "Moon River," his hand at her back, her head on his shoulder. Through the thin fabric of her dress, his fingers felt the scars on her back. He forced down the anger in him, not wanting any reminders of what the cult had done to her.

"I like to dance," she said.

"I know." They'd been dancing several times in the past year.

"Some things you just don't forget." She raised her head, her eyes twinkling. "We dance so well together, Caleb McCain. I must have known you in another life."

He just smiled, wishing that was true—that he was the man in Belle's life. But he was her protector, her friend, and another man was waiting for her. Of that Caleb was certain. But tonight she was his.

Several other men asked Belle to dance and he stood on the sidelines trying to let go. He was just amazed at the change in her. A few months ago Belle was a frightened woman, not wanting anyone to touch her. She was now unafraid of human touch, but she still had issues about her back and didn't want anyone to see the scars.

When Josie surfaced completely, he wondered how she would deal with it.

The auction started and Belle and Caleb took their seats. Gertie's bird-hat was a big hit and Caleb almost choked when it sold for ten thousand dollars. Gertie had obviously gotten the word out.

It was after midnight when they returned to the Parker house. Gertie retired to her bedroom and Caleb lingered for a moment in the living room, not wanting this night to end.

"Are you packed?" he asked Belle.

She sat on the sofa, removing her heels. "Yes. What time do you want to leave?"

"How about eight?"

"That's fine." She rubbed her feet. "I know one thing. I didn't wear heels a lot as Josie."

He grinned. "Probably not as a police officer."

She leaned back. "I can't remember anything about that."

"You will."

"Yes."

There was an awkward pause as they both dealt with an uncertain future.

Caleb was the first to speak. "I better go so you can get some rest."

"Good night."

"Good night, Belle." He said her name slowly, reverently, and probably for the last time. As he walked out, he jerked off his tie. Tomorrow she'd find her family and answers. Tomorrow she might recover her memory completely.

And Caleb would return alone.

THE NEXT MORNING Belle was up early, her few meager belongings packed into a suitcase. She said a tearful goodbye to Gertie and her pets, then went downstairs to wait for Caleb.

Within minutes she was in Caleb's Tahoe headed out of Austin to Beckett. She felt a sense of foreboding and couldn't shake it. Conversation was slow as they took I-35 then the I-410 Loop toward Corpus Christi.

"Have you remembered anything else?" Caleb asked, sensing her nervousness and wanting to put her at ease.

She shrugged. "Not much. Just bits and pieces from my childhood." She turned in her seat to face him. "The rest of it is there and even though I'm still afraid, I'm ready for it all to unfold."

He knew she was. He suddenly realized that his issues with his father were nothing compared to what she'd been through and had yet to face. And he'd never leave her. Until she asked.

"Did you tell your parents where you were going?" she asked, and he knew she wanted to change the subject.

"Yes. I saw them yesterday and they're very happy you're regaining your memory."

She smiled slightly. "You have very good parents."

Belle had met them on several occasions and his parents liked her. She got along well with people. He returned her smile, knowing his parents were great.

"You were lucky to have Andrew for a father instead of Joe McCain."

She always seemed to know what he was thinking.

"Yeah," he replied. "I hope I never forget that."

"You won't." She was quiet for a moment and he glanced at her. Her brow was creased in thought. Suddenly she said, "I had good parents, too." Her eyes were distant. "My father loved my mother since they were kids. My mother's father worked on the Silver Spur Ranch and when my mom was old enough she started working in the main house as a maid."

Caleb didn't think she even realized she was remembering, so he let her talk.

"My father went off to college and it broke my mom's heart, but he came back often to see her. When he graduated, Boone said it was time for him to get married and start producing heirs. He had the bride all picked out and it wasn't Marie Cortez. My father was torn between family loyalty and my mother. In the end, he married Lorna Caraway and my mother left the ranch and never returned."

Caleb waited, but she didn't say anything else. He wasn't sure how much to push. "Was your mother pregnant when she left?"

Belle shook her head. "No. My father couldn't stay in the arranged marriage so he left to find my mother."

"What happened to the first wife?"

She frowned deeply. "She was very angry at my father for leaving her. She was four months pregnant at the time."

There was a tangible pause and Caleb went on pure instinct. "So you have a half sibling?"

She gripped her head. "I suppose. Why can't I remember?"

"Don't get stressed out," he cautioned, turning on US 281 toward Three Rivers. "How about something to eat and drink? I didn't have a thing but coffee this morning. How about you?"

"I had a muffin and fruit with Ms. Gertie, but I'd love a cup of coffee."

They stopped at a small diner in Three Rivers. The trip was three and a half hours and they were more than halfway. Caleb ordered coffee and they sat in a booth.

Belle pulled a Snickers out of her purse. "Want a candy bar?"

"No, thanks." He hid a secret grin at her chocolate fetish. She never went anywhere without chocolate.

The waitress brought coffee and Belle nibbled on the bar, licking her lips. He watched as if mesmerized.

"Her name is Ashley," Belle said suddenly.

"What?" Caleb wasn't sure what she was talking about. He was totally absorbed in her mouth and tongue.

"My half sister, that's her name."

"Oh."

Caleb took a sip of coffee and waited for her to continue.

"That doesn't feel right, though." Belle clutched her cup, and her turmoil tightened his gut.

"Don't push it. We'll be in Beckett soon and hopefully some of your questions will be answered."

Her eyes suddenly sparkled. "You and I have something in common. We both have a half sibling."

"Yeah." He couldn't take his eyes off her face, that light in her eyes.

"I hope my sister is as nice as Eli."

Caleb wished that, too, and he wished all her memories would unfold like a fairy tale. But the stark truth was someone tried to kill her, possibly someone in her own family.

"Lorna is my father's ex-wife." Belle seemed to be remembering tidbits at her own pace. "And I have an uncle—Mason is his name, I believe. And I remember Caddo."

"Who is Caddo?"

"I don't know. I just remember the name and I get a good feeling inside when I do. I must have liked him."

Caleb toyed with his cup. He knew she wasn't married, but little things pointed to a boyfriend, a fiancé maybe. When she'd started remembering in the hospital, she'd said that he'd bought her Egyptian cotton sheets and she'd told him they were too expensive. She could never pinpoint who *he* was, and she hadn't mentioned him since. Maybe Caddo was the man she'd been talking about.

He pushed his jealousy down, keeping her best interest uppermost in his mind. "Could Caddo be a boyfriend?"

She shook her head. "No. It's not that kind of feeling. It's more of a friendship reaction."

That was a relief, but Caleb knew if it wasn't Caddo, it was someone else. And he had to accept that.

Soon they left and Caleb held the door for an

elderly man, puffing on a cigar. Belle twitched her nose as they walked to the car. "That cigar is so strong."

"They'll probably make him put it out," Caleb remarked, getting into the truck.

They turned onto US 59 toward Beckett. The land was flat with scrub oaks, bushes, mesquite and plenty of cacti. This was farming and ranch land enclosed with barbed wire fences.

"Are you okay?" Caleb asked after she remained quiet for several minutes.

"I'm remembering all these names, but I don't feel a connection to any of them."

"You said you came to Beckett after your parents died. The report said you'd been there less than a year so you probably didn't get to know anyone very well."

"Well enough that someone put a bullet in my head. I keep asking myself why. Why would someone shoot me? And why did I wake up in Austin? That's three and a half hours from Beckett."

"We'll find out soon enough." Caleb had no answers for her, he only had the same questions. She was so sweet, so completely enchanting. He couldn't imagine anyone having a grudge against her or wanting to hurt her.

"Yeah." She glanced out the window

"Do you remember anything about your grandfather?" That bothered Caleb the most. How could a powerful man like Boone Beckett not report his granddaughter missing?

The scent of the cigar triggered a memory. "He's a controlling manipulative person." Belle watched the barbed wire fences flash by and Boone suddenly filled her mind. She closed her eyes as a scene became vivid.

"I'm Boone Beckett, Brett's father." The bear of a man standing in her parents' living room introduced himself. He puffed on a cigar and the smoke spiraled around his face. The wind left her lungs and she couldn't speak.

"Did you hear me, girlie?" His voice boomed and she had the urge to step back. But she didn't. Her father had never backed down from him and she wouldn't, either.

She swallowed hard. "Yes."

"I'm here to take my son's body home to Silver Spur."

"What about my mother's?"

His eyes darkened. "Her body will never rest on the Silver Spur. She took him away from his heritage, his family, and I'll never forgive that."

Anger welled in her chest. "She didn't take him away. You forced him to leave by manipulating his life and not allowing him to marry the woman he loved."

"He could have had any woman he wanted," Boone shouted.

"He wanted my mother," she shouted back.

Boone glared at her through narrowed eyes. "Listen, girlie, I'm not arguing with you." He pulled a sheet of paper from his pocket. "Sign this and our business is over."

"What is it?"

"Form to release your father's body to me."

She raised her head in defiance. "My father stays buried next to my mother—forever. That's it."

"What's it going to take. Ten thousand? Twenty thousand? Tell you what—I'll give you fifty thousand dollars and you sign the paper and we're done."

"Get out," she screamed. "Get out and take your money with you."

"Do you know who you're talking to, girlie?"

Her eyes blazed. "Unfortunately, yes."

He stuffed the paper in his pocket. "Since you're Brett's daughter I was trying to be nice. Figured you could use the money. But Brett's body is going home to Silver Spur with or without your approval. All I have to do is get a court order and no judge is going to say no to me."

"Get out and don't come back," she seethed between clenched teeth.

He inclined his head. "You got guts, girl. I'll

give you that, but it's always smart to know when to cut your losses."

With that the memory dissipated. She opened her eyes, staring out at the long expanse of highway. Her thoughts were inward, troubled. Had Boone removed her father's body from the cemetery, from her mother, in Corpus to the Silver Spur Ranch? *Think. Think. Think.* Did Boone separate her parents? She had to know and she struggled to remember what had happened next. But nothing was there.

"Dammit. Dammit. Tell me." She gripped her head with both hands.

"Are you okay?"

Caleb's concerned voice reached her. She blinked, realizing she'd been talking out loud. "Sorry. I was having an insane moment trying to remember something."

"What?"

"When my parents died, Boone came to Corpus, wanting to take my father's body back to the Silver Spur Ranch. He demanded that I sign the papers to release the body. I refused and we had words." She swallowed. "You see, he wanted my father to be buried at Silver Spur, but not my mother. I told him to leave and never come back."

She paused. "I couldn't bear the thought of separating my parents. They were so much in love, yet at times there was a sadness in my father that neither my mom nor I could assuage. He loved the Silver Spur and he missed it every day of his life, but Boone made it intolerable for him to live there. My mother was a Mexican and not good enough for a Beckett."

"Evidently Boone came back."

"I guess. That's what I was trying to recall—if he had my father's body moved away from my mother. I couldn't live with that."

"Do you know how you came to live in Beckett?"

Her head felt heavy with all the memories rushing in. "Yes. I was at loose ends after losing my parents. I needed to get away. Boone kept at me about my dad's body, but I never gave in. Finally he said he'd make a deal with me. He wanted me to come to Silver Spur to see the heritage my father had left behind. If I came and stayed for a while, he'd stop his efforts to move the body. So I went. I wanted to see this place my father talked about all my life." She took a ragged breath. "Boone didn't separate my parents, but we were still arguing about it. Boone and I didn't have the best relationship, and Lorna and Mason seemed to hate me. But I stayed. I'm not sure why."

"Did you live on the Silver Spur?"

"No. I lived in town with a friend of my mom's,

Lencha Peabody. My mother's mother died when she was five and Lencha helped raise her. Lencha and her family lived next door. Oh." She rested her head against the seat with a slight smile. "It's so nice to remember Lencha. She's Mexican with a bit of Karankawas Indian. She's known as a healer and sometimes a witch, but to my mom she was like a mother and I grew up hearing stories about Lencha and her colorful personality. Lencha married a white man, as she called him, Henry Peabody, who was twelve years older and worked on the Silver Spur. He died a few years ago and Lencha was glad to have Marie's child to fuss over and I felt at home with her." She lifted her head. "I'm sure she was worried about me. I wonder why she never reported me missing."

"A lot of this isn't adding up."

She frowned. "Do you think I'm remembering it wrong?"

"No. I think you just have a lot more to remember."

She wrapped her arms around her waist. "The unknown is so scary."

"But it's what we've been waiting for—to identify the unknown. Then it won't be so scary."

She looked at him. "I'm so glad you're with me."

His eyes met hers. "You can count on that."

"You're so nice, Caleb McCain, and I'm sure

a Texas Ranger isn't supposed to spend this much time on one case."

"We don't stop until the bad guys are caught and in jail and soon the person who shot you will be in jail."

"Oh. This is Beckett," she said, glancing back at the city limit sign. "Barely fourteen hundred people live here."

Caleb turned toward the business area. The town was small, with one main street where all the businesses were located. There were no fancy retail stores, just old-fashioned storefronts that had been there for years. It was like a scene from the 1950s with parking in front of stores and parking meters. A blacksmith shop, feed store and beer joint had weatherworn boards that had stood the test of time. The only new building was the post office.

"Until I can do some checking it's probably not wise to let people know you're alive."

"I agree. We can go to Lencha's. I trust her."

"Which direction?"

"Turn left then take Tumbleweed. Lencha's is about a mile on the right."

Caleb followed her directions to a small white frame house with a chain-link fence around it.

"Go around back to the garage," Belle instructed.

Caleb stopped in front of the double garage that had a small truck parked inside. Belle gasped.

"What is it?" Caleb asked.

She pointed to the garage. "That's my parking spot and my car's not there."

Caleb looked at her pale face.

"Evidently I drove away from Beckett."

"Seems like it."

"I need to see Lencha." She opened the door and got out. Caleb followed.

The yard was well kept, but the house needed painting and some outside boards were rotten. There were no close neighbors. Lencha lived on several acres. Farther down were some brick homes then a trailer park.

It was noon, but no one was about. Belle opened the gate and they walked up the back steps. A pleasant scent greeted Caleb and he noticed all the flowering bushes and plants in the flower beds. A huge greenhouse was in back and he glimpsed a large garden filled with all sorts of vegetables and more plants.

Belle knocked but no one answered. "Lencha sometimes gets lost in her own little world," she said, and opened the door. They went into a utility room that held more plants in pots, then into the kitchen. A birdlike woman in jeans and a chambray shirt was at the sink washing dishes.

Long gray hair hung down her back. A squirrel climbed down her back then up again to rest on her shoulder. Caleb blinked, wondering if he was seeing things.

When the squirrel noticed them, she scurried down Lencha's back to the floor, standing on her hind legs making funny noises.

"What's wrong with you, *Chula?*" Lencha asked, looking down at the squirrel. "You've had your lunch, so be quiet. I'm not giving you any more corn. You're fat as a pig now."

Belle smiled at *Chula,* Lencha's pet squirrel. As she stood in the room, soaking up the familiarity, that sense of belonging that she hadn't had until now—*Chula,* the hardwood floor, the Formica table and chairs, the sunflower curtains and the scent of herbs and lavender—all were familiar. Lencha grew lavender in the yard and it drifted to her nostrils and saturated her body. A metamorphosis began to happen. She could feel it. It was like shedding a skin and letting new life in. For so long she'd felt like a mismatched piece of furniture that she'd been trying to fit into rooms where she didn't belong. But this was a part of her and a part of her family.

"Lencha," she said quietly, almost afraid to speak.

"Lawdy, lawdy, will it never stop?" Lencha dried a dish. "People call me a witch and I'm beginning to believe them. How else could I conjure up her spirit and hear her voice so clearly?"

Lencha didn't turn around or acknowledge her presence. She put the dish in the cabinet as if Belle wasn't even standing there.

"Lencha." She tried again.

Chula scratched at Lencha's legs.

Glancing down at *Chula,* Lencha caught sight of Belle, taking in Caleb behind her. "Lawdy, now she's got a man with her." Lencha shook her head as to rid herself of the image. "How long will I continue to see her? I'm too old for my mind to be this active."

Belle finally understood. Lencha thought she was seeing things. She walked closer. "Lencha, it's me. I'm real and I'm alive."

Lencha shook her head. "Go away, Josie, and stop torturing an old woman."

Belle touched her and Lencha jumped back, her eyes big, then in a trembling voice, she asked, "Josie? Josie Marie?"

"Yes, Lencha. It's me."

"Heaven above. *Santa Maria madre de Dios.*" Lencha grabbed her and held her tight. "Josie Marie, you're back. My precious child, you're back." She drew away and stroked Belle's face. "You're back."

"Yes." She gripped the old lady as tight as she

could. Lavender was all around her and a peace-fulness came over her. The past connected to the present just that easily. She wiped away an errant tear and stared at Lencha. "Josie Marie is home."

In that moment she became Josie Marie again. New strength surged through her and the shackles of fear slipped away. Her memory hadn't com-pletely returned, but it would and she could sort out the rest of her life on her own.

Looking at Caleb, she saw a glimmer of sadness in his eyes. Weak, defenseless Belle Doe was no more. She disappeared the instant Lencha called her Josie, and Caleb knew that. She saw it in his gaze.

A moment of dejection swept over her. She brushed it away with a flicker of remorse. She was Josie Marie Beckett, police officer, looking for the person who'd tried to kill her. She wanted justice for what she'd been put through and she'd find all the answers she needed one way or another. Revenge was such a harsh word, but she wanted revenge or something to explain away the nightmare.

Her eyes settled on Caleb. Surviving her parents' deaths, being shot and living without a memory seemed minimal compared to what she had to do now. How would she say goodbye to a man like Caleb?

CHAPTER FOUR

WORDS FELT LIKE A WAD of cotton in Belle's throat and she couldn't force them out. Her eyes clung to Caleb's and she memorized every line of his honed, lean face, the sensual curve of his mouth, the dark hair, neatly trimmed, and those incredible warm eyes.

Before she could speak, Lencha stroked her face, her hair. "Child, where have you been? Why did you leave like that?"

Belle stared into Lencha's gray eyes and saw the worry and concern. She would talk to Caleb later. Now she had to tell Lencha what had happened to her.

"Lencha, this is Caleb McCain, a Texas Ranger."

Lencha turned to Caleb, *Chula* on her shoulder. She studied him openly. "Texas Ranger, hmm? Had a cousin who was a ranger back in the old days when a ranger was all the law we had out here. Nice to meet you." She shook his hand.

"Nice to meet you, too, ma'am." He glanced

at *Chula.* "Don't think I've ever seen a pet squirrel before."

Lencha scratched *Chula.* "Found her as a baby in the backyard. Must have fallen out of a nest. I fed her with an eyedropper and she's been a pet ever since. She's like a cat, but I can't leave her alone in the house or she'll tear up everything." Her eyes narrowed. "So what are you doing with my Josie?"

Josie took Lencha's arm and led her to the kitchen table. "It's a long story…."

Josie told her everything about her ordeal—waking up on Austin's skid row, the bullet in her head, the cult, the memory loss, the struggle back to reality and the kind people who helped her.

"Santa Maria madre de Dios!" Lencha made the sign of the cross. "Child, are you okay?"

"Partly. I still don't remember how I ended up in Austin or what made me leave Beckett."

Lencha jumped up. *"Ojo."*

"No, Lencha…" But Lencha was already out the door.

"Ojo?" Caleb asked with a lifted brow.

She sighed. "It's the eye. The evil eye. It's Mexican—if a person looks at your child and thinks things, good or bad, about them, it can cause high fever, crying or fussiness or something like that. I'm not up on this stuff, but when I was small I had a real high fever and the doctors couldn't keep it down. Mama was worried and called Lencha and she came to Corpus. My mom and dad scoffed at a lot of Lencha's rituals, but were willing to try anything. After Lencha did her thing, my fever was under control within thirty minutes."

Lencha hurried back in, her gray hair everywhere, making her look like a witch. In her hands she carried a brown egg, a sprig of rosemary and a bottle of brackish greenish liquid. She filled a glass with water and brought everything to the table. Saying a prayer in Spanish, she rubbed the liquid all over Josie, even her clothes.

"Lencha!" Josie protested, twitching her nose at the strong scent.

"What is that?" Caleb asked, and Josie met his eyes, not sure how to explain Lencha and her healing methods. But she knew she didn't have to. Caleb was very open-minded, understanding… The pungent smell of the herbs filled her nostrils and stopped her thoughts.

"Basil, rosemary and rue. A *limpia,* a cleanser to expunge evil forces," Lencha replied, taking some liquid in her mouth and spitting it over Josie.

"Lencha," Josie protested again, but Lencha paid no attention to her. She held Josie's head with both hands and said another prayer.

Then she took the egg and rosemary in one hand and rubbed it over Josie's head and body.

"Lencha, this is for babies," Josie protested, "and I'm beginning to stink."

"Shh." In Spanish she said another prayer and broke the egg into the water. "See, the albumen is milky and murky. The evil has been extracted. She made the sign of the cross. "Now, we've broken the spell."

"Lencha…"

Lencha wagged a finger in her face. "Don't scoff at the old ways. They work. This might be a little different, but it will work, too. Someone looked upon you with envy or malice." Lencha touched her face. "How could they not? You're so beautiful, just like my sweet Marie." She took a seat and held Josie's hands. Lencha was known for her healing remedies and Josie suspected that most of the time she made a lot of them up. Belief was a powerful thing, though. Lencha had told her that many times.

Josie glanced at Caleb. He didn't seem surprised or shocked at Lencha's methods. Just interested. After a minute, he spoke. "Maybe you can help us in other ways, too. When was the last time you saw Bell…I mean Josie?"

Lencha nodded. "Remember it well. I do midwifing when I'm needed. Lot of Mexicans here are illegal. The Garcia's daughter went into labor and they called me. They're illegal and didn't want to go to a hospital, afraid of being sent back to Mexico. I was there all night. She gave birth about five and I got home around seven. Josie's car wasn't in the garage and I thought she was at work, but her room light was on and the door was open so I went in. A suitcase was on the bed with some clothes thrown into it and her gun and badge were on the nightstand. I thought that was peculiar so I called Eric and he said Josie left work yesterday to go visit with her grandfather and…"

"Who's Eric?" The name created a mass of confusion inside Josie and she had to know. Or it could be the herbs were clearing her sinuses.

Lencha looked perplexed, then patted Josie's hands. "Child, he's your fiancé. Tall, blond, good-looking guy. Eric Hanson's a lieutenant on the police force here. You two hit it off the moment you set eyes on each other."

A fiancé? She was engaged to be married? To Eric…Hanson. She closed her eyes and tried to see his face, but all she could see was Caleb's. The only man who'd occupied her mind totally. She gritted her teeth and forced Caleb away, but nothing was there. Why couldn't she remember this man she'd loved and was planning to spend the rest of her life with? Panic took root and she slowly calmed herself.

"When was the last time you saw Josie, Mrs.

Peabody?" Caleb's soothing voice brought her back to the conversation. For a long time now, she thought of his voice like a glass of warm milk. When she was small and she'd have nightmares, her mother would give her a glass of warm milk and it would calm her and make her feel safe. That's what his voice did—made her feel safe and secure. As a child, she needed the warm milk. As an adult, she needed Caleb. But soon that dependency would fade. She had to stop leaning on him and accept her life. Accept Eric.

"I saw her that morning before she left for work. She was happy, energetic and excited about finding a girl who was missing. She went to work and I never saw her again." She reached out and touched Josie's face. "Oh, child, I thought I'd lost you like I'd lost your mother."

Even though Marie had never returned to Beckett, Lencha visited often and she'd been one of the reasons Josie had come to Beckett. She was the only link to her mother's family and she wanted to be around someone who'd loved her parents, who had understood what she was going through.

"That old buzzard had something to do with this. I know he did." Lencha's voice turned cold and accusing.

After Boone had pressured Brett into a loveless marriage and Marie had left Beckett, Lencha and

Boone had become bitter enemies. Lencha had put several curses on him, but her curses never fazed the indomitable Boone Beckett.

"Mrs. Peabody…"

Lencha held up a hand. "Please call me Lencha. Mrs. Peabody died when my husband did. I'm just Lencha now."

"Lencha." Caleb inclined his head. "You said Josie was excited about finding a missing girl. Do you remember the girl's name?"

Lencha shook her head. "No. Josie never talked about her cases and she's not one to gossip."

Josie listened with a surreal feeling, as if they were talking about someone else. Nothing was ringing any bells. Except Eric.

She swallowed. "I was going to see my grandfather. What happened after that?"

"Eric said you had a big argument with Lorna and was very upset. You called him and said you were leaving Beckett and never coming back and that you'd call as soon as you reached Corpus. He tried to talk you out of it and asked you to wait until he was off duty, but you wouldn't listen. You even called Dennis Fry, the police chief, and told him you couldn't stay in Beckett any longer."

Complete silence followed those words. Caleb looked at Josie and her olive skin was a sickly white. He wanted to stop the questions, but he couldn't. It was time to keep the answers coming.

"I called your parents' house in Corpus every day, sometimes three times a day, and there was never an answer. Finally the phone was disconnected and I knew something was wrong. You always kept up with the bills."

"Did you do anything?" Caleb asked.

"You better believe I did." Lencha snorted. "Eric and I went out to Silver Spur and confronted the biggest, meanest buzzard around. The type of buzzard who'll pick your bones before you're dead. Big Boone said Josie got a little upset with Lorna and in a few days she'd calm down and come back. When she didn't, I filed a missing person's report with Dennis, but never heard a damn word. I didn't give up, though. Kept bugging the hell out of him."

"And nothing happened?"

"Not until a few minutes ago when Josie walked in. All those potions and spells I've been weaving kept you alive and my precious child is back." Lencha grabbed Josie and they hugged again.

Caleb stood, knowing nothing was adding up. If a missing person's report had been filed, then it should have been in the system. They would have known who Belle was months ago. There were some shady dealings going on and he intended to get some honest answers.

"Do you remember the date Josie left?"

"Sure do. February twentieth." Lencha pulled an old calendar out of a drawer and opened it. "See, I wrote it down."

He stared at the date circled in red. They had the timeline almost correct. Belle had said it was very cold when she'd been taken to the cult's compound. The area had experienced a freezing winter last January and February. She'd been with the cult until mid-April when Eli and the FBI had infiltrated the group. The time from the twentieth until the cult had found her was still a mystery. It couldn't have been long, though—days at the most. It had been almost fourteen months since she'd been missing.

Time to find more answers.

While Lencha was fixing something to drink, Caleb pulled Josie aside. "I'm going over to the police station to see what I can find out, then I'll head out to the Silver Spur Ranch."

"No," she said in a strong voice. "It's time for you to go. I can sort out my life now and I have to stop depending on you."

He saw that determined expression, the stubborn set of her jaw, but he wasn't leaving. "No way." He shook his head. "I said I'd stay until your full memory returned and it hasn't. You know me well enough to know that I always keep my word."

"Yes." She bit her lip.

"I'm not leaving you until we know who tried to kill you. It's not safe until then. Your memory is returning so that shouldn't be too much longer." He touched the frown on her forehead. "Besides Gertie'd have my hide if I left without knowing you were completely safe."

"Okay." She gave in with a slight smile. "I wish I could go with you, but I know it's best if no one sees me for now." She looked down at herself. "And I really need to get cleaned up. I'm beginning to smell."

Caleb grinned. "I thought Gertie was eccentric."

She met his grin with one of her own. "Lencha's a colorful person. Some people call her a witch, but she's not. She just knows how to cure a lot of ailments with remedies from her grandmother. I'm not sure about the evil stuff, and my mother wasn't, either. My mom loved her dearly, but said Lencha liked to put on a show."

Unable to resist, he tucked a stray tendril behind her ear. "Get reacquainted with Lencha and try not to worry."

A pained expression came over her face. "I don't remember Eric and I should. Why…"

"Belle…Josie, please, don't stress over it. It's all going to come back to you." He had the hardest time calling her Josie, but he was trying.

"I suppose."

"See you in a little while." He walked out the door, turning into an investigating ranger, instead of a man whose heart was dangerously close to breaking.

THE POLICE BUILDING was easy to find, a redbrick structure on the end of Main Street with two police cars parked in the side lot. He went in through the front door into a reception room. A green-eyed blonde, somewhere in her thirties, sat at a small desk, answering phone calls.

She hung up. "May I help you?"

"Caleb McCain, Texas Ranger. I'm here to see Chief Fry."

"Oh, oh." She pointed to a door. "He's the first door on the right."

"Thank you."

He walked into a larger room with several more desks. Two police officers dressed in traditional blue were working there. One was blond and Caleb knew he had to be Eric. A hard knot formed in his stomach as he knocked on the appointed door. When he heard an answer, he went in.

A balding man in a starched white shirt was writing in a file at his desk. He raised his head as Caleb entered.

"What can I do for you?" The chief laid down his pen.

Caleb walked forward with his hand outstretched. "Caleb McCain, Texas Ranger. I'm working a case and could use some help."

Dennis stood and shook his hand. In his forties, medium height with a slight pouch, Dennis had a friendly smile.

"Chadwick is the ranger in this county so you must be from another area. Have a seat."

Caleb settled his frame into a vinyl chair. "Yes, I am. I've notified Chadwick that I'm in the area." Rangers were respectful of each other's territory and they worked well together. There was nothing stronger than the ranger bond and brotherhood. Caleb had had a long talk with Chadwick before leaving Austin and if he needed any help all he had to do was call him.

Dennis eased into his chair, the springs creaking from the weight. "What can I help you with?"

Caleb pulled a small photo of Josie from his pocket, one that Gertie had taken. He pushed it across the desk, watching the man's face. "Do you know this woman?"

"Well, I'll be damned. That's Josie Marie Beckett. She used to be on the police force." Dennis leaned back, a sly grin on his face. "But you knew that, didn't you, Ranger McCain?"

Caleb retrieved the photo and slipped it back into his pocket. It was the only photo he had of Belle and he wasn't parting with it. "Yes. I knew she worked here. I'm trying to find out what happened to her."

"I'd sure as hell like to know, too. Damn good officer. She called me at home and said she had to leave and that she was sorry. We haven't seen hide nor hair of her since."

"Did you try to find her?"

"Boone was in here every day demanding results. We sent out bulletins and checked the house in Corpus. Nothing. Josie had a big blowup with the Becketts and I guess she just didn't want to be found." He leaned forward. "So Boone's got the Rangers involved. I hope you find her. It'll get a lot of people off my back, including Lencha Peabody and her curses and her spells."

"Do you remember the date that she left?"

"Late February of last year. The twentieth, I believe."

That was the same date Lencha had given him so he knew the chief wasn't lying or trying to hide anything.

He stood, knowing he wasn't going to get any more information here. He wasn't sure the chief knew anything else. Today was just a fishing expedition. Tomorrow he'd demand answers, especially about the bulletins. "Thanks. I'll be in the area for a few days."

The door opened and Eric stood there.

"Come in," Dennis invited.

Eric stepped in and closed the door.

"This is Texas Ranger Caleb McCain." He paused after making the introduction. "He's looking for Josie."

Eric's blue eyes widened. "Oh, man. I'll help you any way I can. I've been searching for over a year and I'm worried out of my mind."

Caleb stared at this man. Josie's fiancé. He was as tall as Caleb, but there the difference ended. He was as blond as Caleb was dark and his arms were muscled as if he worked out. His voice and his eyes showed genuine concern, and Caleb blocked all the jealousy that lapped at him. Jealousy that surprised him. He never considered himself a jealous person.

"Thank you," was all he could say. "I'll be in touch."

Eric followed him out. "Did someone ask you to find her?"

Caleb turned to him. "I can't divulge that."

"Listen." Eric ran a hand through his hair. "I just need to know that she's alive and okay."

"As I said, I'll be in touch." Saying that he

strolled to his vehicle. He couldn't tell Eric yet. It was too dangerous for Josie. Keeping her safe was his top priority.

HE STOPPED FOR GAS and asked for directions to the Silver Spur Ranch. Turning off the highway, he took a winding county road. The road angled left, and to the right were brown stone arches with The Silver Spur emblazoned across the top. A large spur decorated each end. He drove over a cattle guard and brown board fences flanked him on both sides. The land was flat, inundated with mesquite and cacti, and had a desolate, lonely feel. Oil wells dotted the landscape and cattle roamed among the mesquite. The road seemed to go on and on and then it suddenly appeared—a massive two-story Mexican hacienda constructed of brown stone and a tiled roof. Two wings extended toward the back and barns, metal buildings, pipe corrals, sheds and several more houses were in the distance.

Caleb had heard of political barbecues that had been held here and he could see it was a large impressive operation. He parked in the circular drive and marveled at the large Texas star made from red, white and blue tile inlaid into the rock driveway. A smaller tiled star was at the front door. He rang the doorbell and heard "The Eyes Of Texas" resounding inside the house.

A Mexican maid in her forties answered the door. "May I help ya?"

Caleb removed his hat. "Yes, ma'am. I'm Caleb McCain, Texas Ranger. May I speak with Mr. Boone Beckett, please."

"He no see no one."

"This is about Josie Beckett."

Her black eyes opened wide. "*Si. Si.* Come. Come." He followed her through a large foyer, about the size of his apartment, into a formal living room then into a massive den of leather, silver and stuffed animals. Mounted heads of deer, elk and numerous others decorated the walls along with stuffed ducks and birds he didn't recognize. A chandelier made from deer horns hung from the ceiling. Different types of animal skins covered the floor and in the center of the mahogany-paneled room was another Texas star. Boone loved Texas, that was evident.

The man himself caught Caleb's attention. He sat on a red leather sofa, his cowboy boots propped on a horseshoe wrought-iron and glass coffee table. The silver tips on his boots glinted from the light. A huge TV screen covered one wall and Boone was watching a hunting show, a glass of whiskey in his hand, a cigar in his mouth.

"Mr. Beckett, Texas Ranger to see ya," the maid said.

"Hell, Chadwick. I done told you ten times I don't know nothin' about that dead body found in Sagebrush Creek. He worked for me. So what? A hundred vaqueros work out here and I don't know every damn one of them." He spoke in a bored tone and his eyes never left the TV.

Caleb walked farther into the room. "I'm not Chadwick. I'm Caleb McCain and I'm looking for Josie Beckett."

That got his attention. Boone swung his feet to the floor, set his drink down while clicking off the TV. "Well now, son—" he took a puff on the cigar and blew smoke into the air "—if you find her, you let me know 'cause I want to have a talk with that little gal." His voice projected pompous arrogance.

"When was the last time you saw her?"

Boone shot him a dark glance, chewing on the cigar. "Who in the hell asked you to find her?"

"That's confidential, sir."

"It was that old bat, Lencha. She flies around at night sucking the life out of everyone around her. She said I had something to do with Josie's disappearance, but I did everything I could to find her. The girl had a hissy fit and doesn't want to be found."

"Mind if I have a seat?"

Boone nodded. "Take a load off."

Caleb lowered himself into a red leather chair and crossed his legs, placing his hat on his knee. "What was the hissy fit about?"

"Woman stuff." He grunted, removing the cigar from his mouth. "Been married four times and never understood a one of them. Never will, either. I don't know what the hell they want or need or think for that matter."

"What does that have to do with Josie?"

"I told you—woman stuff. Her and Lorna, Brett's first wife, never got along. Every time Lorna looked at Josie, all she could see was Brett's betrayal. I guess that was too much for Lorna. I wasn't here the night Lorna and Josie got into it, but basically Lorna lost it and told Josie she wasn't wanted here and that Marie was a tramp and a whore. That's when Josie blew her top saying she was leaving and never coming back. No one saw her after that. The vaqueros saw her car leaving, though."

Caleb slowly removed his hat from his knee, uncrossed his legs and leaned forward, gauging his words carefully. "Why did you never report her missing?"

Boone's eyes narrowed. "Because that old bat, Lencha, beat me to it. I hounded that inept Fry every day, but Josie seemed to have disappeared off the face of the earth." The eyes narrowed to mere slits. "Are you implying I had something to do with Josie's disappearance?"

Before Caleb could respond, Boone added with a growl in his voice, "Because if you are, I'll have that badge ripped off your chest with your skin still attached."

Caleb looked directly at him. "Mr. Beckett, if you're so powerful, why haven't you found your granddaughter?"

"Listen, you…"

"Pa, Consuelo said a Texas Ranger is here." A man with light brown hair and blue eyes walked in. This had to be Mason. In his fifties, he was average height and his age was beginning to show with threads of gray in his hair and flab around the middle.

Boone made the introductions. "He's searching for Josie."

"That old busybody just won't let it rest, will she?" Mason seethed under his breath, then he turned to Caleb. "This wasn't the place for Josie and she knew it. If she wanted to come back, she'd be here."

"Maybe she's unable to do that," Caleb's said.

"What?" Mason frowned, as if he didn't understand the answer.

Two blond women strolled into the room. Lorna and Ashley. "Oh. I didn't realize we had company," Lorna said. Her hair hung like a bell around her face and she was dressed in a tan linen suit and heels. Very elegant and sophisticated—everything Boone would want in a wife for his son.

Again Boone made the introductions and Lorna's green eyes turned stormy at the mention of Josie. "No offense, Mr. McCain, but what's your interest in Josie?"

Caleb stood. "Justice, ma'am. Justice."

"Justice." A brittle laugh left her throat. "Has a crime been committed?"

"That's what I'm trying to find out."

"I hope you find her," Ashley spoke up. She was a replica of her mother except her hair was long and held with a clip behind her head.

"Oh, please." Lorna sighed in anger. "Let's don't go through this again."

"She's my half sister," Ashley said, undeterred by her mother's anger. "You always seem to forget that."

"Oh, sweetie, I never forget that. Josie Beckett is not welcome here—ever."

Boone stood to his full height. He was a big man with a barrel of a chest and a presence that demanded attention. "Listen, missy, you don't give orders around here. No one does, but me."

"Pa…"

"Stay out of this, Mason, or you'll find yourself

on the first truck out of here. I want to make one thing very clear, then I don't want to hear one more word about it again. Josie is welcome here any time—day or night. Does anyone have a problem with that?"

"Not me, Pa." Ashley put an arm around his waist and hugged him.

Boone removed her arm. "You're still marrying Richard Wentworth and kissing up won't change that."

"I don't love him," Ashley said stubbornly.

"You don't have to. It's not required. Just do what's expected of a Beckett."

"He's fifteen years older than me."

"You'll adjust."

Tears gathered in Ashley's eyes and she ran from the room.

The tears didn't faze Boone. He flopped down on the sofa. "Now everyone get the hell out of my den and that includes you, ranger man." He clicked on the TV and jammed the cigar into his mouth.

Meeting Boone was unlike anything Caleb had ever experienced before. He lived in his own world where he was king, and with his wealth, he could pretty much make that happen, even with his arrogant personality.

Caleb placed his hat on his head and headed for the door, needing fresh air.

"You find Josie, ranger man," Boone shouted after him.

Caleb kept walking, knowing a response wasn't necessary. In the foyer Lorna caught up with him, grabbing his arm.

"Don't bring her back here." There was a hint of a warning in her voice.

He removed her fingers from around his arm and strolled out the door. Outside, he sucked air into his lungs, feeling thoroughly inducted into the dysfunctional Beckett family.

As he drove away, he could fully understand why Brett didn't want to marry Lorna. She was like a cold fish compared to Josie, and Caleb was sure Josie took after Marie, warm and vibrant.

Through all the tension he could feel an underlying fear. They were all afraid of something. Or of what his investigation might uncover. Deciding which one might have shot Josie was like taking a stab in the dark. Sooner or later the truth would come out, though. He just had to be patient.

CHAPTER FIVE

AFTER SHOWERING and changing into clean clothes, Josie walked into her bedroom and stopped short. Everything was exactly as she'd left it, even the open suitcase was still on the bed. A photo of her parents stood on the nightstand. She picked it up and touched it lovingly. Josie had taken it on their twenty-fifth wedding anniversary. Both faced the camera and her father had his arms around her mother's waist as Marie leaned her back into him. They were smiling, happy. A sob caught in Josie's throat.

She sank onto the bed, holding the photo against her, hoping their love would cause a spark to ignite the rest of her memory. But nothing happened.

Chula jumped onto the bed and crawled up her back. "Oh, *Chula*." She squirmed. "Those claws are sharp." She held the squirrel in her arms, stroking her.

"*Chula*," Lencha called and appeared in the doorway. "There you are."

"She's grown so much," Josie said of the squirrel. "I remember her as a baby. You were wondering what to do with her, but I guess she's made a good pet."

"Yes. She disappears sometimes, but she always comes back." She scooped *Chula* out of her arms. "I'll put her outside for a while."

Josie just sat there, wondering what Caleb was finding out. She didn't have the strength to make him leave and she should have. But she still needed that warm glass of milk.

Nervous, she walked around the room touching her things, a jewelry box her father had given her, lotions, perfumes and makeup. In the drawers were panties, bras, socks, hosiery and T-shirts— all hers. Her officer's uniforms hung in the closet with slacks, jeans and a couple of dresses. All familiar, yet not quite her. *Then whose were they?* She couldn't answer that. All she knew was that the items weren't Belle's. God! She ran her hands up her arms. She had to let go of Belle. But when she did, Caleb would be gone, too. And for now she wasn't ready to do that.

Everything Dr. Oliver had cautioned her about was coming true. Her attachment to Caleb was impeding her full recovery. She was strong enough and smart enough to know that she and Caleb were only friends. They would always be friends. She would never lose that. She leaned against the dresser trying to calm her chaotic mind.

"You okay?" Lencha came back in and sat on the bed.

"You haven't touched this room," Josie said instead of answering.

"Sure I have. Put your gun and badge in a drawer. Dusted a bit." Lencha glanced around. "If I did anything else, that would mean you were gone forever and I just couldn't do it."

Josie knew *that* feeling well. *She wasn't losing Caleb.* She had to make herself believe that.

Lencha studied her. "So, is something going on with you and the ranger?"

Sweet, direct Lencha could read her like a book. "He's a very good friend and he's been there for me when no one else was. He brought me back from the edge of insanity and he showed me that not all people are bad. He has a very good heart."

"And you're in love with him?"

She took a moment to answer, wanting to be truthful about what she was feeling. "Belle was very grateful to him. Josie—" She shrugged. "I'm not completely Josie yet."

"Josie is engaged to Eric," Lencha reminded her.

She raised her troubled eyes. "Was I in love with him?"

"You said you were and he wanted to get

married right away. But you wanted to wait until you and Boone had reached a measure of understanding. You actually wanted the old buzzard at your wedding."

"I did?"

"Yeah, and he was pressuring you six ways from Sunday."

"How?"

Lencha tapped one of the posts of the antique Spanish bedroom set. "Had this shipped from Spain with Egyptian cotton sheets—like we don't have that in this country. Had central air and heat installed in this old house."

Josie lifted an eyebrow. "You allowed him to do that?"

"We went to Corpus one weekend to take care of your parents' house and the old bastard had it installed while we were gone. You repeatedly said no and so did I. Didn't faze him. Not much I could do after the work was done, except put another curse on him. But he's so damn evil they don't even affect him any more."

Egyptian cotton sheets. Those words hung in her mind. They were the first thing she remembered in the hospital. And the central air and heat. She remembered that, too. At the time Caleb had thought she was talking about a husband or a lover, but she was remembering her grandfather and his callous way of trying to make amends for the years of neglect.

Seeing her sad face, Lencha jumped up. "Let's fix supper. How about tacos and chocolate quesadillas?"

Josie looped an arm around Lencha's waist, letting go of the turmoil and accepting the peace she'd found in being home. "A balanced diet if I ever heard one."

CALEB WALKED into the house and heard Belle's laughter. No, *Josie's* laughter. Was he ever going to think of her as Josie? It might take some time. But it was good to hear her laugh. She needed more of that in her life.

"Ranger McCain," Lencha said when she noticed him. "Have a seat. We're fixin' supper."

Josie smiled at him and his pulse hummed like a racing car at the starting line. He was sure her smile had voltage power because it always revved him up with all his cylinders firing in perfect order, ready for the race, ready for the checkered flag. As a kid, he was enamored with racing. As a man he was enamored with Belle…Josie. But that race would never be run.

"We're having tacos and chocolate quesadillas," she said.

"Excuse me?"

"You heard right." Her smile broadened.

"Josie loves chocolate and when she was a kid Marie made chocolate quesadillas for her with chocolate sauce, chocolate chips, white chocolate and nuts all on a large flour tortilla. It's just about ready. Have a seat."

Caleb removed his hat and did as instructed. The tacos were loaded and delicious, but he hesitated over the quesadillas. At the eager look in Josie's eyes, he ate it. He had to adjust his taste buds and it wasn't all that bad.

Taking a swallow of tea, he said, "Tea has an usual taste. What's in it?"

"Just drink it. It's good for you," was Lencha's response.

When Lencha turned away, he whispered, "What's in it?"

"A mixture she makes from herbs. It won't hurt you." And, of course, she smiled and he'd drink and eat anything she wanted him to.

After the meal, Josie followed him into the living room while Lencha went to feed her animals. He sat on the worn brown tweed sofa and she curled up beside him in the corner, facing him.

"What did you find out?"

"Same story that Lencha told us, but Fry said a missing person's report had been filed and it should have been in the nationwide database."

"But it wasn't?"

"No. If it was, we would have known who you were that first week."

She studied the tips of her fingernails. "Someone is lying."

"Yes."

"How did it go at the Silver Spur?"

"Same story. Boone said he wasn't there the evening you came out to see him, but you and Lorna had an argument about your father and mother. Lorna called your mother some names and you stormed out saying you were leaving and never coming back."

Her hands curled into fists and she squeezed her eyes shut. "I don't remember."

"Ashley seemed genuinely concerned about you," he told her, to ease her stress. "And so was Boone."

Her eyes flew open. "He was?"

"Yes. He ordered me to find you."

"Moments pop into my mind like bubbles in a bubble bath and dissipate just as quickly. But the memory of my grandfather is very strong. We had this strange relationship. At first, he seemed to hate me because I was Marie's daughter, then he wanted me in Beckett and he started buying me all these things." She ran her palms down the thigh of her jeans. "He's the one who bought me those Egyptian cotton sheets and had central air and heat installed in this house. Said a Beckett had to have the best. In the next breath he'd say he was bringing his son's body back to Silver Spur and we'd argue. I was determined not to move my father away from my mother." She chewed on the inside of her lip. "I wonder if he had it done while I was gone. I'll have to ask Lencha."

One sentence stuck in Caleb's mind. *Boone had bought her the sheets.* Not a boyfriend or a husband as they'd originally thought when she was in the hospital remembering bits and pieces of her life. Eric hadn't bought them for her. Why did that make him feel so good?

He channeled his thoughts back to the conversation. "I think it's time for you to make an appearance. Today was just a trial run. Tomorrow we'll get more answers and you can find out about your father."

She took a deep breath. "Yes, I agree. It's time."

"Just remember this will be dangerous. Once everyone knows you're alive, the person who tried to kill you could try again."

She nodded. "I know and I'm ready. I want my life back."

Caleb stood, not wanting to think about a life without her. That would come soon enough. "Now, I need to find a place to spend the night. Any motels in Beckett?"

She looked up at him. "You'll stay here. There's an extra bedroom and Lencha won't mind."

"What won't Lencha mind?" the woman asked walking into the living room in rubber boots, *Chula* on her shoulder.

"That Caleb stays here," Josie informed her.

"No. Don't mind a bit. If someone's gonna try to hurt Josie then I want you near. My spells are not as strong as they used to be."

"Thanks. I appreciate it." He wanted to be close, too, just in case someone was that stupid.

Lencha sank into her recliner. "Just remember you'll be sharing the bathroom with two women, so don't embarrass us."

"Yes, ma'am."

CALEB SLEPT SOUNDLY on a featherbed with a strange smell wafting around him. Jars of herbs and bottles filled with all colors of liquid he hadn't a clue about were on the dresser. Items Lencha made cures and potions out of, he was sure of that. At four he awoke with a start and listened. Noise. Someone was in the kitchen. He crawled out of bed and opened the door. Lencha's light was on so it had to be her.

Good God! What was she doing at this time of the morning? Probably weaving spells or something, he thought as he went back to bed. Lencha was as eccentric as Boone. How weird it must be for Josie to be caught between them.

When he finally awoke, he got out of bed and headed for the bathroom, taking a shower, shaving and getting dressed. Josie's door was closed so she still had to be asleep. He walked into the kitchen inhaling the smell of coffee.

Lencha poured him a cup. "You're up early."

"I'm an early riser." He took a sip. "And so are you."

"Yep. Always have been," she replied, taking a bowl out of the refrigerator.

The stuff in the bowl looked weird, like puffed-up or swollen raisins. "What's that?" he couldn't help but ask.

"Golden raisins soaked in gin."

"That's a relief. Thought it was eye of newt or something."

"Don't be cute, Ranger McCain." Her voice was stern, but there was a twinkle in her eyes. "Eat nine raisins soaked in gin every morning for my rheumatism."

"Why not just drink the gin?"

She gave him a look. "It's not the same thing. It's the chemical reaction of the raisins and gin that helps rheumatism. Not an ache or pain in my body."

"I'll remember that for future reference."

"Good. I can cure most things or at least I have

remedies that might help. God gave us natural cures from the plants he put on this earth. All that stuff you get from your doctor is poison." She turned toward the stove. "Making chocolate pancakes for Josie. Want some?"

"Are you kidding?" His eyebrow lifted.

"Not that I'm aware of."

He smiled, and shifted his thoughts to Josie's memory recall. "Lencha, it would be best if you don't give Josie a lot of information about her life. The doctor said it was best for her to remember on her own."

"Figured that out myself, Ranger."

He nodded, sipping on his coffee.

Josie walked in dressed in jeans and white short-sleeved fitted blouse. Her dark hair was pinned at the back of her head. Her eyes were bright and she looked ready to face this day.

He pointed a finger at her, unable to keep a grin from spreading across his face. "You're a chocoholic."

"Yes." She kissed Lencha's cheek. "Guilty. You know my secret."

"You should weigh at least three hundred pounds."

She made a face. "Bite your tongue."

"Sit down, you two, and I'll dish up the pancakes," Lencha ordered. "I made yours plain, Ranger."

"Thanks. I appreciate that." Caleb straddled a chair.

"Coward," Josie whispered, and laughed.

It was so easy with Caleb. She loved teasing him, laughing with him and just sitting quietly by his side. That easy peacefulness would soon be shattered, the moment they stepped out of this house to face the people of Beckett and the Beckett family. Her nerves tingled with a premonition of uncertainty and peril.

By the end of this day she might know the person who hated her so much.

WHEN THEY WALKED into the police station, everything became deadly quiet. The phone ringing sounded like a gun being fired. Eric was the first to respond.

"My God, Josie! It's you." He hurried to her side, but she backed away holding her hands up.

Seeing she was having difficulty, Caleb took over. Dennis stood in his doorway, a shocked look on his face. "Could we speak in your office, please?" Caleb asked.

"Sure, sure. Come in."

As the door closed, Eric begged, "Josie, please talk to me."

"Josie's lost her memory, so you'll have to be patient."

"What?" Eric looked from one to the other in confusion.

Caleb told them what had happened to Josie. Dennis and Eric stared back at him as if they couldn't believe what they were hearing.

His gaze centered on Dennis. "You said a missing person's report had been filed, but there's nothing in the system. The FBI searched and so did the Texas Rangers. Someone is lying."

"I'll get to the bottom of this," Dennis promised.

"So will I," Caleb replied.

Dennis paused briefly, not missing that note of warning in Caleb's voice. "My office is an open book and we'll help you all we can."

"Josie," Eric spoke to her, "you don't remember me?"

She looked at him, tall, blond and handsome just as Lencha had said. But there was no connection, no feeling of recognition. "No. I'm sorry. I don't."

His face paled. "Who would do this to you?"

"That's what I'd like to know."

"When you called you told me about the argument you had at the Silver Spur and said you were packing and going home to Corpus."

"Did I tell you what the argument was about?"

"No, you said you'd explain later and that you couldn't stay here one more minute. It was about six-fifteen and I waited for Carl to come in to relieve me then I hurried to Lencha's to try and talk you out of going. You'd already left. I tried your cell phone repeatedly, but you never answered. Someone had to have shot you about that time." He took a step toward her. "Josie…"

She stepped back. "Please, don't. My focus now is trying to regain my memory. Don't pressure me."

"Of course. Just let me help."

She looked him square in the eyes. "Find out what happened to the missing person's report."

"I'm on it. I'll turn this office upside down until I get to the truth."

"Lencha said Josie was working on a case involving a missing girl," Caleb intervened. "Any idea who that was?"

Eric shook his head.

"Gosh, man, that was a long time ago." Dennis sank into his chair. "But I'll turn over all the files she was working on at the time, but it will take time to pull those cases." He paused. "Does Boone know Josie's back?"

"No, and I'd appreciate it if you didn't alert him. Josie needs to do that herself."

"Yes, yes. I understand."

"Who would have handled the missing person's report in this office?" Caleb asked.

"That's Teri Fields, an officer. She does most of the paperwork."

"May I speak with her, please?"

"Sure." Dennis touched a button on his desk and soon Teri walked in—a tall, attractive brunette with hazel eyes.

Dennis made the introductions.

"Josie," Teri exclaimed, staring openly at her. "You're back."

"Yes," Josie answered quietly.

"Ms. Fields, did you handle a missing person's report on Josie's disappearance?" Caleb came straight to the point.

"Yes. About a month after she'd left." She glanced from Caleb to Dennis. "Is something wrong?"

"No missing person's report has been filed on Josie. She's not in the system."

"That's ridiculous. I did it myself." Her hand shook slightly as she brushed back her hair and Caleb knew she was lying. The first kink in unraveling the truth.

"Ms. Fields, there are records and if you're lying, it will be easy to find." He didn't pull any punches.

"Teri, what happened to that report?" This was Dennis. Obviously he wanted the truth as badly as they did.

"I filed it. With Lencha and Boone in here every

day, why wouldn't I? You told me to. I haven't done anything wrong."

Dennis nodded. "Go back to your job."

"She's lying, Fry, and you know it," Caleb said as the door closed.

"I'll handle this, Ranger McCain, and I'll have answers by the end of the day." He looked at Josie. "I'm sorry for all you've been through and you have my full cooperation in apprehending this person."

"I'd like to have the files as soon as possible," she replied.

"Sure. I'll put Raylene on it right away. Should have them by the end of the day."

They walked into the outer office and no one spoke.

Eric followed them. "Can I come by later and talk to you?"

Josie turned to him and his eyes were eager. For a brief moment an elusive memory floated across her mind then dissipated. "I don't remember you, so please give me time."

"Talking might help to regain your memory."

She clenched her jaw and she knew exactly what she was doing. *Suppressing her memories because of Caleb.* She was still clinging to that security, that safety. Damn. Did Dr. Oliver have to be right about everything? "I have to do this on my own. I hope you understand that."

"Not really, but I'm glad you're back. And I can wait."

"Thank you."

They walked out into the bright sunshine and Caleb unlocked the Tahoe. As they sat in total silence, bubbles of memories floated in her head and quickly vanished. Desperately she tried to snatch them back but they disappeared into the blankness of her mind.

"Belle…Josie, are you okay?"

"I should know these people, but I don't. Flashes of Dennis pinning a badge on my shirt, of Eric smiling at me dart through my mind, but I can't connect them with any feelings. And don't say it will come," she said with a spurt of anger. "I'm tired of hearing that."

Caleb ran his hand over the steering wheel. "Do you feel up to paying the Becketts a visit?"

Her eyes clashed with his. "Nothing can stop me."

He started the engine with a smile. "Just wanted to make sure that fighting spirit was still intact."

"The memory loss gets to me, but I'll connect the dots and soon. You can count on that."

She wasn't looking forward to seeing the

people who'd driven her out of Beckett. That didn't keep her from going, though.

Nothing would.

CHAPTER SIX

TRAVELING DOWN a county road Caleb asked, "Do you remember any of this?" Miles and miles of barbed wire fences, mesquite, cacti and scrub oaks flashed by.

Her face softened. "The first day I came here I saw it all through my father's eyes. He said you either loved this land or you hated it. The dust gets in your hair, your clothes and coats your skin. The wind, you know by name. Some days you curse her and others you say a prayer for the cool breeze that gets you through the searing heat. The loneliness seeps into your soul and becomes a part of you. The vaqueros, the cowboys, are family and they'll die for you. Some people don't understand the pull, the mystique, of the land. Dad said you had to be born here to fully comprehend it." She took a breath. "As I looked at this land that goes on forever with a fascination I didn't understand, I could feel his presence and knew I was doing the right thing in visiting Silver Spur."

"And now?"

"I'm wishing for one of Lencha's spells." Her lips twitched.

He smiled and admired her sense of humor. After she'd recovered from her ordeal at the hands of the cult, that was one of the first things he'd discovered about her personality. She teased, joked and laughed and it was a wonderful thing to watch unfold.

Parking on the circular drive, he turned to her, "Ready?"

She nodded, gazing at the large hacienda and some vaqueros herding cattle in the distance. The first time she'd come here she'd been overwhelmed with emotions. Today was no different.

"Just be prepared for some nastiness from Lorna and Mason."

"Oh, I can handle a little nastiness. I might even retaliate with some of my own."

They walked up the sidewalk to the front door and the wind blew with an eerie calm. Caleb rang the doorbell. A maid opened the door.

"Miss Josie," she exclaimed, her hand against her chest. "Ya a sight for sore eyes."

"Thank you, Consuelo." She knew this woman, her name, but that was all. "Is my grandfather home?"

"In his den. He be so happy."

They followed Consuelo to the large room.

The whole family was gathered, having coffee. They didn't even pause the conversation when the door opened.

Josie glanced around the room at the animal heads, the animal rugs, the silver and leather and the sheer showiness. This room epitomized her grandfather. She'd thought that the first time she'd come here and she remembered that feeling of not belonging, of not being part of the Beckett family. She wondered if she'd felt differently later.

"You do something about that boy," Boone was saying to Mason. "He's starting to get under my skin with his arrogance."

"That's just Caddo. The vaqueros work well under him and he can tame a horse better than anyone I've ever seen with just his voice and his hands. He has an attitude, but he's invaluable on this ranch."

"No one's invaluable out here but me." Boone snorted. "And what's all that chanting and dancing in front of the vaqueros. He ain't no Indian. He's a damn half-breed Mexican."

Suddenly she knew who Caddo was and why they were friends, but she pushed it to the back of her mind, concentrating on the Becketts in front of her.

"Josie," Ashley shouted, finally noticing her. She sprinted across the room to Josie and hugged her.

"Well, I'll be a sonofabitch." Boone rose to his feet, his teeth clamped around a cigar. "Girlie, you got some explaining to do."

"Why did you bring her back here?" Lorna hissed, her eyes on Caleb.

Caleb calmly removed his hat. "Ms. Beckett, yesterday you asked if a crime had been committed and I didn't answer you. Now I can. Yes, a crime has been committed. Someone tried to kill Josie and I'm here to find out who."

Her eyes turned to a frosty green. "Are you saying that someone here would do such a thing?"

"You tell me, ma'am. From our conversation yesterday, you seemed to have a strong motive."

"You bastard, get out of this house." Lorna trembled visibly.

"Consuelo," Boone shouted so loud the chandelier shook.

Consuelo scurried in. *"Si, señor."*

"Take Mrs. Beckett upstairs and give her something to make her more mellow."

"Si, señor." Consuelo took Lorna's arm and tried to lead her from the room, but Lorna jerked away, confronting Josie.

"Why did you have to come back?" Lorna screamed. "You're not welcome here, but you're just like your mother clinging on when you're not wanted."

Familiar scents and sights were triggering Josie's memory and so many feelings swirled around her. But at Lorna's offensive voice, she disengaged from the past and stepped close, restraining herself from slapping her. "I'm never going away, Lorna, so get used to it. If you mention my mother again in that tone of voice, I will slap you."

"You bitch. You bitch," Lorna screeched and a Mexican man hurried into the room to help Consuelo. She jerked and fought, but they managed to control her.

"Mother, please," Ashley begged, following the trio out of the room.

"She's gettin' worse," Boone snapped. "Those doctors ain't helpin'."

"That's because she's continually confronted with the past." Mason's eyes centered on Josie.

She moved toward him, not backing down an inch. "Are you talking about me, Mason?"

"You know how she feels about you."

"Yes. I know how all the Becketts feel about me, and I came back for a reason. Sit down and I'll tell you a story."

No one moved or resumed their seats. In a calm, clear voice she told them the ordeal she'd been through. As she talked, Boone's cigar rolled from one end of his mouth to the other.

When she finished, Boone collapsed onto the sofa muttering, "Dammit. I thought you were just angry and stubborn like your father. I never dreamed you were in any kind of danger."

"She was," Caleb said. "Fry said there was a missing person's report filed, but nothing was in the system and the FBI and the Texas Rangers ran ads in all the big newspapers hoping someone could identify Josie." He twisted the rim of his hat. "Now I'm wondering why no one saw the ads."

Boone's eyes narrowed. "I read the Corpus and Houston papers and I never saw any ads."

"Sometimes you're away and the papers pile up and you don't go through them all," Mason pointed out.

"Yeah. I could've missed it."

"How could everyone miss it?" Caleb directed the question at Mason.

"Hell, man, I don't have time to read papers. I'm busy running this ranch."

Boone took a drag on the cigar. "What does Fry say about all this?"

"He's trying to find out what happened to the missing person's report."

"He'd better or his ass won't be worth squat around here." He glanced at Josie. "Girl, you don't remember nothin'?"

"My memory is slowly coming back. I remember planning to come out and visit with you, but everything after that is a blank." Her eyes met his. "I remember us arguing all the time about my father's body. Did you do anything while I was gone?"

He slowly removed the cigar from his mouth and she saw the tips of his fingers were brown from all the smoking. That was one of the first things she'd noticed about him that day in her parents' living room. That and his abrasive personality, so unlike her father's.

"Well, girlie, when I couldn't find you, I did what I thought was best for my son. His body now rests in the Beckett family cemetery."

The words were like a blow to her chest and she fought to breathe. "How could you? You knew how I felt about that. How could you separate him from my mother?"

"Marie Cortez took him away from his heritage."

"*You* took him away!" Josie shouted, feeling the tremors that shook her body. "With your controlling, manipulative ways! And I'll never forgive you for this. And I'll never rest until his body is back by my mother's."

Boone stood, his eyes hard and unyielding. "I don't need your forgiveness, girlie, nor do I ask for it. Brett's body is in the family plot south of the house if you want to visit it. Your choice."

"You…you…" Words choked her at his blatant arrogance, then she realized they'd be wasted on him anyway. She swung around and ran from the room.

Caleb stared directly at Boone. "This isn't over. I'll be back later for a statement from everyone in this house. I'll keep digging until I find out what really happened here that day."

"Don't give me orders, ranger man."

Caleb didn't blink, his eyes never leaving Boone's face. "We can bounce insults off each other all day, Mr. Beckett, but you can rest assured I will be back and I'll get answers. I would expect, for your granddaughter, that you would want them, too."

Boone shoved the cigar back into his mouth. "Ranger man, once you get to know me you'll be surprised how offensive and nice I can be all at the same time."

"Looking forward to it." Caleb placed his hat on his head. "Mason," he acknowledged, walking out.

CALEB HURRIED to his vehicle. Josie was inside, crying, and his heart wrenched. He knew how much she wanted her parents' bodies to stay together.

He gave her a few minutes, then asked, "What do you want to do?"

She brushed tears away with the back of her

hand. "I have to see his grave. I don't want to, but I need to feel my father's presence."

He started the engine. "Exactly where is this cemetery?"

"Take a right at the end of the drive." Caleb followed her instruction. "Now a left." And there it was enclosed with an eight-foot wrought-iron fence. The big double gates had the Silver Spur logo on it and Beckett in large letters. He parked in front and they got out.

To the left was a small country church. Caleb stared at the white clapboard building with a steeple. A wrought-iron fence also enclosed it and the yard was neatly maintained, with no weeds or cactus inside the fence. Several bushes were planted at the entrance.

"Boone's great-grandfather built the church so the vaqueros could have a place to worship. Now they go to the large Catholic Church in town," Josie explained.

"It's well taken care of," Caleb commented.

"A little piece of Beckett history."

"Mmm." After opening the gate, he sensed her disquiet and looked into her troubled eyes. "Are you okay?"

"No. I don't think I can handle this."

He reached for her hand and closed his fingers around hers. She trembled and at that moment

Caleb wanted to strangle Boone Beckett. Josie had been through enough and she didn't need to see her father separated from her mother.

"Do you just want to leave?" He thought he'd give her that choice.

Her chin jutted out. "No." All the survival instincts he'd witnessed in her since he'd known her were in full force.

Together they walked into the cemetery.

Some of the tombstones were old, dating back to the 1800s, and there were rows and rows of them. "Obviously Becketts have been here for a long time."

"Right after God created earth." The tears in her eyes glistened with humor and he knew she was going to be okay.

"Do you have any idea where it would be?"

"No. We just have to look."

"I'll take this side."

"Okay," she replied. "I'll search in this area."

Caleb walked about twenty feet when he saw it. He blinked and looked at it again. "Josie, over here," he called, not quite understanding what he was seeing.

Josie just stood there, not moving.

"It's okay. Come look."

She shook her head. "I don't think I need to."

She gazed at him across the cemetery and

something in his eyes pulled her forward. He met her halfway and took her hand again, leading her to the grave.

When he stopped, she stared at the tombstone, her eyes opening wide. "Oh my God!" Her fingers trembled against her lips. It was a double head-stone. On one side was written Brett Boone Beckett. On the other was inscribed Marie Cortez Beckett. Boone had both their bodies moved! "Why didn't he tell me? Why would he let me believe…?"

A pickup roared toward them, dust spiraling behind it.

"You can ask the man himself," Caleb said, blinking against the bright sun.

Boone climbed out of the Chevy diesel truck, the sun glinting off his silver belt buckle. He settled a big Stetson on his head and ambled toward them.

Josie took a long breath. "Do you enjoy up-setting me?"

Boone chewed on his cigar. "Maybe. Reminds me of your father."

Josie knew she would never understand this man or his motives, but she was very grateful. "Thank you," she said simply, then asked, "Why did you do it?"

Boone shrugged. "I don't need to explain, girlie. It's done."

"Why couldn't you tell me?"

"Sometimes it's more fun that way. And to set the record straight, no one at Silver Spur tried to kill you."

"How do you know that?" Caleb asked.

"Because if they did, they would be disinherited and no Beckett would risk that."

"Maybe they thought they wouldn't get caught."

"Chickens have a way of coming home to roost, ranger man. Just like the truth." He looked at Josie. "You've been through a bad spell, girl, and if there's any shady dealings going on in Beckett or on the Silver Spur, I'll get to the bottom of it. Close the gate when you leave." He ambled back to his truck.

No explanation. Nothing. That was Boone Beckett, and Josie realized, not for the first time, how difficult it must have been to have him as a father. She glanced at the graves, side by side, as her parents were in life.

She touched the granite stones. "They're together." Unable to stop herself, she threw her arms around Caleb and hugged him. "They're together."

"Yes," he murmured, holding her close against the outline of his hard body. Unashamed, she pressed even closer, loving the way her heart raced at the masculine contact. His musky aftershave filled her nostrils and she breathed in the scent with a sigh of pleasure. His soothing voice and compassionate nature warmed her through and through. He was her haven, her one-of-a-kind man and she wanted to lay her head on his shoulder and let the world slip away. But that was her fantasy world. Reality was waiting.

JOSIE WAS QUIET on the way into town and Caleb left her alone with her thoughts. The past and the present raged inside her and she had to sort through all those conflicting feelings. When he held her, though, none of that seemed to matter. But it did and he had to remember that. He had to remain detached, an outsider, giving her the freedom she needed to accept her life without any encumbrance holding her back. That wasn't going to be easy.

They stopped by the police station and picked up the files. Raylene had them ready, all sorted in a box. Josie didn't get out and Caleb knew the morning had been hard on her.

As he pulled into Lencha's drive, she said, "I think I'll go through the files this afternoon to see if anything jogs my memory."

"I'll go back to the police station to see if I can find out anything. Fry should know by now what happened to the report."

Josie stared straight ahead to the vacant spot in the garage. "Wonder where my car is? Did I drive away in it or…?"

"I'm sure we'll know in the next few days."

"Yeah," she answered in a faraway voice.

That note in her voice twisted his gut. "Bel... Josie."

"I'm fine, Caleb." She opened the door and got out, then retrieved the box from the backseat.

He immediately got out to help her.

She gave him a sharp glance. "It's a box, Caleb. I can carry it."

He frowned. "Are you angry with me?"

"No. Yes." She started toward the house.

He caught up with her. "What does that mean?"

She turned to confront him. "You're too nice, do you know that?" Her eyes flared with the emotions she was feeling. "Be rude, insulting, uncaring or I'm never going to be able to let you go." Saying that she ran into the house, clutching the box.

He gazed after her with his mouth open, then he quickly clamped it shut. Where did that come from? She'd been so affectionate in the cemetery and now... God, what was he doing? He'd given his word to Dr. Oliver that he wouldn't do anything to impede her memory and he'd held her like a lover, not a friend. Damn. Damn. Damn.

His first instinct was to go after her—which is what a nice guy would do. But he had to start detaching himself. He would now.

JOSIE CHARGED INTO the house, slammed the box on the table and flopped into a chair. What was she doing? Caleb didn't need to know how she felt. It would serve no purpose at all. Her emotions were slipping and sliding like a bar of soap on a wet tiled floor.

"Hello to you, too."

She heard Lencha's voice and looked up to see her standing by the sink, a frown on her weathered face.

"Sorry. I'm so mixed up inside that it's making me crazy."

"I'll fix you one of my feel-good tonics."

"The last time you fixed me one of those I had a headache for three days."

"That was the night you got engaged to Eric."

"Was it?" Josie glanced at her ring finger and wondered what had happened to her engagement ring. The cult had probably hocked it cause she never remembered seeing it after she woke up. Through the troubled thoughts she saw Eric smiling, his blue eyes sparkling as bright as the diamond and…just like that the image was gone.

She shifted uneasily. "Lencha, did you know that Boone had both my parents bodies moved to the Silver Spur cemetery?"

"Yes, child, I know." Lencha wiped her hands on a towel and came to the table.

"Why didn't you tell me?"

"You needed to find that out on your own." Lencha stroked her hair. "And I was unsure of what to tell you or not to tell you."

Josie leaned against her, knowing she was right. She had to recover her memory without props. "It's a wonderful thing Boone did."

"Don't get too carried away with gratitude. I'm sure the old buzzard has an ulterior motive."

Josie sighed and grabbed the box. "I'll be in my room for a while."

"Sure you don't want a tonic?"

"No, thanks, Lencha. I just need some time." Time to remember. Time to forget. And time to make sense of it all.

As CALEB DROVE UP to the police station, Mason stormed out and climbed into a truck and sped away, tires squealing. Caleb stared after the truck. Evidently something hadn't gone to Mason's liking and Caleb intended to find out what.

Raylene wasn't at her desk, so he walked into the larger room. The place was empty, except for Teri. She sat at a desk and her eyes were red as if she'd been crying.

He removed his hat and sat across from her. "Afternoon, ma'am," he said.

"Ranger McCain," she acknowledged and quickly sorted through papers on her desk.

Before he could speak, she added, "If you're here to grill me, you can save your breath." Her hands shook and she finally put them in her lap.

He leaned forward slightly. "Do you know what happened to Josie?"

"Yes." She looked away through the lone window with bars to the clear day. "Eric told me."

"And you're nervous and worried. You can't hide it."

She closed her eyes briefly. "I didn't think I was doing anything wrong."

"What did you do?"

She opened her eyes. "I didn't file the report like Dennis asked me to."

"Why?"

"Lencha's half-crazy and Josie had told Eric she was leaving and never coming back. She told Dennis the same thing. She wasn't a missing person or, at least, I didn't think so at the time. She left of her own free will."

"You didn't have the right to make that decision." He tried hard not to grit his teeth at this woman's arrogance and he felt there was more to the story.

"I know, and I'm sorry. I had no idea someone tried to kill her."

Caleb studied his hat, then looked directly at her. "You didn't make that decision alone. Someone asked you not to report Josie missing, didn't they?"

"No." She looked away. "It was my decision."

"Do you think I'm gullible, Ms. Fields?"

Her head jerked toward him.

"Then why didn't you file that report?" His voice was loud and she flinched.

"I told you."

"And you're lying." The tone of his voice didn't change. She was protecting someone and he knew it. Now he had to get her to admit who.

"Please. I take full responsibility."

"Are you willing to go to jail?"

She licked her lips. "I…I…"

"Did Eric ask you not to file the report?"

Her eyes flared. "Of course not. He wanted her found more than anybody."

"How about Mason Beckett, Ms. Fields?"

"What?" That fear in her eyes gave her away. She was protecting Mason.

"Did Mason ask you not to file the missing person's report?"

"What the hell?" Eric stood in the doorway. "You didn't file the damn report?"

Teri got to her feet. "Now, Eric, don't get angry."

Caleb stood, also, seeing that Eric was close to losing it.

Eric jammed a hand through his hair. "Why the

hell would you do that?" Then he nodded his head in realization. "Mason's been stringing you along like his own personal whore and you'd do anything he wanted just hoping that someday he'd marry you."

"It wasn't like that," Teri cried. "Josie was causing so many problems in the Beckett family and she left voluntarily. You even said that…and…Mason thought it best to keep it that way."

Eric grabbed her arm and jerked her forward. "You stupid bitch. Every day I waited for news and you hadn't even put her name in the national database of missing persons. You stupid bitch. I could strangle you with my bare hands."

Caleb pulled Eric away. "Calm down."

"Stay out of this, McCain," Eric warned, jerking away.

The two men eyed each other. "Listen, I was there when they brought Josie to the hospital and I've been with her ever since. I have enough anger to go around, but anger doesn't solve anything." Caleb glanced at Teri. "She's only a pawn. I'm after the person who did the shooting. The law will take care of Ms. Fields."

Teri moaned.

"What's going on?" Dennis asked as he walked in.

Caleb gave him the gist of the story.

"Goddammit. In my office," Dennis said to Teri.

Eric swung away, then whirled back. "I'm sorry I lost it."

"It's okay. I've done that, too."

"I keep thinking this all could have been avoided."

Caleb placed his hat on his head. "The person who shot Josie left her for dead, thought she was dead. Not sure that could have been avoided, but we could have placed her with her family a year ago."

And I never would've gotten to know her.

"Please, see if you can get her to talk to me," Eric pleaded.

Caleb nodded. "I'll try. She's feeling her way right now so be patient with her." He looked at Fry's door. "Tell the chief I'll be back later."

He walked away with a sense of guilt and dread. He didn't feel so nice at that moment. He felt jealous that Josie had once loved Eric and when her memory returned she would again.

How did a nice guy accept that?

With a lot of pain.

CHAPTER SEVEN

SITTING CROSS-LEGGED on the bed, the files scattered around her, Josie read through each one. Faces and events flashed in her mind. Theft case. Billy Bob Eastep reported his truck missing, stolen right out of his yard. After a day of searching, she found Billy Junior had taken the vehicle for a joyride with friends to Corpus. Breaking-and-entering case. Louann Krump said someone was breaking into her house. It took a week of stakeouts to discover that Louann's daughter's boyfriend was climbing through the window to visit. She could see many of these people's faces clearly and remembered details about each case.

Josie threaded her fingers through her hair and picked up another file. Cattle rustling case. Cattle were disappearing from some of the smaller ranches. She and Eric spent a month camped out on lonely dirt roads, waiting. Finally they caught the Wilby brothers red-handed.

Those nights were long, but they had ways to pass the time. They…she grabbed her head to stop the memories. For the first time she didn't want to remember, but the past and Eric were there…just waiting. Why was she so afraid?

WHEN CALEB WALKED into the kitchen, a sharp smell greeted him. Lencha stood at the stove, stirring something in a big pot. Her long gray hair hung down her back. He had visions of witches and brews from stories he'd read as a kid.

"What's that smell?"

Lencha turned to look at him. "A friend of mine has diabetes and I'm making her a batch of my homemade cure."

Caleb peeked into the pot. "What is it?

"I don't give away my secrets," Lencha told him. "Since you're Josie's friend, I'll tell you the basics—boiling the leaves of the cacti with a few secret ingredients."

He shook his head. "You're a wonder, Lencha."

"Been called worse." Her gray eyes narrowed on him. "And in case you're thinking it, Ranger. I'm not a *bruja*. I just know some secrets passed down from my ancestors. In the old days, there were no doctors out here. My great-grandmother was a healer and I help people when I can. Still not a clinic here. Big Boone tried to set one up and is still trying to work something out with a doctor in Corpus. The old *bastardo* will get a cut of the profits would be my guess. Now people either go to Corpus or Laredo, the rest look me up."

"They're lucky to have you."

"The Mexicans trust me."

"I do, too, Lencha." He grinned. "And I never thought you were a witch."

The corner of her mouth twitched.

"But you could probably scare the crap out of me with very little effort."

Lencha chuckled. "That's what it's about—the power of the mind. If a person believes I can help them, I usually can. Skepticism and negativity kills just about everything, even good health."

"As I said, Lencha, you're a wonder, and you can doctor on me anytime."

Silence followed and Caleb thought about the newspaper ads about Belle that had run in all the big newspapers. This had been at the back of his mind since their visit to the Silver Spur. How could everyone have missed it? He had a copy of the ad in his briefcase and he hurried outside to get it.

"Lencha, I have something I want you to see."

"Sure." She walked to the table and he laid the paper in front of her.

"Do you know that woman?"

Lencha peered at the photo. "No. Should I?"

"That's Josie. We ran the ad soon after she was rescued from the cult."

"That's not my Josie."

He looked closely at the picture. Josie's hair hung limply around her face. Her eyes were sunk in her head and her features were slim, almost anorexic. That's how she'd looked then and staring at the photo he suddenly knew why no one recognized her. It didn't look like the real Josie. At the time, they didn't realize she was a shell of her former self. But it explained why no one answered the ads.

"This is how Josie looked when they found her?" Lencha asked.

"Yes," Caleb replied.

Lencha touched the photo. "My poor child."

Caleb patted her shoulder. "She's fine now." He looked around. "Where is Josie?"

"In her room going through those files."

Caleb picked up the paper, strolled down the hall and stopped in Josie's doorway.

Sitting in the middle of the bed, her dark hair hanging loose, she looked as beautiful and mysterious as the first day he'd met her. And her face was troubled just as it had been then. As traumatized as she was, he still recognized her real beauty.

Files were scattered around her and he knew what must be bothering her. He stepped in. "Hi. How's it going?"

She looked up and for a moment he was lost in the darkness of her eyes, that come-hither warmth that seemed to be a part of her. "Good and bad," she replied. "I'm remembering, but not anything about that night."

He moved a couple of files and sat on the edge of the bed. Placing his hat beside him, he turned to face her. "I figured out why no one answered the ads about you."

"Why?"

He placed the photo in front of her.

"Yikes. That doesn't look like me."

"At the time it did." He hadn't looked at the photo in a while and he never realized how much she'd changed in the last year. No wonder no one recognized her—not even her family.

She studied the picture. "I look…"

"Traumatized."

"Yes." She wrapped her arms around her waist and he knew she was forcing herself not to think back to that time, right after she'd been rescued.

"Did you find out anything at the police station?" she asked, as if she needed to get her mind on something else.

Dr. Oliver said she could handle things and Caleb didn't want to keep anything from her. He told her about Teri, the missing persons report and Mason.

Her brow knotted together. "Yes. Teri was seeing

Mason." She pushed back her long hair. "He has this bad-boy image that some women seem to like. When he was nineteen, he killed a man in Laredo in a bar fight. Had to spend some time in prison before Boone could get him released. Ever since, he's been meaner and wilder than ever. He's well-known among the female population around here and a few husbands have tried to kill him." She paused. "But why would he not want me found? Especially if Lorna and I had this big argument and I said I wasn't coming back."

"A lot of this doesn't make sense."

She frowned. "I wish I could remember that night."

"It was probably traumatic and you're still blocking it."

"I suppose," she mumbled in a faraway voice.

A plate with a single slice of chocolate quesadilla sat beside her. "You're finishing the quesadilla?" he asked to change the subject.

A smile rippled over her lips and she picked up the slice. "Want a bite?"

"No. I…" She held the piece to his lips and his heart accelerated to an alarming speed at the light in her eyes. He took a bite without a second thought. She then took a bite and there was something sensual about her eating after him. Even the way she chewed was sensual; his eyes were fascinated by the movement of her mouth and throat. He knew at that moment that his feelings for Josie were going to be very hard to control.

She licked her lips. "You have chocolate on the corner of your mouth."

He ran his tongue around his mouth.

She shook her head. "No. Still there." She licked her forefinger and wiped the corner of his mouth, removing the chocolate.

Her touch was wet, warm and as sensual as anything he'd ever experienced. When she put the finger in her mouth to taste the chocolate from his lips, he knew he had to kiss her, to taste her sweetness. Nothing else mattered at that moment. He didn't even hear a warning. He leaned forward and she met him halfway.

Before their lips could touch, an earth-shattering chant ripped through the house. "Ah ye, ah ye, ah ye, ah yeeee, Josie Marieee!"

"Caddo," Josie cried and jumped off the bed, running for the back door.

Caleb followed more slowly, getting his emotions under control.

"Loco," Lencha muttered, looking out the window as Caleb entered the kitchen.

He joined her and saw a man somewhere in his early thirties astride a brown-and-white paint stud. In tattered jeans and worn boots, his shirt was unbuttoned revealing a bronzed chest. His head was bare and his long dark hair hung around his face. Riding bareback, he circled in the pasture chanting, "Ah ye, ah ye, ah ye, Josie Marieee!"

"Who is he?" Caleb asked, his curiosity getting the best of him. But he knew this had to be the man Boone was talking about—the half-breed.

"The spawn of the devil." Lencha clucked her tongue and went back to stirring the pot.

"What do you mean?"

"Go outside and meet him and you'll understand." Lencha didn't even turn around.

Josie flew through the gate and Caleb watched as Caddo trotted forward and held out his hand. She placed hers in his and he pulled her up behind him and they galloped away into the endless land, plumes of dust obscuring them from view.

Walking outside and shooing chickens away, Caleb wasn't worried, just curious. Who was Caddo? Spawn of the devil. That didn't tell him a whole lot. But obviously he was someone Josie trusted. Another step in completing her memory, in finding herself, her true personality. He didn't expect this to be easy, but he never realized how deeply he'd come to love Belle. Damn. Josie. She was Josie Marie. When he finally accepted that, he could go on with his life.

He leaned his forearms on the board fence,

waiting. Soon he saw the dust and the horse and riders racing for the house. Caddo pulled up short and Josie slipped to the ground, her hair in disarray, her eyes shining. Swinging his leg over, Caddo jumped to the ground without making a sound.

The first thing Caleb noticed was that he was tall and his skin was browned by the sun, not race.

"Caleb, this is Caddo, my friend," Josie introduced them.

Caddo shook his hand with fingers like steel—callused steel. Caddo was used to work, that was evident. As Caddo looked directly into Caleb's eyes, Caleb received a jolt. He had startling blue eyes. *Beckett eyes*. It was no question that Caddo was a Beckett and as Caleb studied him he knew who Caddo's father was. Mason. Caddo looked just like him, except for the darker hair.

"Josie Marie says you lawman, Ranger."

"Yes."

"You find *bastardo* who tried to kill Josie Marie and Caddo'll string him up for the coyotes to feast on."

The man didn't smile or flinch. He was dead-serious.

"The law will take care of him."

Caddo reached for the horse's mane and swung onto his back. "Law out here means squat. Only Boone Beckett's law." The horse pranced around, ready to run. Caddo patted his neck with a gentle hand. "Ranger, Caddo make his own kind of law." He nodded to Josie, kneeing the horse. *"Adiós, prima."* Then he was gone.

Josie raked her fingers through the long tresses, trying to straighten her hair. She sank onto a bench by the garage.

"So that's Caddo," he said, easing down by her. "Obviously you remember him."

"Yes." Her eyes followed the dust. "I met him the first day I came here. I had a flat and while I was fixing it, he jumped the fence on his horse and scared me to death. I didn't know if he was going to murder me, rape me or what, and my gun was in the car. I soon found Caddo was a gentle yet different type of person. When he rode away, he said, *'Adiós, prima.'* I knew that meant cousin, but I didn't know why he thought we were related. Then I met the Becketts."

"It's uncanny how much he looks like Mason."

She lifted an eyebrow. "You noticed, huh?"

"Yep."

"Everybody sees it, but Boone. All he sees is the Mexican part."

"What is Caddo's story?"

"When Mason got out of prison, he was wilder and meaner than ever, but he was like a magnet to women, as I already told you. Caddo's mother,

Theresa, was no exception. She was eighteen, very pretty, and married to a man in his forties. Her family worked on the Silver Spur, as did her husband. When Mason set eyes on her, that was it. They had an affair and when Caddo was born with those blue eyes, her husband left her and the Silver Spur. Theresa died in childbirth when Caddo was five."

There was silence for a moment. "I'm guessing Mason was the father of the child."

"Lencha said Theresa never saw anyone else. After her death, Caddo lived from family to family, but basically he's been on his own since then. The Becketts provide him a house and he rarely stays there. He lives out on the prairie with the elements and the animals. No one ever made him go to school all that much so he has very little education."

"Does Mason claim him?"

The eyebrow lifted again. "What do you think?"

"I think not."

"You got it, but Mason marked Caddo for the world to see."

Spellbound, Caleb watched the chickens scratch in the grass. For the first time he wondered if he looked like Joe McCain. Could people tell by looking at him that he was Joe's son? Althea had said many times that he and Jake were lean and lanky like Joe. But what about the face? He had his mother's brown eyes, but the angles and planes of his features were not hers. He'd never thought about it before and he had to admit he probably did favor his father. That was a sobering thought. He didn't want anything from Joe McCain—not even his DNA. And he was betting Caddo didn't want anything from his father, either.

"Does Caddo know that Mason is his father?"

"Caddo knows everything and he pushes Mason's buttons any way he can, just daring Mason to fire him or force him off the Silver Spur. Mason never crosses him and pretty much gives him free rein. Because if there is anyone wilder and meaner than Mason, it's Caddo."

"That's why Mason was taking up for Caddo this morning?"

"Yes. Mason doesn't want Boone to find out about Caddo's paternity. He fears he'll be disinherited, so it all remains a secret—to Boone."

"Boone has to be deaf, dumb and blind not to know."

"Or he chooses to ignore it."

Caleb leaned forward, his elbows on his knees, his hands clasped. "I'm trying to figure out what this has to do with you."

"Me, too. I've remembered almost everything, except that night."

He turned his head to look at her. "And Eric."

She looked away. "And Eric."

Caleb took a breath, not wanting to talk about this, but also knowing he had to do what was best for her. "Eric was very upset about what Teri had done and he asked me to try and get you to talk to him." He paused. "Why won't you?"

Raising her arms, she gathered her hair in both hands and looped it over her shoulder. "You want me to be honest?"

"Nothing else."

Her eyes held his. "Because…when I remember Eric, my feelings for you will change." She swallowed visibly. "And that's what has kept me going for the last year, kept me sane and kept me focused."

When she said honest, she meant gut-wrenching honesty. A part of him reveled in her answer, the other part knew it was wrong. They couldn't cling to something that wasn't meant to be.

"That's what you meant about me being nice."

"Yes. You've been my haven and I'm not sure I can give you up."

Being nice was hell. Now he had to do what he'd just told himself—what was right for her. "Let yourself remember, Josie. You don't need me anymore."

"I wish it was that easy," she murmured, then jumped up and sprinted into the house.

He sucked air into his lungs. No, it wasn't going to be easy, and whatever happened he was never going to be the same again. He thought of leaving, but he couldn't do that until Josie was safe. Eric could take over, but he had started this and he had to finish it. No matter how painful it was to him.

The sun began to slowly sink into the western sky, dimming the horizon for a second in a kaleidoscope of reds, oranges and yellows. Breathtaking. He could feel the allure, the mystery of wide-open spaces and the pull of something he couldn't define or explain. And he was getting in too deep to think straight.

He slowly stood and made his way to the house.

THEIR SUPPER WAS SOMETHING Caleb had never eaten before, but it was tasty and he ate it. Mainly because Josie was eating it. As Lencha took *Chula* outside and he helped to clear the table, he said, "I'm not even asking what that was."

She grinned. "Just be thankful it wasn't pig feet, calf tongue or *menudo*."

He set his plate in the sink. "Lencha is a very unusual person. She told me she's not a *bruja*."

"She doesn't like to be called that, but she knows a lot of the rituals. All the Mexicans trust her and her healing methods. Some of the white folks, too. She's helped raise a lot of children, including

Caddo and me. She has six of her own scattered across the country. When you grow up on the Silver Spur, you either love it or yearn for freedom. Lencha made sure all her children chose freedom."

He leaned against the cabinet. "So Lencha raised your mother?"

"My grandfather, Rafael, was the foreman of Silver Spur under Boone's daddy, Enos. Rafael traveled a lot with him to choose cattle appropriate for Silver Spur. On a trip to a large ranch in South America, Rafael fell in love with the rancher's daughter, Joscelyn."

"That's who you're named after?"

"Yes. And my mother."

"So they married?"

"Yes, and he brought her to Texas, but she was never happy here. She loved Rafael, but she missed her home, her family. She lost a little boy a year younger than my mother. He fell off his horse and cattle trampled him before my grandfather could reach him. He was only three and Lencha said Joscelyn grieved herself to death."

Josie wiped the table with a dishcloth. "She died when Marie was six and Lencha and her family lived next door. My mother lived with my grandfather and cooked and cleaned the house, but Lencha kept an eye on her, helping her. Lencha hoped that one day Marie would marry one of her sons, but when Marie was fourteen she started working in the summertime in the Beckett house. Once she and Brett looked at each other, that was it. There never was another man for her."

He folded his arms. "Did Marie have healing powers like Lencha?"

She gave a slight smile. "No, nor did she want to. She left the Silver Spur, trying to put her Mexican heritage behind her. She worked as a maid during the day and took night courses at a junior college to better herself. When my father joined her in Corpus, it was the happiest day of her life. She tried to get him to go back to face his responsibilities, but he refused. He…" Her brow wrinkled in thought. "There's a reason he wouldn't. I know there is, but I can't remember."

Caleb moved toward her, hating to see her go through all this. A knock at the door stopped him.

Seeing her distress, he said, "I'll get it."

Ashley stood on the doorstep. "May I speak with Josie, please?" she asked.

Before Caleb could decide if this was wise, Josie said from behind him. "Come in, Ashley."

Caleb stepped aside and Ashley walked in. "I just wanted to let you know that I don't feel the same way as my mother."

"Have a seat." Josie gestured toward the sofa and the sisters sat down side by side. Caleb took the overstuffed chair, watching them. Two sisters as different as night and day—one dark, the other light.

"My mother has a hard time dealing with the past," Ashley said. "She's never gotten over my father's betrayal and in the past few years it seems to have gotten worse."

Father's betrayal. The phrase rolled around in Josie's head but it didn't sound right—didn't sound like the father she was remembering.

At Josie's silence, Ashley touched her arm. "Josie, you're not the cause of the past and neither am I."

Josie nodded. "We're just the results of it."

"When you first came here, I tried to hate you because you had Brett as a father and I didn't. But as soon as we met there didn't seem to be any hate at all, just a curiosity about each other."

"We talked a lot about Brett Beckett," Josie replied, suddenly all those talks coming back. Though she remembered something still didn't feel right.

"I'd never met him. I'd just seen him in photos, but everyone told me I had his eyes."

"Yes." Ashley had the Beckett blue eyes. That didn't bother Josie. She had the eyes of her Mexican ancestry and the love of her father.

"I hope we can still be friends."

"Me, too." Josie tucked her hair behind her ear. "Right now I'm struggling to remember what happened to me. Once that happens, I'm not sure what my life will be like."

And that's what she was afraid of. Josie suddenly recognized the truth. Something in her life had been so horrible and it was safer to suppress it—safer to cling to Caleb and his security. But she was stronger now and she could face her past.

Ashley touched her arm again. "I'm so sorry for all you've been through. I could never survive anything like that. You're so strong. I wish I were more like you."

Josie remembered that Ashley was completely controlled by her mother and Boone. She went away to boarding school at an early age and spent a lot of time in Europe. At thirty-two, she was the most shy and insecure person Josie had ever met, especially when she was at home on the Silver Spur around the Becketts.

Josie gave a small smile. "Still trying to have a life of your own?"

"Yes." Ashley grimaced. "I planned to spend the summer in Switzerland with a friend, but Pa is insisting that I marry and settle down. I don't love Richard Wentworth, but he's wealthy and has clout in Austin. Pa says I need to learn to use power because the Silver Spur will be mine one day and I have to think about my heritage." Her cheeks flushed as she'd realized what she'd said. "I didn't mean to offend you."

"No offense taken. I have no interest in Silver Spur," Josie told her. "And I'll tell you the same thing I told you before. Until you stand up for what you want, you'll always be under Boone's thumb."

"I wish I had your strength."

"When you want something bad enough, you'll find the strength."

The truth of those words echoed in Josie's mind. *She wanted her own life back.*

"Like my father," Ashley whispered.

"Yes, like our father," Josie corrected.

There was a moment of awkward silence, then Ashley stood. "I'm glad you're home and safe."

"Thank you."

Ashley walked out and Josie stared at Caleb. "Something's not right."

Caleb moved to sit by her. "What? You doubt her sincerity?"

"I don't think so. I don't have bad feelings toward her. It's what she says that makes me uncomfortable."

"It probably has to do with your father."

"Yes. I'm sure it does." But Josie wasn't sure. What was it that bothered her about Ashley?

Before she could add anything, there was a knock at the door again. Caleb got up to answer it.

"Eric," he said in surprise.

"I'd like to speak with Josie."

Josie's first instinct was to go to her room, but she couldn't keep avoiding this conversation. She had to talk to Eric, her fiancé.

"Come in," she called, and Caleb opened the door wider.

Eric hurried to her side. "Josie, I'm so sorry for what Teri did. I just keep thinking I should have double-checked to make sure it was done. I feel it's all my fault."

"I think I'll check on Lencha," Caleb said, heading for the back door. "She's been outside for a while."

Josie couldn't have loved him more at that moment, but he didn't have to leave. Nothing was going to be said that he couldn't hear. She had to start to break those ties, though.

"It's not your fault," she told Eric as Caleb left. "That wouldn't have stopped me from getting shot. Someone wanted me dead."

"I can't believe that." He sat by her and she was comforted by his nearness. She didn't even have the urge to move away.

She pulled back her hair to show him where the bullet had gone in—a small spot on the left near the temple where her hair would never grow again.

"Oh God!"

"I'm very lucky to be alive. They said it was a .22 caliber pistol and the shot was fired from a distance. That's the only reason I'm probably still alive."

"Oh, Josie."

She stared at his handsome face and tried to force the memories, their love, to the surface. But that blank void was still there. Letting go of Caleb was going to be harder than she'd ever imagined.

Eric watched her. "You still don't remember me, do you?"

"I'm remembering bits and pieces. It's like a puzzle and soon I'll have the full picture."

"I'll be here and I'll give you all the time you need."

"Thank you." She twisted a strand of her hair. "Do you remember any missing person's report I was working on? Lencha said I was excited about finding a girl who was missing."

"No. I'd been gone two weeks and had just gotten back into town. My father broke his ankle and I went home to Three Rivers to help out. We talked several times, but you never mentioned a missing girl."

"What did we talk about?"

"Mostly about setting a wedding date."

"Did we?"

"No." He sighed. "You were still battling with Boone over moving your father's body and you didn't want to get married under those circumstances."

She flung her hair back to keep from fiddling with it. "He had both bodies moved while I was gone."

"I know. I hope you're pleased about that."

"Yes. They were both born on the Silver Spur and that's where they should rest, but I couldn't move one without the other."

"I understand." His hand reached out to touch her, but suddenly he pulled it back and she was glad. They were talking in an easy, comforting way that was familiar. She wasn't ready for anything else.

He reached into his pocket and pulled out several chocolate kisses. She stared at the wrapped chocolate and remembered. Smiling, she took one and unwrapped it.

"You used to bring me candy kisses."

"Yes." His voice was excited. "And you kept them in your desk drawer."

"My chocolate fix during the day."

"You're remembering."

"Slowly, yes, just give me some time." Wonderful memories were filling her head bit by bit, but a big chunk was still missing.

"Like I said, I'll be here."

"Thank you, and thanks for the candy."

Eric left soon after and she got ready for bed. Caleb didn't ask anything about Eric and she could feel a bit of distance between them.

Let yourself remember, you don't need me anymore.

How she wished that was true—that letting go would be easy. But she'd spent the last year with the most incredible man and a part of her was always going to need him. Was it possible to love two men and someone not get hurt? Even she knew that answer was no. She just didn't want that person to be Caleb. But how could itnot be?

CALEB LET THE WOMEN have the bathroom first. He made a call to check in with his office and talked to Tuck for a few minutes. Then he called Beau to let him know he wasn't coming home just yet. His brother would tell the rest of the family.

Removing his gun from his belt, he laid it on the dresser. He unbuttoned his shirt and sat down to take off his boots. Josie had been quiet after Eric had left and he didn't question her. She didn't need that kind of pressure. Her memory was returning and soon all the pieces would fall into place. And he would return home alone.

That's the way it had to be.

As he yanked his shirt out of his jeans, the sound

of a gun firing echoed through the house. In a split second, his gun was in his hand. His one thought was to protect Josie.

CHAPTER EIGHT

HE FLUNG HIS DOOR OPEN at the same time that Josie opened hers. She held a gun in her hand and all she had on was a T-shirt.

"What happened?" he asked.

"Someone fired a shot through my window. I'll check the front, you get the back."

Clearly she didn't need protecting. She'd shifted into her officer's training in a heartbeat.

"What the…" Lencha came out of her room, her gray hair as wild as her eyes.

"Stay in your room," Josie shouted. "And away from the window."

Josie ran down the hall, dropped to the floor and crawled to the door so as not to be seen through the window. Caleb headed for the back door. In a few minutes they met back in the kitchen.

"Anything?" she asked. Her voice was different. Eager. Excited. It held no fear at all.

"Nothing," he told her. "Everything's quiet, except I could hear *Chula* in a tree."

She charged down the hall to her room. They both stared at the mess. The bullet had come through the window facing the road. Shattered glass lay on the hardwood floor.

Josie placed her gun on the nightstand. "I was getting ready for bed when the glass exploded and the bullet whizzed right past me. The bullet is probably lodged in this wall."

Caleb caught her arm as she started toward the wall. "Josie?"

"What?" She looked at him.

"You're…you're very calm."

She blinked. "I'm a police officer. I've been trained to do this and for the first time it feels right. Adrenaline is pumping through my veins. This is what I do."

"Someone just tried to kill you—again." He hated to point that out, but he wanted her to be careful.

"Yes. This person has now made a move and next time I will be ready."

"Please be careful."

"I intend to and I intend to nail this bastard."

He watched her closely. "Have you remembered anything else?"

"No. But I'm not afraid anymore."

He could see that. Her eyes were as bright as he'd ever seen them and he became acutely aware that all she had on was a T-shirt. And he wore only his jeans.

But Josie's mind was clearly on the business at hand. She yanked up the phone and called Eric.

"I'll get dressed," he said.

"Oh." She glanced down at herself. "Guess I better do the same."

"Coast clear?" Lencha peeped out her door, a shotgun in her hand.

"Yes," Josie answered. "I reported the shooting so Eric is on his way over."

"I'll put on the coffeepot."

Caleb barely finished dressing when he heard Eric's voice. They dug the bullet out of the wall and Eric put it in a plastic bag to send to the lab. The shooter was getting nervous. Making mistakes.

Caleb and Eric cleaned up the glass and taped plastic around the window until it could be fixed. Lencha went to bed and the three of them sat around the table, drinking coffee, talking about their next move. Caleb and Josie would visit the Becketts and Eric would start an investigation. Both Caleb and Eric were worried about Josie being a moving target. And they were worried about Lencha's safety, too, since she lived in the house.

"I'll have a guard put on the house," Eric said. "That will make us all feel better."

"And Josie should go nowhere without one of us with her," Caleb added.

She made a face at this, but complied.

Plans made, excitement over, they retired for the night. Caleb couldn't sleep, though. Too much coffee and too much going on in his head. Who would be this stupid? To openly try to kill Josie now?

Josie was taking this well. Actually the frightened Belle he'd known had all but disappeared and the fiery, strong and resourceful Josie had emerged.

That's what he wanted—had been working toward for a year. He rolled out of bed in pajama bottoms, deciding to get a glass of water. He heard a noise and was instantly on the alert. Voices—Josie's and Lencha's. He moved down the hall and spotted them in the living room.

Josie lay on the sofa on her stomach and a sheet covered her to the waist. Her back was bare and from the lamp he could see the outline of her breast and the smoothness of her olive skin. But his attention was on her scars—deep, diagonal ridges. The cult leader had beaten her with a board and a rope and he'd left his mark. Deep anger boiled inside him.

The doctors had told him about the scars and he'd felt them through the fabric of her dress when they'd danced, but he'd never seen them.

Lencha knelt on the floor and began to rub cream from a jar into the raised ridges. She chanted in Spanish, engrossed in her task, her gray hair all around her. Caleb turned and went back to bed, not wanting to intrude or make Josie feel uncomfortable. If Lencha could make the scars go away, then he was all for it.

He fell across the bed thinking, as he had so many times, that Josie had to be strong to survive what she'd endured. Not only had she survived, but she'd overcome the trauma. He went to sleep with visions of her smile in his mind.

"YOU HAVE MAGIC FINGERS," Josie murmured as Lencha rubbed her secret salve into her skin.

"That's what it'll take to get rid of these scars. Lawdy, child, why didn't you tell me about these sooner? And I wouldn't have seen them tonight if I hadn't walked in on you undressing."

"It's not something I like to talk about."

"*Dios!* Child, you're stubborn. This scar tissue has to be broken up and we have to do this every day."

"Mmm." Josie was half-asleep as her body relaxed at Lencha's gentle pressure. She'd been so revved up and she knew she'd discovered an important part of herself tonight—the cop in her. As soon as she'd heard the shot, she'd instinctively known what to do. She didn't cower in fear. She didn't feel any fear at all. Josie Marie had surfaced in a heartbeat.

She felt good about that and she wasn't ever going to cower again. She was fighting back. One thing was very clear—the person who'd shot her was still in Beckett. But who? That part of the picture was still blank, but it wouldn't be for long. From all she'd read and from what Dr. Oliver had told her, being in a familiar place was the catalyst she needed to trigger her full memory. The shooting, the trauma, would be the last piece to fall into place. Her mind's defense mechanisms would finally give way because she was strong enough to handle it.

Her eyes grew heavy and she smiled as she remembered the shocked look on Caleb's face as he saw her with the gun in her hand.

Josie Marie Beckett was back. Weak, helpless Belle was fading and she felt a moment of sadness—maybe Caleb was right. She wouldn't need him much longer.

THE NEXT MORNING was hectic. Dennis called and wanted them at the station. After filling out a report, Dennis decided they needed to check for any unusual tire tracks on the road. Caleb, Eric and Josie did a thorough investigation of the area and found where someone had pulled over into the ditch in front of Lencha's house. On a long shot, Eric had a tire print made and it was late afternoon by the time Caleb and Josie drove out to the Silver Spur. Caleb had called ahead so the Becketts knew they were coming.

Josie had attached her gun to her belt that morning. She wasn't back on the police force, but she wore it anyway. Caleb and Eric were doing everything to protect her, but she had to protect herself, to be on guard and stay focused.

They walked into the den where Boone and Mason stood at the built-in bar.

"Want anything to drink?" Boone asked. "Just name your poison."

"Answers," Josie replied. "I would like some answers."

"Whoa, girl." Boone held up a hand, his voice projecting to the next county. "You come in here packing heat and all revved up with that light in your eyes. I done told you there's no criminals here."

"Point taken, Boone, but—" her eyes swung to Mason "—before I leave here Mason is going to tell me why he had Teri not file the missing person's report."

Boone downed a shot glass of whiskey. "She better be lying, boy."

"She's not," Mason said matter-of-factly. Boone's ire never affected Mason. Boone's money did. "I didn't see any need to waste officers' time in looking for someone who wasn't missing. Josie made it plain she was leaving and never coming back and Lencha is loony as a bat."

"Why was I leaving and never coming back?" Josie asked just as calmly. "What happened here that day?"

Mason slammed his glass onto the counter. "I already told you and I'm getting tired of this interrogation."

"And I'm getting tired of the lies." Josie stood her ground.

"No one's lying to you," Mason shouted. "Get your damn memory back and you'll know that."

He charged past her, but she wasn't through. "Most of my memory is back. Do you want to talk about Caddo?"

Mason swung around, his eyes narrowed to tiny slits. She had his full attention.

"Caddo?" Boone asked. "What the hell has that half-breed done now? I told you, Mason, to fire his damn ass. Let him go terrorize someone else's ranch for a change."

"Caddo stays on the Silver Spur." Mason's voice was hard and unyielding. And there was something else—almost like fear. Fear of losing Caddo. Did he actually care about his son? That was a staggering thought.

"Now you listen here, boy, I don't understand

your loyalty to this half-breed. He's scary as hell sometimes. Howling with the coyotes and chasing the wind."

"He's different, but he saves this ranch time and money and I'm not losing a hand like that. I don't care if he wears heels and a dress in his off time, he gets the job done."

"Now don't get your britches in a knot."

Again Mason was fighting for Caddo. That meant he had to care something about him, but Josie also knew that Mason would never admit it, never let on to Boone. His inheritance was at stake.

"Can you tell us where you were about ten-thirty last night?"

Josie was glad when Caleb took over the questioning. She needed a reprieve.

"He was drunk on his ass." Boone spoke for him. "Felipe and Pablo carried him upstairs about eleven. Why?" Boone walked to his chair and sat on the edge, a cigar in the corner of his mouth.

"Someone took a shot at Josie last night."

"Dammit. What's Dennis doing about this?"

"Do you or Mason own a small caliber pistol?" Caleb asked instead of answering.

"Sure do." Boone took a puff on the cigar. "Cabinet over there is full of all kinds of guns. You're welcome to look."

Caleb didn't move, as Josie knew he wouldn't.

If anyone had used the gun, it wouldn't be in plain sight.

"I'd like to ask Lorna a few questions."

"Well, ranger man, all you're going to get out of her is some muttering and moaning. She's been sedated since yesterday."

"And Ashley?"

"She's in her room, pouting. Does that better than anyone I know." Boone blew plumes of smoke into the air. "Any more questions?"

"Not today, but tomorrow I'd like everyone present and fully conscious. Josie's life is at stake and this person has to be stopped."

"My sentiments exactly, ranger man."

Josie walked toward the door.

"Josie." Boone's voice halted her.

She turned to face him.

"I know you think I'm hard, crude and a lot of other things, but you're my granddaughter, just like Ashley. No one here would hurt you. You're a Beckett. Never thought I'd admit that, but you are." He removed the cigar from his mouth. "Lorna might want to hurt you, but she hasn't got the nerve. You're like your father—strong, spirited and stubborn as hell. I saw that in you the first time I met you. You're a Beckett, girl. Don't ever forget that."

She didn't know what to say so she nodded and walked out. Caleb met her at his vehicle.

"You okay?" he asked.

She shivered. "It's almost surreal. When I first came here, I waited and waited for him to admit that. Now that he finally has, I'm not sure how I'm supposed to feel. It's not like I thought it would be."

"Because so many doubts are connected to it."

"Yes." She smiled slightly, knowing she could count on Caleb to put things into perspective.

Before they could get into the Tahoe, a squad car drove up behind them on the circular drive. Josie thought it was Eric, but Dennis climbed out.

"Get any information?" he asked.

"No," Josie replied.

"I got a call so I better see what the big man wants. Catch you later."

As they drove away, Caleb remarked, "I guess Dennis is pretty much in Boone's pocket."

"Yes. As Caddo said, Boone is the law in Beckett."

"Does Dennis have a family?"

"Yes. Rhonda—that's his wife's name." She knew that without having to think about it. As Dr. Oliver had said, some of her memory would return without her being aware of it. "They'd been trying to have a baby for years. She had several miscarriages, then a stillborn baby. Finally they decided to adopt. The paperwork had all been done and they brought the baby home, then the mother changed her mind. They had to give the little girl back. Rhonda and Dennis were devastated, but the agency promised them another baby. That was fourteen months ago, so I'm sure they have the baby by now. I'll have to ask Dennis about it."

"Dennis has a family to support and he'll do anything to keep his job."

"Oh, yeah. He kowtows to Boone, but I always felt he was an honest man."

"That's good…"

A boom sounded and the car swerved. "Hold on," Caleb shouted. Then another boom and the car spun round and round and ran through a fence, mesquite and a ravine. The car bounced and jerked and had them holding on for dear life. The last thing she heard was Caleb scream, "Josie!" Then everything went black.

WHEN JOSIE WOKE UP she felt disoriented and didn't know where she was. Then she saw the shattered glass of the windshield and a mesquite limb poking through. They had an accident or something. Caleb! She turned to see him slumped over the steering wheel. She smelled gas. Oh, God! She quickly unbuckled her seat belt and her head throbbed from the movement.

They had to get out of the car.

"Caleb!" she shouted. He didn't move. She

reached over and shook him, but still he didn't budge. A wave of dizziness assailed her. She had to stay conscious. *Focus. Focus.* She threw herself against her door and it opened. Stepping out, the dizziness became worse. She held on to the car, side-stepping cactus, to get to Caleb. All the while she prayed his door would open and that he was okay.

She gave it one hard yank and when it swung wide, tears stung her eyes. "Caleb!" she shouted again, but still he gave no response. Unclipping his seat belt, she slid her hands under his armpits and tugged, careful to balance his head against her chest. Tugging and pulling she managed to get him out onto the ground. Then she dug her heels in and dragged him as far away as she could. When her breath burned in her chest and her arms gave way, she collapsed backward, sucking air into her lungs.

After a second she scrambled to her knees, bending over Caleb. He had a bruise on his forehead. Her heart stilled. Was he breathing? Unbuttoning his shirt, she placed her hand over his heart. She picked up a strong pulse immediately. Thank God. She kissed his forehead with her trembling lips.

"Caleb! Caleb! Wake up!"

A coyote howled in the distance and Josie glanced up. It would be dark soon and this was no place to be. Animals, unfriendly and dangerous, would be foraging for food. They had to get back to the ranch. But how? The dizziness became intense and she sank back on her heels.

Darkness slowly began to blanket the land and Josie knew she had to do something. The ranch was about five miles away. In daylight they could walk it, but not at night in their conditions. They had to wait it out.

The car hadn't exploded and she needed to get what she could out of it to survive the night. She struggled to her feet and made her way to the vehicle. The smell of gas was still strong. She took a deep breath, forcing herself to be quick and ignore the pounding in her head. A flashlight was in the glove compartment and she grabbed it along with her purse. She snatched two jackets from the back, then moved away as fast as she could.

Rolling up a jacket, she tucked it under Caleb's head. He moaned and her pulse tripled in speed.

"Caleb?"

He came to in a rush. *Josie Belle was in danger!* He had to do something, but his body wouldn't move and he felt pain shoot through his head. "Josie…"

"Shh." He felt her touch and he relaxed. She was alive.

It took a moment then he opened his eyes and stared into the darkness of the night. "Oh, oh."

"Try not to move," Josie said. "We had an accident."

"What happened?"

"I don't know."

He took a couple gulps of air and rose to a sitting position. His head throbbed for a second then stopped. "Are you okay?" he asked quickly.

"We both hit our heads, but otherwise, I think we're fine. The car smells of gas and I'm not sure it's drivable. We're stuck here for the night."

He looked at her and saw she was calm and in control. "You're remarkable."

"I'm shaking and scared out of my mind."

He wrapped an arm around her and pulled her close, the feel of her was all he needed.

"I got a flashlight and the jackets out of the car. Our biggest worry are the animals foraging for food—wild boar, bobcats, deer, coyotes, not to mention snakes, ants and lizards. The light will keep most of them away, but with the ants, lizards and snakes, we'll have to take our chances."

He reached for his cell phone on his waist and winced. "Try to see if you can get a signal."

Josie poked out the number for the police station. "Nothing. Damn! When Dennis leaves the Silver Spur maybe he'll notice the break in the fence."

"We can hope," Josie replied, her voice doubtful.

"We could fire a shot into the air," Caleb suggested, "but I'm not sure it would be heard."

"It would, but no one would care. Shots are fired all the time out here."

Caleb sighed. "Then we better find a place for the night." He pushed to his feet, staggered a bit, then regained control.

"Probably by that gnarled mesquite." She stood also and followed him to the tree. Taking the light, he looked for ants and the like. She dropped the jackets and they sat down, their backs to the tree.

"Do you think someone shot at us?" she asked quietly.

"I don't know. That person would have to be waiting for us, knowing we were out here."

"Yeah."

"Someone is afraid of what you'll remember."

"And they're determined that I die before that happens."

He wrapped an arm around her. "As I said before, none of this makes any sense. If I was going by the book, all the evidence points to Lorna and Mason. But they're too obvious, too open."

She rested her head on his shoulder and Caleb clicked off the light. "We need to conserve the battery. I'll turn it on at intervals to keep the animals away. Try to get some sleep."

"Are you kidding? I'll never be able to sleep out here. A rattlesnake might wrap itself around my throat or my foot." She shivered. "No way."

"With head injuries we need to stay awake anyway. We can talk."

"Are you serious?"

"What?"

"Men never want to talk."

"I'm different, I suppose. I had a mother who encouraged me to talk." He rested his chin on her head.

"That's where you and Eli are so different. He closes up like a clam."

"But Caroline has a way of opening him up."

"Mmm." Her hand splayed across his chest and silence mingled with the night sounds of crickets, barks and howls.

Even though danger lurked behind the darkness, Caleb felt a peacefulness he couldn't describe. Maybe it was the night. Or maybe it was just holding Josie Belle, which was how he was beginning to think of her.

"My mother knew what kind of man Joe McCain was, cold and never sharing any part of himself. She was determined that her sons wouldn't be like that. Every day after school, we had to tell her the good and bad parts of our day. Beau could go on and on— guess that's why he's a lawyer. Sometimes I'd wish for a switch to turn him off."

A chuckle left her lips. "You have a good relationship with your brothers."

"Yeah." He caressed her arm. "Even Jake—and I was almost thirty when I met him. It's good to have us all back together."

"Did you ever meet your father?"

"Once." He leaned his head against the tree. "My mom sent Beau to the feed store for birdseed and I went with him. Joe McCain was there and Beau pointed him out, and Beau, sometimes having more nerve than common sense, walked up to him and said, 'Hi, Dad.' Joe whirled around and replied, 'As long as you're with that woman, you're no son of mine. You're a bad son.'"

"He called Beau a bad son?"

"Ridiculous, isn't it? Beau is about as good as they come, but since he chose to go with my mother Joe always referred to him as the bad son."

"Did he say anything to you?"

"No, but he looked at me with the strangest look in his eyes."

He stopped speaking and Josie prompted, "What happened next?"

"Nothing, Beau pulled me away and I was as eager to get away from him as Beau was. But I was thinking about Caddo and how much he looks like Mason. Maybe Joe looked at me and saw his own image that day. Maybe he finally knew I was his son."

Caleb thought about all the years he agonized over the fact that Joe denied who he really was. But if Joe admitted it, he would also have to admit the truth about himself. He was a liar, a cheat and a jealous unstable man.

"Maybe he did, but his pride wouldn't let him admit it."

"He died a short while later. Beau, with his big heart, went to the funeral and Mom said I could go if I wanted. I chose not to and I've never regretted that decision."

She touched his face. "You were lucky to have Andrew in your life."

"Yes." He clicked on the light. "In all the years I was growing up he never raised a hand to me or even raised his voice. And I gave him plenty of opportunity."

"I can't believe that."

"I was a typical teenage boy." His thoughts went back. "One time I was playing baseball in the front yard with my friends. I guess I was about nine. I hit the ball and it sailed right across the street through Mrs. Finney's window. All the kids were scared of Mrs. Finney. She walked with a cane and always wore a scowl and she didn't like kids in her yard. We all ran into the house and hid out in my room."

The wind blew through the mesquite and he pulled her closer. "That night Dad set the ball on the table and asked, 'How did this get into Mrs. Finney's living room?' I didn't lie. I told him the truth. He said, 'What do you think we need to do about this?' I replied, without having to think about it, that I needed to apologize to Mrs. Finney and replace her window. He smiled and hugged me.

"Andrew taught me about responsibility and love and he taught me that a man didn't need to raise his voice or get angry when something went wrong." Caleb took a breath. "When I played ball in high school, he taught me that winning was great, but it didn't teach a man a lot. In defeat a man learned what he was made of, and there was never any shame in doing one's best. At sixteen and seventeen that didn't mean much to a kid who wanted to win every time. Years later I knew he was trying to teach me that I wasn't always going to win in life."

"You get all your kindness from Andrew."

"Yeah." And sitting under a canopy of stars he knew that he wasn't going to win this time. He wasn't going to walk away with the heroine.

Josie Belle belonged to someone else.

CHAPTER NINE

THE GROUND WAS HARD and the May evening grew chilly as the wind whistled through the mesquite. A coyote howled in the distance and answering howls echoed around them. Bright stars glittered above, beautiful in a way Caleb had never seen before. He felt as if he could pluck one right out of the big sky and hold its warmth in his hand.

Josie snuggled into him and he shut off the light. Suddenly all those conflicting feelings about Joe McCain seemed to dissipate. He didn't miss a thing by not knowing his biological father. He had so much more in his true father, Andrew. Andrew's teachings about right and wrong would give Caleb the strength to walk away from Josie when the time came.

"Oh." She jerked upright.

"What?"

"Something ran across my leg."

He quickly snapped on the light to see a fuzzy

tail disappear into the thicket. "I think it was a raccoon or a fox."

She shivered. "I'm not that fond of wild animals." She reached for her purse. "How about a candy bar?"

He laughed out loud and something rustled in the bushes. "Do you always carry chocolate with you?"

"Never know when a girl might need a chocolate fix." She handed him one and they ate in silence. Then she said, "Hope Lencha's not too worried. I'm sure she's called Eric by now and he's probably looking for us."

"I don't know how far off the road we are. We'll be hard to find in the dark. Our best bet will be to just leave the light on, hoping Dennis or Eric will see it."

"Yeah. Eat all that chocolate and don't drop any crumbs or the ants will find us. I put the wrappers back in my purse."

"Very wise."

She was quiet for a moment and he could almost feel the wheels turning in her head. "What are you thinking?" he asked.

"About the future. The person who shot me. My memory. And you."

"Me?" He lifted an eyebrow.

"Yes." She snuggled into him once again and

his arm instinctively went around her. "And how much I'm going to miss you and your voice."

"My voice?"

She told him about the warm milk and how his voice made her feel, especially when she was so afraid.

"You can always drink a glass of warm milk with chocolate in it." He was trying to be flippant, but inside his heart felt heavy.

"It won't be the same." She looked at him and slowly kissed the corner of his mouth. "Kiss me, Caleb."

"I don't think…"

"Please."

He couldn't resist her plea. He took her lips with a fiery hunger fueled by a year of glances, touches and yearnings. His hand slid under her blouse to her breasts then traveled to her back and caressed the scars. Pulling him closer, Josie's hands ran through his hair as the kiss went on, taking them on a journey of emotions that flowed through both of them. This journey would demand its own reward—total fulfillment.

"Caleb, make love to me," she whispered into his mouth. For a brief moment he ignored the warning in his head and tasted her tongue, her lips, her mouth and let himself feel everything that he shouldn't. *She belonged to someone else.*

Drawing his mouth away, he gulped in deep breaths of the night air and his hands stilled. He couldn't do what she'd asked. He couldn't do that to her, to himself, or Eric. Her emotions were precarious. His weren't. Once her memory returned, she would regret this lapse.

"Josie…"

"Shh." She placed a finger over his lips. "Don't be nice."

"Josie Belle." His breathing was so labored he felt as if he was having a heart attack. And in a way he was. He cupped her face, forcing the words out. "Our making love will only complicate things."

"I like it when you call me that." She twisted a button on his shirt.

He caught her hand, thinking that no man should be this nice. No man, especially him. He wanted her more than he wanted his next breath, but… "Josie…"

"I know." She sagged against him.

"Once you remember more about your relationship with Eric, you'll regret this lapse." His voice sounded hoarse.

"I'll miss you."

That note in her voice twisted his gut that much more. "But not for long."

"Mmm."

But I'll miss you forever.

CALEB WOKE UP as sun threatened to burst through the horizon. An array of colors from gold, to oranges, reds and yellows lit up the eastern sky and bathed the land in a soft light.

Somewhere toward morning he and Josie had fallen asleep. He looked down at the dark head on his shoulder and treasured this time out of time with her. It would be their last.

A menacing growl caught his attention and he turned his head slightly to see a wild-looking dog a few feet away. The shaggy hair along his spine was raised and his lips curled back, brandishing his sharp teeth. Caleb reached for his gun on his right side, but Josie was lying against it.

At his movement, she stirred.

"Be still," he whispered, fearing the dog was about to attack.

She lifted her head, saw the dog and smiled. *"Zar,"* she called, but the dog didn't budge, nor did his eyes leave Caleb.

"You know this dog?"

"He belongs to Caddo, who can't be far behind." She sat up, brushed her hair from her face and looked around.

Silently Caddo appeared through the thicket riding bareback and leading another horse. *"Zar, abajo,"* he said to the dog, then he jumped to the ground.

Caleb and Josie scrambled to their feet. Josie staggered and gripped her head. Caleb caught her. "You okay?"

"Just a little dizzy."

Caleb's body had aches and pains he didn't want to think about.

As Caddo reached them, Josie asked, "How did you find us?"

"The sky, the stars tell Caddo."

She arched an eyebrow. "You saw the light."

"Uh-hmm. Whole Silver Spur look for you." Caddo glanced at the wrecked vehicle. "Someone no want you alive, *prima*."

"I know. Can you please help us get back to the ranch?"

"*Si*. Brought horse." The blues eyes narrowed on Caleb. "You ride, Ranger?"

"You bet," Caleb responded. "But first I'd like to take a look at the car."

Caddo and Josie followed as Caleb gave the vehicle a once-over. The left back tire was blown out, basically a rim and shreds of rubber were left. The right front tire on the opposite side was the same. At first Caleb thought that someone had shot the tire, but with both tires being the same that would mean there had to be two shooters on opposite sides of the road. He doubted that, but someone must have tampered with the vehicle. But when? And who?

"We go," Caddo said. "People are worried." He handed Caleb the reins of a chestnut mare, and Caleb was glad to see it had a saddle. Caddo swung up on his paint in one fluid movement, then held out his hand to Josie.

Caleb put his foot in the stirrup, mounted the mare and took off after Caddo. Caddo knew the trails through the thicket, and they sailed across desert as if it were firm earth. The dust from the paint's feet stifled Caleb at times, but he kept pace with the other horse. They crossed two dry creeks, then the horses splashed across a shallow one. Caleb never paused. He kept following, knowing somehow that Caddo was testing him.

They came upon a large herd and the *vaqueros* shouted with joy when they saw Josie and Caddo. Caddo shrieked a chant and rode faster, scattering the cattle. A Mexican settlement, where the *vaqueros* lived with their families, loomed ahead. Caddo didn't slow down as they galloped through. Squawking chickens scattered, and Caleb glimpsed shacks and houses, women working in gardens and hanging out clothes. Barns and outbuildings were in the distance and Caleb knew they were getting close to the big hacienda.

Caddo cleared a fence, and Josie's hair flew

behind her. The chestnut mare took the fence without hesitation and soon Caddo slowed as bigger barns and a show arena came into view. The ranch house was now clearly in sight, big and imposing.

The ranch was larger than Caleb had ever imagined. Oil wells pumped to the left and to the right. Cattle grazed as far as he could see. Soon the wrought-iron fence that enclosed the house was only a few feet away. Caddo dismounted and opened a gate, then he mounted again and they rode to the front of the house.

Josie slid to the ground, her hair in disarray. "Thanks, Caddo."

Caleb swung out of the saddle, knowing he'd probably be aching from head to toe tomorrow. He handed Caddo the reins.

"*Mucho* good, cowboy." Caddo's white teeth flashed.

"Yeah." Caleb ran a hand through his disheveled hair. He had no idea where his hat was. "Did I pass the test?" There was no doubt in his mind that Caddo wanted to see what he was made of. They could have traveled the road they'd ran off of the night before. But somehow Caddo had his own route planned.

"*Sí.*" The teeth flashed again.

Zar trotted up, his tongue hanging out of his mouth.

"Adiós, prima, Ranger." In a flash Caddo was gone, the dog running behind him.

Caleb stared into Josie's dark eyes and she was smiling. He melted from the warmth, as did all his aches and pains.

"I learn more about you everyday, Caleb McCain."

He winced. "Tomorrow I might need some of Lencha's gin and raisins, mostly the gin."

At the mention of Lencha, they were quickly brought back to reality. He tucked her hair behind her ear. "Ready?"

"Yes. We have to let everyone know we're okay."

"And figure out who's hoping we're not."

The door swung open before Josie could ring the bell. *"Dios,"* Consuelo said. "Come. Come. Mr. Boone fit to be tied."

They stepped inside. Lorna and Mason were descending one of the two spiral staircases that curled to the top floor of the house. Josie stared at the couple, their heads close together, whispering. At that moment everything fell into place and Josie remembered that night, the argument. Her head throbbed as painful, disturbing memories crowded in on her. She held her head with both hands, frowning, waiting for the pain to stop.

"Josie." She heard Caleb's voice and she took a

deep breath. Anger rolled through her like a hurricane. She sucked in another breath and marched into the den. Her day of reckoning had arrived. She knew the answers now and someone was going to tell her why they thought it necessary to kill her.

Boone jumped to his feet when he saw her. "Damn, girlie, you gonna give me a heart condition. I've been up all night worried about you." He looked at her bedraggled appearance. "You're filthy and your hair looks as if rats have nested in it. What happened? That old witch has been calling, threatening everything under the sun."

Caleb explained about the wreck and it gave Josie time to get her thoughts straight. She didn't worry about Lencha. She knew Caddo would get word to her. Now she had to deal with what she remembered about the night she'd been shot.

The phone rang and Consuelo interrupted. "It's Mr. Eric, *señor.*"

"Tell him they're safe and at the house."

"*Sí, señor.*"

Mason and Lorna walked into the room and Josie forced herself to remain calm. *Don't overreact. Take it slow.* But her nerves were coiled into springs ready to explode.

Mason shoved his hands into his jeans, his expression bored. "So they found you."

Caleb explained about the wreck again, then

stared directly at Mason. "The tires were tampered with."

Mason poured coffee from a silver pot for him and Lorna. "Don't look at me. I haven't been near your car."

"But you're afraid of what I'll remember, aren't you, Mason?" Josie had the perfect opening and she took it.

"Of course not." But his eyes gave him away. He didn't look at her as he took a swallow from his cup.

Lorna took a seat on the sofa, placing her china cup carefully on an end table. "Josie, we're getting a little tired of these theatrics." She was in control today, but she wouldn't be for long.

"Me, too, Lorna, so I'll cut to the chase." She took a breath. *Slow. Take it slow,* she kept repeating to herself, trying not to be overwhelmed by the memories crowding in on her. "I remember what happened here that afternoon."

Complete dead silence followed her words. She saw surprise in Caleb's eyes, but fear was evident in everyone else's—even Boone's.

Lorna rose to her feet, her control slipping. "Mason, do something."

"Yes, Mason, do something," Josie said, walking closer to him. "Do something about the secret you've kept hidden for over thirty years."

"You don't know what the hell you're talking

about. You're getting as loony as Lencha." He tipped up his cup with a nervous hand.

"My father did not betray his family, his birthright." She remembered it all and she shouted the words and they vibrated off the walls, just like her insides were vibrating with anger. "You betrayed him. Your own brother."

"What are you talking about, Josie?" Boone demanded, smoke from his cigar spiraling around his face.

"Are you going to tell him or should I? One way or another the truth is coming out *today*. Neither my father's name nor my mother's will be dragged through the mud one more minute."

"No one will believe you," Lorna said, her composure still holding.

"A DNA test will confirm it."

Lorna's eyes flashed with fear and she bit down on her trembling lip.

"Okay. I've had enough," Boone said, his teeth clamped around the cigar. "Josie, what the hell are you talking about?"

She took a deep breath and looked at her grandfather. "Brett is not Ashley's father. Mason is."

"What!" He spit the cigar onto the floor and no one made a move to pick it up.

Josie raised her eyes from the rug to Boone's face. "Brett found out Lorna was four months pregnant and they'd only been married for two. He knew he wasn't the father, but he didn't know who was. After that, he couldn't stay in the marriage. Everything he loved he gave up because he had morals and values. The Silver Spur meant the world to him, but once he knew the truth he couldn't stay here. He had to find the only woman he'd ever loved. In my teens I heard my parents talking about Brett's first marriage and I wanted to know about it. My father told me that Ashley wasn't his and how he didn't want me growing up thinking he'd leave a child behind. He would never do that." She paused and no one moved or spoke.

"That day I came out here to talk to you and you weren't here. You'd told me my father's things were in a room upstairs and I could go through them if I wanted. I decided to do that while I waited for you. I didn't know which room it was and when I opened a door, I got the shock of my life. Lorna and Mason were in bed together and I suddenly knew who was Ashley's father. I slammed the door and ran away. Mason caught me in the den and threatened me. I told him what I thought of him and that he didn't have to worry. I was leaving and never coming back."

"Is this true?" Boone demanded of Mason.

"Pa, I…"

Boone backhanded him across the face. Mason

staggered, but he didn't go down. He held a hand to his red cheek. "The first one's free, Pa."

Boone hit him again. "You bastard. You sneaky, cheating bastard. Brett belonged here. He should be running the Silver Spur today, but he left and you knew how that affected me. You…"

"Yeah, Pa. I know." Mason's voice was low, gritty. "Brett was the golden boy, your favorite. If you'd given me half the attention you gave him, maybe I wouldn't be so damn messed up."

"My fault, huh? You were wild, boy, from the day you were born. Never could do anything with you."

"Did you ever try?" Mason shouted, then threw up his hands. "What's the use. I'm outta here."

Boone grabbed his arm. "You're not going anywhere. I lost one son and I'm not losing another. You will stay and face this and you will tell the goddamn truth. Do you understand me?"

Lorna sank onto the sofa and began to cry silently. "Please, Ashley must never know."

Boone turned on her. "Missy, I thought you loved Brett. I forced him to marry you for that reason."

"I did."

"Really? Is that why you slept with his brother? And obviously still are."

"Mason was fun and…I'm sorry. I was young and stupid. Ashley doesn't need to know."

"She's grown up thinking her father didn't care about her and that will stop."

"Boone, please."

"*Consuelo!*" Boone shouted. Lorna's plea fell on deaf ears.

Caleb moved to Josie's side and she needed his presence.

"*Sí, señor.*" Consuelo appeared.

"Get Ashley down here."

"Boone, please," Lorna continued to beg. "She'll hate me."

Josie never wanted Ashley hurt, but she didn't see any way to stop it now. Secrets had to be exposed so they could all start living again.

Caleb touched her hand and whispered. "Have you remembered who shot you?"

"No. I just remember that day and running to my car, crying." The rest was still a blank and she kept trying to bring it up, but like so many times, it wasn't there.

"Now let's have more truth." Boone pinned Mason and Lorna with a sharp glance. "Did either of you shoot Josie to keep this secret?"

"I swear, Pa. I didn't. She said she was leaving and I knew she was mad enough to leave for good and that was fine with me. That's the reason I stopped the missing person's report. She left voluntarily."

"I hate guns." Lorna grimaced. "I don't even know how to fire one."

Josie stepped closer to her, looking her in the eye. "Why do you hate *me* so much? You know the reason my father left."

Lorna twisted the diamond on her finger. "I loved Brett, but he didn't love me. And you're just a reminder of everything I couldn't have. Marie had her hooks in him and she just wouldn't let go."

"Excuse me?" Josie resisted the urge to slap her.

At Josie's tone, Lorna took a step backward. "Figuratively, of course. I was the one who drove Brett away. Are you happy now?" The green eyes blazed with renewed anger. "You've destroyed my whole life, just like your mother did."

"My mother didn't destroy your life. *You did.* When are you going to admit that?"

Lorna clamped her lips tight.

"She left because she couldn't stay here after my father married you. She didn't call, write or get in touch with him in any way. He made a choice and she respected that. You betrayed him in the worst way. And to make it even worse, you blamed my mother. You still do."

A sob left Lorna's throat. "I can't lose my daughter. Please, say something to Boone. You don't want Ashley hurt, do you?"

She didn't, but she felt powerless to stop anything now. And she wasn't sure she wanted to.

Ashley had to know that Brett wasn't her father and that he hadn't betrayed her or Lorna. That was uppermost in Josie's mind—to right the wrongs that had been done to her father.

Suddenly Josie felt drained and just wanted to get away. But this wasn't over. If Mason or Lorna hadn't shot her, then who? There were only two Becketts left, Ashley and Boone. Boone had no motive. That left Ashley. Could she have overheard what had happened that day? Josie glanced at Caleb and saw the same thoughts were going through his mind.

From the start Ashley never seemed to have any animosity toward Josie. Could that have all been a facade?

Consuelo hurried back into the room. "Miss Ashley's not in her room. She left a note." She handed it to Boone.

He read for a second, then, "Dammit!" erupted from his lips. "The whole damn family is falling apart."

"What does it say?" Lorna asked.

He read:

"Dear Mother and Pa, I've decided to leave and try to make it on my own. Please don't try to find me. I will not be forced into an arranged marriage. Hope you understand. Love, Ashley."

"No, no, no," Lorna sobbed into her hands.

"Go upstairs," Boone ordered. "I'll take care of this. Consuelo!"

Consuelo escorted Lorna out of the room as Eric and Dennis rushed in.

Eric ran to Josie and stopped, staring at her dirty jeans, blouse and tousled hair. "What happened?"

She told them about the accident.

"What are you doing about this, Fry? Step up the damn investigation before my granddaughter gets killed."

"Yes, sir. We'll guard her until this person is caught."

"And I better see some damn results—like tomorrow."

"I'd really like to go home now," Josie said, and walked toward the door. When she remembered what had happened that day with Lorna and Mason, she just knew one of them had shot her. Now, they were back at square one.

She felt defeated and alone.

Would the nightmare ever end?

CHAPTER TEN

ON THE DRIVE TO LENCHA'S, Caleb, Eric and Dennis discussed what had happened. Search parties were sent out early in the morning but had had no luck. Josie listened to everything they said, but she didn't hear much of it. She was still disappointed. When the memories of Mason and Lorna had come back so suddenly, she was excited, determined to get one of them to admit that they'd shot her. Lorna and Mason were deceitful and without morals but Josie believed them—her leaving was enough for them.

So who? Could Ashley have hated her that much? Josie's thoughts went back to that day. Running to her car was her last memory. She'd been packing, so she'd made it back to Lencha's. If Ashley had come by and wanted to talk, Josie would have gone with her. But where was Josie's car? Could Ashley have disposed of it? That would have taken a conniving, manipulative person. That didn't describe the Ashley she'd known, but sometimes people could be deceiving.

When they reached Lencha's, Eric asked to speak to her privately, but she refused, saying she just wanted to be alone now. She hugged Lencha, who checked the bruise on her head. Dennis suggested that a trip to the emergency room in Corpus wouldn't hurt. She and Caleb both refused and Josie went to take a bath.

Caleb watched her go with a troubled expression.

"She's not good," Lencha remarked.

"No." Caleb sagged into a chair, his head throbbing a bit, but he wasn't worried about himself. He was worried about Josie Belle. "She remembered what happened that night at Silver Spur and she thought it was Lorna or Mason who shot her. It wasn't, and she's struggling with the knowledge that it's someone else."

Lencha sat down. "Caddo told me about the accident. Did that bring back her memory?"

"I think so."

"So what was Lorna and Josie arguing about?"

Caleb told her the whole story.

"Lawdy! Mason is Ashley's father, too?"

"Yes."

Lencha shook her head. "Marie never said a word. Of course, after she left, I only saw her two or three times a year and her and Brett were tighter than two lovebugs. If he didn't want her to mention it, she wouldn't."

"Brett told Josie in her teens when she overheard them talking about Brett's first marriage. He wanted her to know that he'd never leave a child of his own."

"Uh, uh, uh." Lencha wagged her head. "Mason needs to be neutered. No telling how many more kids he's spawned."

Caleb only grinned.

"I bet Big Boone is reeling in those expensive boots."

"He's received a knock, that's for sure," Caleb replied.

Lencha pointed a bony finger at him. "Mark my words, Ranger. Brett told that old *bastardo* why he was leaving. Brett was honest, loyal and he wouldn't have left otherwise. Big Boone knows everything and he's a cunning buzzard. He'll never admit it, though. Likes being the injured one, revels in it."

"Josie said Brett didn't know who the father was. He only knew he wasn't."

"And it's Mason. His own brother." Lencha's head bobbed up and down. "Bet that almost stopped Big Boone's ticker."

Caleb thought about it. Boone seemed to have his pulse on everything that happened in Beckett, the Silver Spur and in Texas. Could he have known from the start about Ashley? Mason and

Lorna had been sleeping together for over thirty years in Boone's house. How could that slip by Boone? He sure had the good ol' Texas boy act down. From the little while that Caleb had known him, he knew nothing slipped by Boone. So who was fooling whom?

Chula scratched at the door and Lencha let her in. As Lencha walked back, the squirrel climbed up her jeans and rested on her shoulder. Lencha stroked her, then *Chula* climbed down her blouse to get nuts out of her apron pocket.

Caleb smiled at the squirrel's antics, but questions beat at him. He leaned forward. "Lencha, do you think it's possible that Boone knew all along that Mason was Ashley's father?"

"Wouldn't put nothin' past that man."

Me, neither, Caleb thought, and headed for the bathroom. Josie's door was open and she lay in her robe curled up on the bed. His heart lurched. He'd seen her like this before in the hospital when she wouldn't let anyone get near her. Stepping into the room, he saw that she was asleep, her damp hair over her shoulder. He relaxed. She was just exhausted, as he was.

He knew he had to investigate this more deeply, and he had the resources. He intended to thoroughly check out the Becketts, but his laptop was in the Tahoe. He had to retrieve it. Calling his captain, he reported what had happened. After assuring the captain he was okay, Caleb was told since his car was state issued, a wrecker would tow it back to Austin for repairs.

He then called Beau and Eli to let them know they were okay. Beau would tell the family and Eli would make sure all the rangers knew he was fine. He also phoned Chadwick, the ranger in the county, so he'd also know what was happening. The rangers were an extended family and Caleb assured Eli and Chadwick that he didn't need any help.

Taking a quick shower, he checked the bruise on his temple—a slight lump, tender and blue. He'd received worse playing ball. He dressed and called Eric, then he took a peep at Josie. She was still out. That's what she needed now—rest.

In the kitchen, he asked, "Lencha, may I borrow your truck?"

"Sure. Keys are in it."

"Thanks. Tell Josie I've gone to get stuff out of the Tahoe. Eric will be by to watch things while I'm gone."

A gray eyebrow darted up. "Does Josie know this?"

"No. She's asleep, but I have some things I need to do and Eric will guard her. Plus there's a guard outside."

Caleb went out the door, knowing he was doing

the right thing by giving Eric and Josie a chance to talk. That's what a nice man would do—back off. For the first time he wished he wasn't so nice.

As he headed for Lencha's truck, a silver Z71 Chevy pickup pulled into the driveway. It was a new four-door cab and Caleb knew by the look that it was loaded. The windows were slightly tinted and he couldn't see the driver.

The door opened and a man got out. Caddo. Caleb did a double take. Caddo's shirt was buttoned, and he wore a hat, his long hair in a ponytail. He looked like an ordinary cowboy. But Caddo was anything but ordinary.

"Ranger," he said as he walked toward Caleb. "Need wheels?" He jabbed a thumb toward the truck.

Caleb scratched his head, realizing he still didn't have his hat. "A good-looking truck," he replied. "Should I ask where you got it?"

Caddo grinned. "No steal. Mine. Hardly ever use it. Rather ride a horse."

Caleb wondered why Caddo would buy a truck like that if he wasn't going to use it.

As if he was psychic, Caddo added, "Gift from my Papa."

Caleb lifted an eyebrow. "Really?"

"Sins of the father cost *mucho*. But Caddo no need nuthin'—not even the name of a Beckett."

The tone of his voice sent a shiver down Caleb's spine and Caleb knew a day of reckoning was coming for the Becketts. Lies, secrets, denial and betrayal would destroy them and he didn't want Josie caught in the cross fire.

"You take." Caddo handed him the keys.

A white pickup stopped at the road with the Silver Spur logo on the door. A Mexican was driving, the windows were down and loud mariachi music played on the radio.

Caddo shouted something in Spanish and the man immediately turned off the radio.

"Caddo, I…" But Caleb was talking to thin air. Caddo was halfway to the truck and soon the white vehicle disappeared out of sight.

Caleb let out a breath. He needed a vehicle and now he had one. Throwing the keys up, he caught them, then slid into the leather interior. He turned the key and it purred like a kitten and it drove like a luxury sedan. As he headed for the accident site, he tried to figure out why Mason would buy Caddo a fancy truck. It meant absolutely nothing to Caddo. Maybe it meant something to Mason, but for the life of him he couldn't figure out what because he didn't think the man had a conscience.

As Caleb turned on the road leading to the Silver Spur, he drove slowly, trying to find the spot where they veered off the road. He missed it the first time, then finally found the break in the fence. He wondered why the searchers couldn't find it last night, but the darkness could have impeded their efforts.

The truck had four-wheel drive so he drove through the ditch and the broken fence and followed the torn-up grass. The vehicle was about a half a mile from the road. He got out to inspect the car once again, but he couldn't tell much about the blown-out tires—there wasn't much left.

He gathered his things out of the vehicle and found his hat. A grin spread across his face. He felt naked without it. Placing it on his head, he noticed the jackets and Josie's purse were back inside. Caddo. He'd come back and rescued the items because they'd left them under the tree this morning. Caddo was quite a personality.

Caleb climbed into the Chevy truck thinking he could identify with Caddo's pain. They both had fathers who wouldn't claim them and Caleb's never would. He was dead. In some strange way he didn't need that anymore. Maybe it was looking at the situation from another point of view. In any case, when he got home to Waco he was going to make sure Andrew knew how much he loved him.

For Caddo, his life was here on the Silver Spur seeing his father every day, knowing the line of father and son would never be crossed. He would never be claimed as a Beckett.

When he reached the road, he turned toward the ranch. In the closest corral, he noticed a piped enclosure with a galvanized walking wheel to exercise horses. Boone stood inside looking over a horse. Caleb drove in that direction. Stopping the truck a few feet away, he climbed the fence to look at the horse. Two men were inside with Boone and the horse, one Mexican, the other white. Caleb had seen neither before.

"What do you think, ranger man?" Boone asked, stroking the animal. The short, thin Mexican held the horse by the reins.

"Good-looking horse." The magnificent gray mare had black markings, a long slim neck and graceful lines.

"Arabian. What do you think she cost?"

"Wouldn't even hazard a guess."

"More than you make in a year."

That was a little dig to let Caleb know that Boone had the money to make his life very miserable. Boone was used to buying people or destroying them. Caleb wondered why the man saw him as a threat, as someone who needed to be bought or destroyed.

"May I speak with you?"

Boone paused for a second, then replied,

"Sure." Then he said something to the Mexican who led the horse into the stables. There was a breezeway between the stables and corrals with tables and chairs and a bar. Obviously a place where Boone could sit with guests and watch the horses being given a workout. Caleb met him there, as did the other man. Cool air wafted around him and he looked up at the large fans that circulated some kind of air-conditioning. Only the best for Boone Beckett.

"This is Hal Garver, my ranch manager." Boone introduced the other man and they shook hands. In his forties, his hair slightly thinning, Hal wore a starched shirt and Dockers with boots.

"I'm glad to hear Josie's okay," Hal said. "She's a sweet girl."

"I'll tell her." But Caleb had no idea if Josie remembered this man.

"Don't you have work to do?" Boone interrupted with his usual tactlessness.

"Yes, sir." Hal headed for the stairs on the side, which evidently housed Silver Spur offices.

"Drink?" Boone asked Caleb from the built-in bar.

"No, thanks." There was ice water on the table. "Water's fine." He poured a glass and sat down, placing his hat on the table.

Boone brought a bottle of bourbon and two shot

glasses. "Just in case you change your mind," he said, sinking into a padded chair. He proceeded to light a cigar and blew puffs of smoke into the air. "Nothin' like good whiskey and a Cuban cigar." He picked up the shot glass with a sly grin. "Unless it's a willing woman."

Caleb let that good ol' boy humor slide, trying to gauge how to start this conversation. "You ever play poker, Mr. Beckett?"

"Sure."

"I've played a time or two myself and one of the first things I learned is how to read people, their body language, facial expressions and voices. Can learn a lot just by the inflection of a word."

"What's your point, Ranger?"

Caleb took a drink of water and set the glass very carefully on the table, then lifted his eyes to Boone's. "You knew Brett wasn't Ashley's father."

"Really?" Boone didn't move a muscle.

"From what I've learned about Brett Beckett he wouldn't have left here without telling you why."

Boone laid the cigar in an ashtray and downed the whiskey in the shot glass with one swallow. "Yeah. He told me, but I didn't believe him. I thought he'd found an easy way to get out of the marriage and that didn't wash with me. He'd married Lorna and he now had responsibilities. I told him to stop making up lies and mooning over that Mexican girl and live up to those responsibilities like a man."

"What did he say?"

"He said he couldn't do that. I told him he'd better or he could kiss his inheritance goodbye. He walked out the door and he never came back." Boone poured another drink of whiskey.

"When he didn't come back, didn't that tell you that he wasn't lying?"

"Well, Ranger, Lorna's father was a congressman in Austin with a lot of clout and I had a lot of business irons in the fire and I needed that clout. And how was I supposed to tell the man that his daughter was less than perfect. Get my drift?"

Caleb nodded.

"When the girl was born with Beckett blue eyes, I figured Brett was lying. He just wanted out of the marriage. Didn't have a clue she was sleeping with both my boys."

"Didn't you?"

The loaded question hung between them and the two men eyed each other. Finally Boone laughed out loud and downed the drink with one swallow. He wiped his mouth with the back of his hand. "Damn, ranger man, you just keep pushing your luck."

"It's hard for me to believe that Lorna and Mason could be sleeping together in your house and you not know about it. It's been going on over thirty years."

"It's family business, ranger man, so I suggest you keep your nose out of it." The words were spoken with a warning, but Caleb ignored it.

He leaned back in his chair. "I'm just wondering why you haven't insisted on them getting married. They're both single."

"Well, now, that's hard to explain." Boone rubbed his jaw. "And I don't feel I owe you an explanation. Or anyone for that matter."

"Playing tough isn't going to help, sir." Caleb kept going, pushing as far as he could to get answers. "This family is falling apart and only the truth will save it." He paused. "Why haven't you insisted on them getting married?"

Boone picked up his cigar and took a puff. "Mason's a womanizer and wouldn't give up his women. Lorna had standards for him to live by and he refused. Didn't keep the sexual attraction from surfacing now and then. Hell, she's a woman and he's a man. What else can I say?"

As Caleb started to speak, Boone held up his hand. "Before you ask, I didn't know Mason was Ashley's father." Their eyes locked and Boone's turned to a color of steel. "Are you calling my bluff, Ranger?"

"Nah." Caleb leaned forward. "The cards are on the table and there's not much left to lie about." He twisted the glass, focusing on it for a second, then slowly raised his eyes. "Except who shot Josie."

"Look at my face, Ranger, and listen to my voice. I don't have a clue. If I did, he wouldn't be breathing."

"Maybe it's not a he."

Boone poured another shot of whiskey. "Now I think we're getting to the crux of what you want to talk about."

"Do you know where Ashley went?"

"Nope. Never thought she had that much guts, but she was seeing this guy in Switzerland." Boone studied his cigar. "She doesn't have it in her to kill anyone."

"Jealousy makes people do crazy things."

"Yeah." Boone took a puff on the cigar. "When you find her, bring her back to Silver Spur, but leave the boyfriend behind."

Caleb got to his feet. "I just want to question her. If she's innocent, what she does with her life is up to her."

Boone's eyes narrowed through the smoke. "I don't guess you heard me, ranger man."

"I heard you, Mr. Beckett, but Ashley has enough problems to face without me or anyone forcing her to do anything."

Boone chewed on his cigar. "You and I see life a little differently."

Caleb placed his hat on his head. "Everyone sees life different than you."

A robust laugh erupted from Boone's throat. "You got that right, Ranger. What are you doing with Caddo's truck?" He slipped the last part in while he was still smiling.

He knows, Caleb thought. He knows Caddo is Mason's son. And like the sly devil he was, no one would ever know that.

"He loaned it to me."

"Mmm." He poured another drink and Caleb walked away wondering why Boone wasn't drunk on his ass. The man could hold his liquor. He took everything Boone had said with a grain of salt, but he had a feeling it was as close to the truth as he was going to get.

Life was a game to the man and he had to win at all costs, even at the loss of a son. Caleb pitied him. He had so much, yet so little.

Before he could reach the truck, Mason rode up on a light brown sorrel and dismounted, frowning at the truck and Caleb. He stormed toward Caleb, his spurs jangling.

"What the hell are you doing with Caddo's truck?"

"Your father just asked the same question." Caleb wasn't deterred by Mason's anger. He was actually shocked by it. The man had a big interest in Caddo, whether he wanted to believe that or not. "Since my vehicle is out of commission, Caddo loaned this one to me."

"Oh." The wind seemed to ooze right out of his chest.

"Very nice gesture in my opinion."

Mason's frown deepened. "Is there some hidden meaning behind that?"

"No. Just that Caddo comes off as a bit radical, but he has a good heart."

"He is radical and Josie keeps trying to see him for someone he isn't."

"Oh, I think Josie sees him for who he is."

The eyes darkened. "Just watch your back around him."

"I always watch my back when I'm on the Silver Spur."

"Listen, Ranger." Mason got into his face and Caleb stood his ground, unblinking, unmoving. "Take Josie and get the hell out of Beckett."

"Why are you so afraid of Josie?"

"I'm not afraid of her." He all but spat the words into Caleb's face. "Her coming here has caused nothing but pain."

"Yeah. It's hell when secrets get exposed."

"Ashley doesn't need to know about the past," Mason shouted. "And now she's gone, God knows where."

"And you blame Josie for that?" He couldn't conceal the disgust in his voice.

"Brett made his choice years ago and his kid has no right coming back here." Mason turned toward his horse.

"This isn't about Josie. It's about Brett," Caleb said, and Mason stopped in his tracks. "The favorite son. He had everything, even the woman you loved."

Mason swung around, his face creased with resentment. "I wasn't good enough for her or her father, but it didn't stop her from trying to tame the bad boy. Sleeping with me didn't change her mind about Brett, though. She didn't know she was pregnant when she married him. When Lorna found out, she tried to pass the baby off as Brett's. But big brother wasn't stupid. I didn't know it was mine until after Ashley was born and I figured out the dates."

So much heartache and deception, and it only seemed to get worse. The Becketts took dysfunctional to a new level.

"Why didn't you marry her then?" was all Caleb could say.

"Because she wanted to make me into Brett. She wanted me to change. Mason, the bad boy, wasn't good enough to be a husband or a father to Ashley, but I'm good enough to sleep with. Now ain't that a kick in the pants?"

Mason was in love with Lorna. Probably had been since he'd met her and love had certainly made a fool of him. But he didn't seem inclined to change that.

Caleb tipped his hat back slightly. "You have the perfect motive to kill Josie. That would end all your problems and keep the secrets intact."

"But I didn't do it."

"No." Caleb looked into blue eyes as cold as anything he'd ever felt, but the coldness couldn't hide the truth. He'd been a lawman for a few years and his instincts told him Mason hadn't tried to kill Josie. "But I'm wondering why."

Mason's hard expression changed and Caleb suddenly knew. "Because she's Brett's daughter. You couldn't kill your brother's child."

Mason didn't deny it. "Doesn't mean I didn't want to. Someone just beat me to it."

The Becketts took stubborn to a new level. Mason wasn't going to admit there was any good in him and probably most people would agree.

"Now Ashley's gone," Mason added, "and Lorna's never going to forgive me. So take your investigation somewhere else and stay the hell out of our lives." With that, Mason stormed to his horse and rode away in a cloud of dust.

Caleb squinted against the sun toward the corral and saw that Boone had watched the whole exchange. He tipped his hat and got into the truck and headed toward town feeling as if he was leaving another world. A world where Boone ruled and nothing was what it seemed.

His goal now was to keep Josie safe and to find Ashley. From the start he'd told himself that this case didn't make sense. And he wasn't sure Ashley could help shed any light on the situation. When Ashley had talked to Josie, she seemed more concerned about her freedom than anything else. If she'd been planning anything nefarious, she was a very good actress. But he'd still check her out.

As he reached Lencha's, darkness was once again throwing a blanket over the land, cooling and comforting in its own way. He opened the door and stopped short. Josie and Eric were at the table, talking and laughing.

CHAPTER ELEVEN

"CALEB," JOSIE SAID. "Join us. We're going over the cases I was working."

It took him a moment to catch his breath. He thought he was ready to let her go, but obviously he was wrong or it wouldn't hurt this much seeing her with Eric. Removing his hat, he pulled out a chair and sat down.

"Find anything significant?" he asked, his voice sounding odd even to him.

"Not really," Eric answered. "We were talking about the Krump case. Mrs. Krump said someone was breaking into her house. The screen on a dining room window was off every morning. Josie and I couldn't figure it out. Nothing was ever missing in the house. So Josie staked out the place and she called me for backup when she saw a man removing the screen and entering the house. We found the man in bed with her eighteen-year-old daughter. It was plainly consensual, but Mrs. Krump was furious. It turned out to be a boyfriend of the daughter and we had to keep him in jail until Mrs. Krump cooled off. When she found out her daughter was pregnant, she wouldn't press charges. Two weeks later Josie and I were invited to the wedding. That's about as exciting as it gets around here."

Josie stuffed the files back into the box. "We have to be missing something. This is just petty stuff."

Eric got to his feet. "I have to return to the station, and I'll see if there's anything that wasn't put in the box. See you later." He paused by Josie's chair, and she looked up.

"Thanks, Eric."

"No problem," he replied, and headed for the door.

Josie continued to stuff the files into the box with a shaky hand. Caleb caught both her hands between his. "What is it?"

"Nothing." With one toss, she threw her hair back.

"You and I have known each other for over a year and there's nothing you can't tell me. What's bothering you?"

She leaned back in her chair. "Eric is so patient and understanding and I want to feel something, but I don't."

"Don't work yourself up. It will come like all the rest." He took a breath. "You were getting along very well when I walked in."

"That was business. It's the personal things I don't remember and I'm tired of thinking about it." She threaded her fingers through her long hair. "Lencha said Caddo loaned you his truck. You've been gone a very long time."

"I went back to the Silver Spur."

A light entered her eyes. "Did you find out anything? Do you know where Ashley is?"

He told her about his talk with Boone and Mason.

Her eyes darkened. "So Boone knows everything."

"That's hard to say. He doesn't openly admit to anything."

"But he knew Brett wasn't Ashley's father?"

"He admitted that your father told him why he couldn't stay in the marriage, but Boone didn't believe him. Or it suited Boone's purposes not to believe him."

"I don't understand what all this means."

"I think it means we're looking in the wrong place."

"What about Ashley?" She sighed.

"Boone said she has a boyfriend in Switzerland."

"But you don't think she's involved, do you?"

Caleb thought about it for a minute. "I wish I could say no for sure, but I can't. After I talk to her, I'll know more."

"And Mason admitted he couldn't kill Brett's child?"

"He admitted that he wanted to, but by the look in his eyes I knew he couldn't and he didn't deny that. I don't believe he had anything to do with your shooting." At her troubled expression, he added, "I met the ranch manager and he seemed genuinely glad you were okay."

She glanced up. "Hal?"

"You remember him?"

"Yes. He was very nice to me when I first came here, a friendly face in a sea of enemies. He's something of a loner, his life seems to be managing Boone's affairs. How he does that I'm not sure because Boone treats him like dirt."

"Doesn't Boone treated everyone that way?"

"Mmm."

She stood and paced around the kitchen. "You said we're looking in the wrong place. Where else do you have in mind?"

"There's enough motives at Silver Spur to get a lawman excited, but that's too easy, too pat." He touched the box. "Someone became angry at you about something and my feeling is it has to do with a case."

"But there's nothing there. All of these cases were resolved peacefully."

"There's still the missing girl Lencha mentioned."

She twisted a strand of hair around one finger. "I wonder if Lencha understood me correctly. Sometimes she gets lost in her own world. And Eric doesn't remember a missing girl."

"Next step—intensify the search for Ashley. Then look through more files. Dennis has been very cooperative so that shouldn't be a problem."

Josie touched the bruise on his forehead and frissons of warmth shot through him. He tried to block that feeling, but he had a suspicion that nothing on this earth was ever going to change the way he felt about her.

"How's the head?"

He looked into her eyes. "Fine. It throbbed a bit when I was talking to Boone, but I think it was his voice. How's yours? Remembered anything else?"

"No. It just throbs a lot."

He rose and they stood inches apart, the scent of her hair, lavender and something he couldn't define, did a number on his senses. Clearing his throat, he said, "A good night's rest will help both of us." He glanced around. "Where's Lencha?"

"Got called out to help with a birth." She walked toward the refrigerator. "How about a sandwich?"

They ate in silence and Caleb soaked up every nuance, every movement, every glance, knowing that soon they would be his last. Her memory could return at any second and then she wouldn't need him anymore.

Just as he'd told her.

How long, he wondered, before he stopped needing her.

THE RINGING OF THE PHONE woke Josie. She squinted at the clock—5:10 a.m. Who would be calling this early? It didn't matter, Lencha would get it. She was always up early. But it kept ringing and it finally dawned on her that Lencha was still out helping with the birth.

She reached for the phone. "Hello."

"Josie, it's Ashley."

Josie sat bolt upright. "Ashley, where are you?"

Instead of answering Ashley replied, "I need to see you, please." There was a note of desperation in her voice. Josie looked up to see Caleb standing in the doorway in nothing but his pajama bottoms. Her heart rate was already breaking records. How much more could she take? She took a deep breath and motioned Caleb into the room.

"It's Ashley," she mouthed.

Caleb walked in and sat on the bed and she wished he hadn't done that. Those broad masculine shoulders were too close, too tempting, too...

"Josie, are you there?"

She brought her chaotic thoughts back to Ashley. "Yes, I'm here."

"I need to talk to you."

"Where are you?"

"I'm in the park. Meet me there and please come alone."

Josie gripped the receiver. "I can't do that. Caleb will be with me."

"Okay, but I want to talk to you alone."

"Ashley…"

"Just come. I'll be by the swings." The phone went dead.

"She wants to meet in the park," she told Caleb.

"Why can't she come here?"

"I don't know. She sounds funny." Josie swung her feet to the floor.

"This isn't safe," Caleb said.

"I know, but maybe this will tell us what we need to know."

"I don't like it." Caleb ran a hand through his dark hair, causing it to stand on end and making him that much more attractive.

She swallowed and stopped her wandering thoughts. "I told her you would be with me, and we can handle this."

Caleb shook his head. "I'm calling Eric for backup, just in case something goes wrong."

"Okay, but ask him to keep out of sight."

Josie quickly dressed and met Caleb in the kitchen in less than five minutes. "Did you get Eric?"

"Yes." Caleb grabbed his hat. "I told him where we'd be and he's going in his own vehicle."

Backing out of the drive, Caleb asked, "Where is this park?"

Josie gave directions. "Beckett actually has a very nice park with a pool and tennis courts donated by Boone. He's also donated a lot of money to the schools."

"Good ol' Boone."

"He's very generous." She gathered her hair and curled it into a rope and clipped it behind her head. "What do you think this means?"

"Ashley's scared and we'll soon find out why." Caleb parked at the curb. "You stay here until I can locate her and make sure it's safe. And keep the doors locked."

Josie started to protest, but knew he was only looking out for her. He walked toward the benches by the swings and someone emerged from the shadows. It had to be Ashley and Josie wondered what they were taking about. It wasn't quite dawn so she couldn't see the figures clearly. Caleb motioned to her and she got out and ran toward them.

She stopped a few feet away. Ashley's blond

hair was tousled and her clothes were wrinkled and dirty. Josie had never seen her like this.

Ashley sprinted to Josie and Caleb made no move to stop her, so Josie wasn't alarmed. Ashley grabbed her in a bearlike hug. "I'm sorry, Josie. I didn't know who else to call."

Josie had no idea what she was talking about, so she led her to one of the benches and sat down. Caleb stood a few feet away. "Why do you need to talk to me?"

Ashley wiped at her eyes with the backs of her hands. "I can't seem to stop crying."

"What's wrong?"

"Everything." She blinked away more tears with a hiccup. "I was taking your advice."

"My advice?"

"About making a stand to live my own life. I gathered up all my jewelry in case I needed to hock it and planned to meet Hans in Boston, then we'd fly to wherever we wanted and start a new life."

"But you didn't do that?"

"No. I left a note and packed a suitcase. I was going down the back stairs when I heard all the loud voices, so I went to see what the argument was about and…"

Now Josie understood. Ashley heard that Brett wasn't her father. Ashley had nothing to do with shooting her. She was just caught in the middle of an ugly family secret. She hugged Ashley. "I'm so sorry."

"Brett isn't my father." Ashley hiccupped into Josie's shoulder. "This man I'd loved and hated all of my life wasn't even my dad. My father was right in front of me all the time. I don't even know my mother. Or him. How could they do this to me? How could they?"

"I don't know." Josie stroked her hair, wanting to comfort her in some way. "Where have you been?"

Ashley drew back, wiping tears from her wet face. "I stumbled to my car and I was crying so bad I couldn't see and I ran into a gate. Caddo saw it happen and when he noticed how upset I was, he drove me to his house and parked my car in his garage. I didn't want anyone to know where I was. He's listened to me cry all night."

"You've been with Caddo?" That shocked Josie even more.

"Yes."

"I didn't even know you knew Caddo."

"Everyone who lives on Silver Spur knows Caddo. He taught me to ride and I've been teaching him to speak better English. We've always had a connection. I thought it was because we were cousins, but we're…we're…sister and brother." She buried her face in her hands and began to cry in loud sobs.

Caddo stepped out of the night and Caleb reached for his gun, then relaxed when he saw who it was. Caddo walked straight to Ashley and sat by her.

"Stop this," Caddo said in his deep voice. "Caddo's tough." He beat a fist against his chest. "You're tough, too."

Ashley quieted down immediately. There was definitely a connection. "He's right," Josie said. "You're stronger than this."

Ashley wiped away tears again. "Yes, I am. I'm leaving, but I had to let you and Ranger McCain know that I didn't shoot you. Caddo said I was now the main suspect. I would never do that. Please believe me."

"We do," Caleb replied. "I'll be right back. I have to let Eric know everything's okay."

"Please don't let him know I'm here," Ashley begged. "It will get back to Pa and he'll make me come back."

Caleb nodded and walked off.

"Where will you go?" Josie asked.

"I was going to meet Hans." She hiccupped again. "But when he found out I wasn't coming with the Beckett money behind me, he suddenly wasn't interested anymore."

"*Bastardo,*" Caddo uttered.

Caleb returned and Josie tried to find the right

words or a solution to Ashley's problem, but to her, only one thing was going to make any of this better. "Ashley, running away isn't going to solve anything. Until you speak to Lorna, you're going to have this sore on your heart that will never heal. Confront her, tell her how hurt and mad you are. That's the only way you'll be able to live your life with any peace."

Ashley's face hardened. "I can't. I hate her."

"Tell her then. Let her know exactly how you're feeling."

Ashley trembled. "They'll make me stay and I can't. I have to get away from here."

"Ranger McCain and I will go with you and if you don't want to stay Caleb will make sure you're able to leave. You can trust him. I have for a very long time and he's never let me down."

Her words were like a cool breeze on a hot day, sustaining and bolstering Caleb. He sincerely hoped he never had to let Josie down.

"You'd go with me?" Ashley asked as dawn appeared suddenly, bathing the park in a golden light.

"Yes," Caleb answered without any hesitation.

"Boone will force me to stay. He might even lock me in my room."

"Not while I'm around." Caleb glanced at Caddo. "And I'm sure Caddo will be around for backup."

"*Si.*"

"I know a place in Austin where you can stay until you get your head straight." Caleb knew Gertie would take her in.

As if reading his mind Josie said, "Yes. Ms. Gertie is a doll and she loves company."

"I don't know." Ashley tucked her straggly hair behind her ears. "I might want to be on my own."

"It's your choice," he said.

"Okay." Ashley took a long breath. "I want to talk to my mother."

They all stood. "Caddo and I will follow you in my car," Ashley added.

"Deal," Caleb answered. He and Josie walked toward the truck as Ashley and Caddo headed for the car.

Josie stopped as a slim woman entered the park with a baby in a stroller. "Just a minute," she said, and hurried toward the woman. Caleb quickly followed.

"Rhonda," Josie called, and the woman turned and looked at her with bewilderment in her green eyes.

"Oh, my, it's Josie," Rhonda said, her expression clearing. She hugged Josie. "Dennis said you were back and well. We all wondered what had happened to you. It's so good to see you."

Josie knelt by the stroller. A little girl with blond

hair and honey-brown eyes smiled. "You have your baby. Oh, my. She's so precious. How old is she?"

Rhonda knelt by Josie. "She had her first birthday two months ago. Dennis and I are so happy. We finally have our baby and we named her Jennifer. I always wanted a daughter named Jennifer and now I have her. We call her Jenny. Isn't she adorable?"

"Yes." Josie touched the baby's cheek and she smiled, showing off her new teeth. "I remember you were waiting for her."

"Yes. The adoption agency finally came through." Rhonda touched her arm. "I'm so sorry for what happened to you. I can't believe you survived all that."

"Thanks." Josie stood. "My memory's slowly returning and soon I'll have my life back."

"I'm glad." Rhonda glanced at Caleb.

Josie made the introductions.

"You're in the park very early," Caleb commented.

"I know." Rhonda heaved a sigh. "We live right across the street. Jenny is teething and she kept Dennis and me up most of the night. She loves the park and I'm hoping she'll tire herself out and fall asleep so I can get a couple of hours rest."

"Hope it works."

They said goodbye and walked to the truck.

Once inside, Caleb said, "So that's Dennis's wife?"

"Yes. She was always very friendly to me."

Caleb pulled up in front of Ashley's Mercedes and they headed toward Silver Spur. Josie was very quiet.

"What are you thinking?"

"That everything is a dead-end and we're no closer to finding out who shot me than when we arrived. You're right, as dysfunctional as the Becketts are, they didn't have anything to do with my shooting."

"Yeah. But nevertheless we seem to get more entangled with their lives."

She glanced at him, a slight smile on her face. "I hope you realize we're heading into the eye of a hurricane."

He nodded. "Day of reckoning for Mason."

"And Boone. Things he's been denying he may now have to face and admit out loud."

"Mmm. I hope Ashley is up for this."

"I hate that she has to go through this, but she has a protector and I don't mean you and me."

"Caddo," he said before she could finish.

"Yes. And how weird is that?"

"I'd say it's right. I know the feeling. Eli, my half brother, has covered my back many times, sometimes without me knowing. I always feel stronger when he's around me."

"And you didn't meet him until you were both grown?"

"Yes. But that connection, that bond, was there."

"Like it is with Ashley and Caddo."

"Mmm." He turned onto the Silver Spur road. "Except Joe McCain was dead and so was Eli's mother. We didn't have that family interference or disapproval. We just had our own feelings to build on."

"And Mason is very much alive," she said.

"As is Lorna."

"As I said, batten down the hatches, this is going to be a rough-and-rowdy, take-no-prisoners kind of visit."

He heard her lighthearted words, but her voice told another story. She was worried. For Ashley. And Caddo. They were close, related by blood, and that bond was there, too.

"It was nice having a sister," she said in a faraway voice. "Even if I knew it was a lie."

He glanced at her. "Were you tempted to tell Ashley the truth when you first came here?"

"No. She was always so sweet and I couldn't do that to her. But it got to me when she kept asking questions about *our* father, wanting to know him better."

They pulled into the circular drive. "I was angry with Lorna, though," Josie continued. "I told her that she knew Brett wasn't Ashley's father and it was wrong to let Ashley go on believing that lie. She went into one of her rages and ordered me out of the house." She stared at the large hacienda. "Like Boone says, truth, like chickens, comes home to roost. Today's a time for truth."

CHAPTER TWELVE

THEY MET ON THE STONE walkway to the front door. Josie linked her arm through Ashley's. "You okay?"

"No. But as long as you're with me, I'll be okay." Ashley glanced at the men behind them. "And Caddo. And Ranger McCain."

Ashley opened the door without ringing the bell and they walked into the foyer. "Where's Caddo?" Ashley asked anxiously, noticing he wasn't with them.

"He slipped away," Caleb replied.

"He's never been in the house and I guess it makes him uncomfortable. But I know he's here. It's uncanny the way he seems to be able to appear and disappear at will."

They followed Ashley into a part of the house Caleb hadn't seen before. It was a large sunroom facing an even larger pool. The room was done in navy, yellows and greens and flowers and plants seemed to be everywhere. A buffet was spread out in silver chafing dishes. Lorna and Mason sat at a table, eating breakfast. The scene looked like a picture out of a magazine of a happy family. But there was nothing happy about this couple—or this family.

Lorna glanced up. "Ashley, darling." She pushed back her chair and ran to her daughter.

Ashley stuck her hands out, preventing Lorna from hugging her. "Don't touch me."

Lorna was taken aback and had a moment to really see her daughter's appearance, with her wrinkled, dirty clothes, and her hair in rattails around her tearstained face. "Look at you. You're a mess. What happened? Did someone hurt you?"

"Yes. Someone hurt me," Ashley answered in a very clear voice.

Mason got to his feet, anger evident in his eyes. "Who?"

"You hurt me," Ashley stated without faltering. "You both have hurt me."

"Darling, what are you talking about?" Lorna asked. She appeared to be in complete control of herself today. "We would never hurt you."

"Oh, please, Mother. I know the truth and you can stop lying and pretending."

Lorna paled and Mason looked away, his anger suddenly gone.

Boone walked in from the kitchen, a cup of coffee in his hand, munching on a soft taco.

"Didn't know we had company." He took a seat at the table. "Found your way back, huh, Ash?"

"I'm not back. I only came because Josie made me."

"Josie giving you orders these days?" He squinted at them as he took a sip of coffee.

"Josie's the only one who cares about me," Ashley told him.

Boone set his cup down very slowly. "I don't remember Josie paying for any of those fancy schools."

Caleb thought he'd never met a more cold-hearted man. Boone and Joe McCain certainly had something in common.

"I never asked you to do that."

"Your mother sure did."

"Boone, please." Lorna shot him an angry stare. "Now, girl…"

"I'm only here for a minute," Ashley interrupted, her eyes on her mother. "Why did you lie to me all those years? Why did you let me believe Brett Beckett was my father?"

"Oh, darling, it was a very difficult time."

"Tell me!" Ashley shouted.

Lorna twisted her hands. "My father and Boone had business dealings and they wanted Brett and me to marry. I'd been in love with Brett since I'd met him, so I didn't have a problem with it. Brett did. He was in love with… Marie Cortez."

Josie stiffened beside him.

"Brett wasn't giving us a chance and I knew he'd forget about her once we were married. He still refused and Boone forced him. I wanted our marriage to work. I…"

"Is that why you were sleeping with his brother? To make your marriage work?" Ashley's words were sharp and insolent.

Lorna put a hand to her forehead. "Darling, please…"

"Is it?" Ashley persisted.

"I started seeing Mason to make Brett jealous. That's all it was."

Mason clenched and unclenched his hands, but he never said a word.

"It was more. You were pregnant with his child, which you tried to pass off as Brett's."

Lorna stuck out her chin. "Brett kept wanting to go to the doctor with me, but I kept finding excuses. The pregnancy had made me very weak and he thought something might be wrong with the baby, so he went on his own. That's how he found out I was farther along than I'd told him. That was it for him. He wouldn't listen to me and he didn't even want to know who the father was. He just wanted out of the marriage."

Silence filled the room. Josie stood as still as a statue.

"Why didn't you marry Mason before I was born?"

"Because I was still married to Brett. I was determined to never give him a divorce and Boone hired a lawyer to make sure it never happened. After a year, we thought Brett had given up. Boone was on a trip to South America to look at some cattle and I took you and a nanny on a cruise to just get away. While we were away, Brett pushed it through somehow. We were never sure how he did that, but the divorce was final and I didn't have any strength left to fight it."

Josie suddenly knew why the divorce went through. She'd overheard her parents talking about it. Brett had found a judge who disliked Boone and his heavy-handed tactics. Boone's lawyer tried to stop it, but the judge granted it. Her parents were married soon after.

"Why would you even want to fight it?" Ashley asked. "He was in love with someone else."

Lorna's eyes darkened. "Do you know how that felt? At night in his sleep he'd call her name and I hated her. She ruined my life."

"Excuse me?" Ashley said, and Josie clamped her lips together. Ashley had to fight this out with her mother. "*You* ruined your life by trying to hold on to a man who didn't want you. And you've ruined mine by lying to me. Take responsibility for what you've done."

Lorna flinched and seemed unable to speak.

"Why couldn't you have married Mason and made everything right?" Ashley kept on.

An agonized laugh left Lorna's throat. "You remember your grandfather. Can you see him letting me marry a man with a record? A murderer. His career would be in shambles."

"Grandfather's been dead for ten years. Why haven't you married Mason since then?"

Lorna touched her forehead with a trembling hand. "It's hard to explain…."

"So you kept lying to me and sleeping with Mason when the need arose. Do you know what kind of woman that makes you?"

Lorna whimpered deep in her throat.

Ashley turned to Mason for the first time. "Why did *you* never tell me? Didn't you want me to know that you were my father?"

The hard lines of Mason's face cracked a bit. "I respected Lorna's decision."

Ashley gasped in disbelief. "Mason Beckett respecting anyone's decision is a laugh. You just didn't want me, either." Her voice broke on the last word and Lorna reached out for her.

"Darling…"

Ashley jerked away. "Don't touch me."

"Enough," Boone bellowed, finishing his breakfast and getting to his feet. "You're a Beckett. That's all you need to know, girl. Now get upstairs and get cleaned up. You look like hell. And I don't want to hear any more of this nonsense. They lied to you, but now you have the truth, so get over it. You've had a helluva good life."

Ashley stood her ground under the crude orders. "I'm not going upstairs, but I am leaving. I'll live my own life, my way."

Boone eyes narrowed at the unexpected disobedience. "Don't force my hand, girl."

"I'm not fourteen years old and you can't force me to stay here," Ashley said in defiance, her jawline rigid.

"Wanna bet?" His eyes narrowed. "Now get upstairs before I lose my patience."

Caleb moved forward. "I promised to take her out of here when she's ready." He looked at Ashley. "Are you ready?"

"Yes," Ashley replied.

"Like hell!" Boone yelled in anger. "Ranger man, you're on my turf and what I say goes here. Take Josie and get out while you can."

"Ashley goes with us." Caleb's words rang loud and clear in the large room.

The steel in Boone's eyes glowed like fire. "Are you calling my bluff?"

"Yes, sir."

"You're a fool, Ranger. I can have twenty vaqueros in here just like that." Boone snapped his fingers. "They'll take you out in the blink of an eye and your body will be found somewhere on the prairie, buzzards picking at your bones." The glow of his eyes leveled on Caleb. "You got five seconds to leave—without Ashley."

Caleb stared back at him, unblinking, unmoving as the seconds ticked off.

"Pablo!" Boone shouted.

"*Sí, señor.*" Pablo appeared from the kitchen.

"Tell the vaqueros I need a job done—now."

"*Sí, señor.*" Pablo backed out.

"*Pronto!*" Boone hollered after him. "You still got time to leave, ranger man. It's always wise to know when you've been beaten."

"You're not scaring me, Mr. Beckett."

"It's okay," Ashley spoke up. "Just go, please. I don't want them to hurt you."

"I made you a promise and I'm keeping it."

Josie touched his arm. This was getting out of control. She didn't want Caleb hurt, and even though Boone was mostly a lot of hot air, she was beginning to feel a little afraid. There'd been bodies found in Sagebrush Creek and Eric always thought it had something to do with the Silver Spur. Nothing could ever be proven, though. Boone was the law here.

Caleb's muscles were tight and Josie knew he wasn't backing down or budging. How many vaqueros could she and Caleb take on? She was mentally calculating when Pablo rushed back into the room, looking flustered.

Boone looked behind him. "Where's the boys?"

"They no come, *señor.*"

"Why the hell not?"

"Caddo say no and vaqueros no cross him."

"Who the hell is Caddo to be giving orders?" Boone's face turned red in anger. "This is my land and I give the orders."

"Pa, let it go," Mason said.

"Like hell. I want that half-breed off this land *now.*"

"He'll take every vaquero with him, then who's going to work this ranch?"

"Where would they go? And who in the hell's side are you on anyway?"

Josie saw him before anyone else did. Caddo jumped from the second floor balcony, which looked out onto the sunroom. He landed squarely on his feet, his eyes as blue and heated as Boone's. Chills crept up her spine. The day of reckoning had more than arrived.

He wore faded Wrangler jeans and had a knife attached at the waist. His chest was bare, his long hair hanging around him. If he'd had war paint on his face and chest no one would have been surprised. It was as if a character from an old Western had come to right a wrong.

For a split second everyone was speechless. Then Caddo spoke to Mason. "Whose side you on, big man?" Evidently Caddo had been listening to every word from his perch upstairs. Ashley had said Caddo'd never been in the house, but Josie was betting he knew it like the palm of his hand.

Caddo was angry, that was very clear from the glint in his eyes to the veins popping out on his neck. Josie wasn't sure what was going to happen next. Mason seemed to have turned to stone.

"Get the hell out of this house," Boone screeched.

"Come on, Caddo," Ashley said. "Let's go."

"No," Lorna screamed. "Don't go near him. He's barbaric and you don't know what he'll do. He could hurt you."

Ashley gave a small smile. "Caddo won't hurt me. He's my brother."

And the walls of secrecy came tumbling down. Quietly. But everyone heard them, crumbling, exposing the unspoken secret of the past. Everyone stood in stunned silence.

"Sonofabitch!" Boone collapsed into a chair, the open truth more than he could stand.

"Oh, I'm sorry." Ashley feigned regret. "Wasn't I supposed to say that out loud?"

Lorna rounded on Mason. "Look what your sleeping around has done. How could you do this to our daughter? To us? That's the very reason I'll never marry you. You can't be trusted to stay away from the Mexican tramps."

Mason grabbed Lorna's face in one hand, his fingers cutting into her cheeks. She tried to jerk away, but he held her tight. "Don't say one word about Theresa. You know nothing about our relationship. She never used me like you did and she loved me just like I loved her. I was crushed the day she died in labor with our second son. I promised her I'd take care of Caddo and I have." He released her and stepped back, curling his hands into tight fists.

Lorna rubbed her face, her eyes glittering with hate.

"Pa made raising him out of the question, but I saw to it that someone was always there for him."

"How did Boone force you not to raise your own son?" The words slipped out before Josie could stop them.

Mason swung to Josie. "By his arrogance and narrow-mindedness. He told me repeatedly that if he caught me with any Mexican girl, he'd disinherit me. I knew he meant every word because of what had happened with Brett. I couldn't risk everything I'd worked my whole life for. Your coming here opened old wounds and created family tension. You knew one of my secrets and I just wanted you to leave and never come back. I'd do anything to protect Ashley."

Josie swallowed the gigantic lump that had formed in her throat. "Are you saying you tried to stop me by shooting me?"

"Goddammit, how many times do I have to tell you and the ranger that I didn't shoot you? I just wanted you away from my family before any of this came out. But you couldn't let it be, could you? You…"

Caddo removed the knife from its sheath and moved toward Mason. Mason paused and Caleb stepped closer.

Caddo pointed the knife at Mason. "I could stick this between your ribs into your heart. You'd feel nothin'. But Caddo no do. He has honor." He beat his chest with his other fist. "Not from Beckett blood. From Karankawas's. My ancestors are proud and honorable. Caddo need nothin' from you. You're a coward. You no hurt Josie, Ashley. *Sí*." Caddo shoved the knife back into its sheath and headed for the door.

"Wait," Mason called.

Caddo stopped, but he didn't turn.

"Never thought of myself as a coward and I've never been afraid of much of anything. Loved a woman who thought I wasn't good enough to be a father to our child. Theresa loved me for who I was, but Pa took that away from me and I wasn't man enough to stand up to him." He took a deep breath and faced Boone. "If Caddo leaves here, so do I."

"Good riddance," Boone muttered, pouring whiskey into his coffee.

"Mr. Beckett." Caleb walked over to him. "Take a good look at everything you're losing. Your sons disobeyed your rules by falling in love with Mexican women, but look at your grandchildren. Caddo is as fine a man as I've ever met. And you yourself said Josie has fire and spirit. This is an opportunity to become a family. Don't let your pride stand in your way."

"Don't preach to me, ranger man. Just get the hell outta my house." Boone's steely resolve was evident in his eyes and voice.

Caleb didn't budge. "My father never claimed me. He denied who I was right up to his death. But I was lucky. I had a mother and a stepfather who gave me everything he couldn't. Never realized how lucky I was until I came here. If you let your son and grandchildren go, you'll die heartbroken and lonely. Take it from me. I know. My father died a broken man."

Boone took a gulp of the coffee.

"You're a powerful man, Mr. Beckett. Just how powerful are you?"

The corners of Boone's mouth twitched. "Not too damn powerful at the moment, ranger man." Josie's grandfather knew when to cut his losses. That's how he became so powerful.

Boone rose to his feet. "I need a strong goddamn drink." He spun toward the den and stopped, turning to look at them. "Ashley, if you want to leave, go ahead. I'm gettin' too old and too tired to try and make my kids understand about their heritage. No one seems to care about that, but me. So go, but know that you always have a home here." He glanced at Josie. "No one here tried to kill you. I hope you find out soon who did. And like Ashley, you have a home here, too. Caddo, not sure about you, boy. Might take me a while. Mason, in my den. Now!" With that he was gone.

Josie looked around. Caddo was gone, too. Maybe he could disappear at will.

Mason followed Boone, and Josie stood staring at Lorna, needing more answers. "Why do you hate me so much?"

"Go away, Josie," Lorna said with a wave of her hand. "Haven't you gotten what you wanted?"

"What I want is the truth. Why would you hate someone who had nothing to do with making your life turn out the way it has?"

"I was so afraid you'd tell Ashley the truth," Lorna shouted. "I wanted you away from here before that could happen. Just like Mason did." Her voice lowered. "And you look just like Marie and brought back all those memories I want to forget. You don't belong here. I don't think you ever will."

"Until my full memory returns, I'm not sure where I belong."

Lorna looked at her manicured nails for a second. "I am sorry for the pain you've been through. I wouldn't wish that on anyone—not even Marie's daughter."

Josie wasn't too sure about Lorna's sincerity, but decided they'd all been through enough for one day.

"Ashley, please, we need to talk," Lorna pleaded with her daughter.

"I'm not ready."

"We'll go on a trip, a cruise, anything you want. I'll tell you everything you want to know and I won't lie to you ever again. I can't change the past, so please let's work together on the future."

Ashley wavered for the first time. Josie could tell by her hesitation.

"I'm not ready," Ashley said again. "Not sure if I'll ever be. But, please, do something for me."

"Sure. Anything." Hope kindled in Lorna's eyes.

"Stop lying to yourself," Ashley told her mother.

"I'm not sure what you mean."

"I'm talking about Mason. After all these years, you're still sleeping with him, so it has to be more than just sex. Admit that to yourself. And to him." Saying that, she walked toward the front door.

"Ashley…" Lorna called, but Ashley never stopped.

Josie looked at Lorna's defeated expression. "My father didn't deserve what you did to him and his life and I should hate you. But oddly all I feel for you now is sympathy. I hope you listen to your daughter."

Josie walked away feeling no victory. Too much had been lost to experience any kind of victory in someone else's pain. She and Caleb met Ashley outside. Ashley was talking to Caddo by her car.

"If that offer is still open about staying with the woman in Austin, I'll take you up on it," she said to Caleb.

"Sure. I need something to write the address on."

Ashley got a pen and paper from her car. Scribbling on the paper, Caleb said, "We'll call and let her know you're on the way."

"Thank you." Ashley blinked against the morning sun. "Right now I just feel lost and I have to find my way to who I really am."

"You might find your way back here," Josie said.

"Maybe." Ashley looked at the hacienda. "When I would go away to school, I couldn't wait to get back home. Now I can't wait to get away." She smiled at Caddo. "Remember, every night at nine I will be calling."

"*Sí.*" Then a smile broke out on his face. "Yes. I will be waiting. Go with God, sister." He nodded to Josie and Caleb and strolled toward the barns. A Mexican rode to him, leading the paint. Caddo swung up on his back and in a flash he was gone.

Ashley hugged Caleb then clung to Josie. "I'm sorry you still don't know who tried to kill you. I'd stay, but I'd be no help whatsoever."

Josie drew back. "Go and find some happiness. You deserve it."

"We all do," Ashley replied as she slid behind the wheel. A moment later, she was driving away from Silver Spur.

Josie climbed into the truck. In an upstairs window, she noticed a curtain pulled back. Lorna. She was watching her daughter leave. How that must hurt. As Josie had told Lorna, all she felt for the woman was sympathy. In trying to manipulate other people's lives, she'd lost everything. Josie found no joy in that. Lorna's life would now be very lonely. She'd spend her days waiting for her daughter to return.

"Hey, over there. You okay?" Caleb's sweet voice reached her.

"Yes. I was just thinking how sad all this is. How the people we love, we hurt the most."

"That's very sad," he replied. "It makes me think about the years I brooded over a father who didn't want me and how that must have hurt Andrew. He was there loving and caring for me, but I kept thinking about the man who didn't care at all."

"I'm sure Andrew understood."

"Yeah. But when I return I'm going to make sure he knows how much I love him."

"You are so special, Caleb McCain. And fearless."

He lifted an eyebrow at that.

"What would you have done if twenty vaqueros had swarmed the room?"

He smiled. "Fight like hell. And I knew Caddo wasn't far away."

"Poor, sweet Caddo. I don't know what his future holds."

"Time will tell," Caleb mused, staring at the wrecker coming toward them. Caleb stopped to speak with the driver.

The man was looking for the Tahoe and couldn't find it. Caleb drove to the spot and saw to it that the Tahoe was hooked up and pulled back to Austin.

Sitting and waiting, Josie's mind went over all that happened. One thing stood out very clearly. The Becketts hadn't tried to kill her and she still didn't know who had. The shooter was still out there. Watching. Waiting. Goose bumps popped up on her skin as her old friend fear made a brief appearance.

Caleb slid behind the wheel.

"You should be going back to Austin, too," she said. "You have a job and you need to return to it." Although she felt that moment of fear, she also knew she could take care of herself. Her dependency on Caleb had to end and his leaving would be a start.

He started the engine. "I'm not going anywhere until I know you're safe."

"But that could take a long time."

"I don't think so. Your memory is almost complete. Just give it a little more time, and you're not getting rid of me."

She knew he was going to say that. That's the kind of man he was. She should have insisted. Why didn't she?

CHAPTER THIRTEEN

LENCHA WAS FEEDING the chickens when they drove into the yard. Shooing away the hens, she hurried to the truck.

Getting out, Josie looped an arm around her thin shoulders. Out of the corner of her eye she glimpsed the guard parked at the road, keeping an eye on Lencha.

"Just wanted to let you know I'm okay and that Caleb and I are going over to the police station for a while. I didn't know if you were back or not and I was going to leave you a note."

"Got back about six and you were gone. Where you been, child?"

"It's a long story. I'll explain tonight." Josie kissed her cheek. "See you then."

"Take that guard with you. I don't need him," Lencha called.

Josie just shook her head.

"Take care of her, Ranger," Lencha shouted to Caleb.

"Yes, ma'am."

Josie climbed back in the truck and they drove to the station. Eric had called and said he'd pulled a lot more files from the last two months Josie was in Beckett.

"Something has to be in one of those cases," she said. "But I don't know if I'll recognize it."

"The missing girl is going to be the key," Caleb replied.

"Yes. Now we just have to find the file." She glanced out the window, feeling a sense of desperation. "This is taking too long."

"But we're narrowing the list of suspects and that's good."

"Yes, but it's getting very discouraging."

Caleb parked at the station and handed her his phone. "Call Gertie. That should cheer you up."

Their eyes locked for a minute. He always knew what to say to her. She quickly poked out Gertie's number.

Martha answered. "Martha, this is Jos—Belle." She stopped herself just in time, realizing Martha wouldn't know who Josie was. "May I speak with Ms. Gertie, please?"

In a second, Ms. Gertie was on the line. "Belle, darlin', are you coming home?"

"No, Ms. Gertie." A part of her wanted to say yes and leave all this pain behind her. She was stronger than that, though. "My memory hasn't fully returned, but I'm sending someone your way. I hope you'll let her stay with you awhile."

"Who, darlin'?"

Josie told her Ashley's story.

"Of course she's welcome here. I'll have Martha prepare a room. What is Boone thinking? Has he lost all his good sense? No, I take that back. He never had any to start with."

"This isn't about Boone," Josie told her. "It's about Lorna and Mason and how they lied to Ashley for so many years."

"I'll take very good care of her," Gertie promised. "I miss you so much. This house is very empty without you."

"Thank you." Josie swallowed and changed the subject before she burst into tears. "How are the girls and Harry?"

"Pampered and spoiled and they miss you, too."

I miss you, too. And she couldn't believe how much. That life was familiar to her. Comfortable. Safe. Everything that Beckett wasn't. No. She wouldn't settle for safe or allowing herself to go backward. She had to remember everything to be whole again.

"How's Caleb?" Gertie asked, penetrating her thoughts.

"Helping me as usual." She glanced at Caleb

and smiled. He was familiar, too. He… No, she wasn't doing that, either.

"Mmm. He's a good man. I don't worry so much about you while he's there. I hope you'll come home soon."

"I don't know. My life is topsy-turvy right now."

"You just take care."

"I will. Bye."

She clicked off and stared at the phone, experiencing a moment of regret. She would never be Belle again.

"Josie?"

She looked into Caleb's worried eyes.

"What did Gertie say?"

"Exactly what we expected her to. She'll make Ashley feel very welcome just like she did me."

"Then why the sad face?"

"She called me Belle and…"

"What?"

"It's hard to explain."

"Try."

"As Belle I had these wonderful people who cared about me. As Josie I don't feel any of that and I miss it."

He reached out to touch her cheek. "I'm still here, Josie Belle."

She loved the way he called her that. She supposed she was part Belle and part Josie. Maybe always would be. Her head tilted toward his hand, needing his touch, his voice. But she shouldn't. It was unfair to him. She had…

Eric tapped on the window. "Everything okay?"

They drew apart and got out. Josie felt a moment of sadness, of loneliness, and she quickly shook it away.

Inside, Eric said, "Got the forensic back on the bullet fired through Josie's window. Came from a small .25 caliber pistol. Now all we have to do is locate the gun, which is a million-to-one shot. The gun is very popular, sold in gun shops all over the country."

Caleb looked through the report. "The gun that shot Josie was a .22 caliber. Our shooter likes small guns." He laid the file down. "Did you put it in the system?"

"Yes," Eric replied. "But the odds are slim of it being used in another crime."

"Yeah, but it doesn't hurt to try. We might get lucky."

The rest of the day they read through files. Dennis helped, too. By six o'clock they were exhausted and frustrated. No file disclosed a missing girl and neither Eric nor Dennis remembered the case.

"Josie." Dennis leaned back, flexing his arms. "Maybe you need to talk to Lencha again to see if she can remember anything else because clearly we didn't have a missing person back then. This is a small town and if someone was missing, everyone would know about it, especially me."

Josie heaved a sigh of frustration. "I'm sorry, Dennis, to take up all this time. But it's the only clue I have." She rose and stretched her shoulders. "It's time to quit for the day and I'll go home and talk to Lencha again."

"Anything I can do?" Eric asked eagerly, and she looked into his blue eyes searching for the light that would lead her to the answers about their relationship, about her life. But that part of her mind was still blank.

"No, thanks. I need to be alone and think. Maybe something will come back to me."

"Just be careful," Eric warned.

"I will."

She and Caleb rode back to Lencha's in silence. There wasn't anything left to say and she could feel her emotions balancing precariously between anger and tears. She refused to give in to either and she refused to lean on Caleb one more minute. But, oh, she wanted to.

In the house she had one goal—to jog Lencha's memory. "Please think back to that day," Josie begged her. "Put garlic around your neck, chant, stir something in a pot, whatever it takes to remember exactly what I said the last time you saw me. My life may depend on it."

Lencha went outside and Josie and Caleb stared at each other in puzzlement. In a minute she came back with a string interwoven with garlic, peppers and something that Josie couldn't identify. Lencha looped the strand around her neck.

At the smell, Josie took a step backward and bumped into Caleb. Her back felt his broad chest and his hands lightly clutched her elbows. She didn't move away. The urge was strong to lean into him and let him wrap his arms around her and… She could preach to herself day and night about Caleb, but nothing was getting through. The only way to accomplish that was to remember— that would wipe away her dependency on him.

She focused on Lencha, never really expecting her to use garlic or anything else to remember. She just wanted to get her attention. Now Lencha had hers.

Wrinkling her nose, she said, "That's a little strong."

Caleb cleared his throat and she forced herself not to smile.

"Awakens the senses, the mind," Lencha said, closing her eyes and breathing deeply several times.

"And the dead," Caleb whispered for her ears only and they both stepped back farther.

Chula scratched at the door and Caleb let her out. Even the squirrel wanted fresh air.

"What happened that morning?" Josie asked.

"I was eating my raisins when you walked in winding your hair in that loop thing you do. I gave you a cup of coffee and you said you knew I had put something in it, but you didn't even care. You'd had a lead on a case and you might need a little extra energy."

Lencha stopped and took several deep breaths.

"What lead?" Josie said, barely audible.

"A phone call. You said you were expecting a phone call about a missing girl and you had to get to work."

"And," Josie prompted in desperation when Lencha stopped speaking.

Lencha opened her eyes. "Nothing. You left and I never saw you again until you walked in here with the ranger."

"Dammit." Josie sank into a chair. "Why is everything a dead-end?"

Lencha looked at Caleb, then went outside to put away the smelly strand.

"We're missing something," she said. Jumping up she ran to her room and grabbed the box of files. She spread them out on the bed, looking at each name carefully, trying to jog her memory.

"Give it a rest for the night," Caleb suggested from the doorway.

"I can't. I have to keep looking."

He walked into the room. "It's a waste of your time."

She blinked. "What?"

"Sometimes older people remember things the way they want and I didn't pay too much attention to Lencha's memory of the last time she saw you. But we keep coming back to it. Now I'm not sold on the garlic and peppers and whatever, but she seems pretty clear about that morning."

"What's your point?"

"I'm certain you were working a missing person case and I'm just as certain you'll never find the file."

She shook her head. "I'm not following you."

"Whoever shot you destroyed the file."

"Oh." She grabbed her cheeks. "Of course." Why hadn't she thought of that? Suddenly she knew they were on the edge of finding the truth.

"It's the only thing that makes sense."

"But it doesn't explain why Eric and Dennis don't know anything about the girl."

"No."

She took a long breath. "Then let's find out."

He caught her arm as she made to walk past him. "We've been with them most of the day and neither has a chink in their story. I want to do some checking tonight so I'll have some hard facts, then we'll talk to them tomorrow."

"What facts? What are you looking for?"

"Background on both men to see if there are any skeletons in their closets."

"I'm engaged to Eric," she said, her voice sounding anxious.

"Try to get some rest. Maybe Lencha can give you something."

She glared at him. "Caleb McCain, this is the first time I've wanted to hit you. I'm not some sniveling, weak-kneed woman who needs to be sedated."

He held up both hands, as if to defend himself. "I'm sorry. I didn't mean it that way. I'm just worried about you."

She knew he was and that one thing saved his hide.

He grinned. "I'm retreating now to my own room."

As his door closed, Josie picked up the files and stuffed them back into the box. This seemed to be a ritual she'd been doing since she'd returned here. Where was the missing file and who'd destroyed it? Why hadn't Eric or Dennis known about the case? Surely she discussed it with them. Could they both be involved? Could they both be afraid of what she'd remember?

With the files tucked away in the box, she lifted

it and stopped. A piece of paper lay on the bed. She set the box on the floor and picked it up. A telephone number was scribbled on it—nothing else. She recognized the area code for Corpus. She studied it for a long time, but it wasn't a familiar number or one she remembered. The paper must have fallen out of one of the files and she had no idea which one. She laid it on her dresser wondering if it meant anything.

Lencha had said that she was waiting for a call. She gritted her teeth in frustration and went to help Lencha with supper. Caleb was busy on his laptop so she carried him a plate and went to take a bath.

Brushing her hair, she couldn't take her eyes off the paper. Following an instinct, she grabbed the phone and dialed the number. The person on the other end might be able to give her some answers. It rang and rang, then an answering machine came on, "You've reached the Williams'. Leave a message and we'll call you back."

Josie hung up. Williams. She knelt on the floor and flipped through the box of files. No Williams, but there was a Willis. Could the number have been misfiled? Yes. Yes. Yes. She remembered seeing it the first day she'd searched. The number was in the Willis file and it meant nothing to her. It still didn't, other than there could have been a Williams file.

Speculation and grasping at straws—that's

what she was doing. Her head pounded and she held it with both hands. Oh God! The pain was severe, like sharp pins darting through her head. It hadn't hurt like this in a long time. When she'd first experienced the pains, they frightened her. But Dr. Oliver had assured her they were normal—part of the healing process.

She got up and stretched out on the bed, the pain growing intense. It eased for a moment and she flipped off the light and curled into a ball, needing sleep more than anything now.

CALEB WAS FRUSTRATED. He had nothing. Eric and Dennis checked out with stellar reputations; there wasn't so much as a traffic violation on either. Even Dennis and Rhonda's adoption was legal. No secrets anywhere. Damn. Damn. Damn. He got up and paced. Who was this mysterious person who wanted Josie dead? What secret did Josie uncover? Who was the missing girl?

He stopped in his tracks as something Dennis had said came back to him. *This is a small town and if someone was missing, everyone would know about it.* What if the girl wasn't from Beckett? That would explain no one knowing. Maybe a friend called Josie, needing help. Maybe…

He darted across the hall to Josie's room. The light was out and she was sound asleep. He watched her for a moment, then backed away, letting her rest. It was what she needed now. Going back to his room, he began a missing person's check for young girls, dating from eighteen months ago for the surrounding towns and Corpus. He worked on into the night.

JOSIE TOSSED AND TURNED in a dreamlike state as voices tortured her. Was she dreaming or sleeping? She fought to make the distinction.

"Are you Josie Marie Beckett?"

She heard the anxious voice clearly. "Yes."

"This is Mae Williams from Corpus. I knew your father."

"Oh."

"He was a good detective and I could trust him. I'm hoping I can trust you, too."

"How did you get my number?"

"Frank Colson, a cop friend of Brett's gave it to me. He said you might be able to help me."

"What's this about?"

"My daughter is missing and I need help."

"I'm not sure how I can help you. I work in Beckett now."

"I know—that's why I'm calling. My daughter left for Beckett over two weeks ago and hasn't returned."

"I can file a missing person's report."

"No." The scream jarred Josie almost to wakefulness, then she floated back to the conversation.

"Why not?"

"Boone Beckett is the law there and I've heard the man is ruthless. Brett never trusted him."

"Does my grandfather have something to do with this?"

"I don't know. My daughter got herself into some trouble and I don't know who to trust or who to blame."

"Why are you calling me?"

"For help. Could you look for her confidentially? I'm willing to pay you. I just need someone I can trust."

"I'll see if I can help and you don't need to pay me. What's her name?"

"Oh, thank you. Her name is Tracy and she's seventeen years old. I'll give you my number so you can get in touch. Call me anytime. I'm worried sick. Please keep this confidential. My daughter's life depends on it."

The voices faded away into a deep dark void. A piercing pain shot through her head and the voices started again.

"Josie, I got a call from her and she's scared to death. I gave her your number and told her she could trust you and that you would help her. She said she'd call you."

"Where is she?"

"She wouldn't tell me."

"Mae, none of this makes any sense."

"I know. Tracy has been acting so strange lately and she won't talk to me. She only said she got herself involved in something she can't get out of."

"With whom?"

"She said someone powerful who wouldn't hesitate to kill her."

"Mae, this is Beckett and there's only one powerful person here. That man is my grandfather."

"I'm sorry, Josie. I didn't even know Tracy knew him."

"So give me a clue as to what's going on. I don't have a good relationship with my grandfather, but I know he doesn't hurt seventeen-year-old girls."

"Unless Tracy was blackmailing him or something."

"Pardon me? What type of girl is Tracy?"

"She's always been a problem child. My husband and I could never do anything with her. Then my husband died and things got worse. Tracy was angry all the time. She left home when she was fifteen and moved in with a boyfriend. They were arrested for trying to extort money from a wealthy man. I hired an attorney for her and she got off with a six-month sentence. I wanted her to come home but she wouldn't. Then she called and said she was in deep trouble again, but she knew a way out. A profitable way out."

"But it didn't happen?"

"No. She called in a panic and said she was going to Beckett and if she didn't return, I'd know she was dead. I tried to talk her out of it, but Tracy wouldn't listen. I waited and waited and she never called and she wouldn't answer her cell. That's when I finally called Frank for help. He and Brett helped me when Tracy was fourteen and ran away. They brought her back and tried talking to her. Your father kept checking on her and I got to know him. When I told Frank Tracy had gone to Beckett, he said he couldn't help, but that Brett's daughter now worked on the police force there and I could trust you."

"So evidently Tracy's somewhere in Beckett hiding out?"

"I hope."

"I'll wait for her call and I'll find her and deliver her to your doorstep. But you have to promise to get her some help."

"I will, and thank you, Josie."

Josie, Josie, Josie.

Her name echoed through her mind and she fought to capture it, to stop it. But the dream took over and the voices continued.

"Miss Beckett, this is Tracy Williams."

"Yes. I've been waiting for your call."

"My mother says I can trust you."

"Yes, you can."

"But you're a Beckett and you're on the police force."

"You have to trust me."

"You haven't told anyone about me, have you?"

"No, Tracy. I promised your mom I'd bring you home. So tell me where you are and I'll come and get you."

"Alone?"

"Yes. Alone."

"I'm in a deer cabin on County Road 249. Hurry. I don't think I have much time."

"I'm on my way."

"Hurry."

CHAPTER FOURTEEN

STILL IN A DREAMLIKE state, Josie crawled out of bed and slipped into her jeans. Walking into the hall, she paused at Caleb's door, then she hurried through the dark house, and out the back to Lencha's truck.

Starting the engine, she headed for County Road 249. She knew the way. It was late and no cars were on the road. She turned off the highway and took a dirt track that led to the deer cabin.

Hurry.

The track was overgrown with brush and mesquite and they scratched against the pickup as the headlights shone the way into a small clearing. Then she saw it—the cabin. It had burned to the ground. No! Nothing was left but ashes and a chimney.

She was too late.

Josie pushed open the door and stepped out. As she did, a searing pain shot through her head and she sank to her knees. In that instant she woke up.

She looked around at the darkness and the head-lights leveled on the pile of ashes.

Where am I?

Suddenly dawn crept up on the horizon, lifting the darkness and illuminating the early morning. A rabbit scurried from the bushes and darted away. She rose to her feet and held on to the truck door for support. *She remembered.* The darkness of her memory had lifted.

Oh, God! She remembered!

The day she was so angry at Lorna and Mason she drove to town, breaking the speed limit. Taking a moment, she called Eric and told him she was going home to Corpus and she'd explain later. He wanted answers, but she was so angry she wasn't ready to give them. Then she called Dennis, severing her ties in Beckett.

Lencha wasn't home so she'd have to explain to her later. She removed her gun and badge and placed them on the nightstand. Her job here was over. She wouldn't be returning. She hurriedly threw clothes into a suitcase. Then her cell rang. It was Tracy. Since the girl hadn't called all day, Josie assumed she'd changed her mind. Tracy sounded desperate and Josie tore out the door to help her. She'd given Mae her word and she was going to Corpus anyway so she'd just take Tracy with her and deliver her to her mother.

She'd made the same trip as she just had, except she'd spotted smoke from the highway. Pressing down on the gas pedal she flew down the road and braked to a stop not far from the burning cabin. Flames leaped and roared from the back of the building.

Wrapping her arms around her, she could feel the tremendous heat of the fire as if it was that day. She'd jumped out of her car screaming Tracy's name. Sprinting to a window she could see a girl lying on the sofa, her face tilted sideways. Josie didn't know if she was alive or dead.

She tried the front door, breathing heavily, frantic to get to Tracy. As she opened the door, the flames drove her back. She needed something to cover herself and dashed back to her car and grabbed her jacket. She heard an explosion, felt a paralyzing pain in her head, then total, dark oblivion overtook her.

Oh my God! Oh my God!

Her hands trembled against her face. Josie never saw the shooter. Her breaths came in gulps and it took a moment for her to realize what all this meant. She'd been waiting to see the face of the person who'd shot her and left her for dead, but she'd never known who that was. She'd been shot trying to save Tracy.

Questions ran through her mind like angry

soldiers looking for a target. But there were no answers. She heaved a painful breath, knowing one thing. Her life was still in danger. And she had to get back to Caleb.

By EARLY MORNING, Caleb had a list of names. He wanted to show them to Josie, but he'd wait until she was awake. He slept for a couple of hours, then took the list to Josie's room, hoping a name would jog her memory.

She wasn't in bed, but he wasn't alarmed. She was either in the kitchen or the bathroom. In the kitchen, Lencha was drinking a cup of coffee at the table with *Chula* on her shoulder.

"Where's Josie?"

"Still asleep."

"No. I just checked."

"Bathroom then."

Caleb hurried to the door, getting a bad feeling in his gut. "Josie," he called. There was no response, so he opened the door. The room was empty.

Where was Josie?

He ran outside and called her name over and over. She was nowhere in sight, but he noticed Lencha's truck was gone. He phoned the police station to see if she'd gone to visit Eric. She hadn't.

Since Caleb was there at night, there was no guard. Damn. What had happened? Caleb grabbed his hat. "Lencha, I'm going to the police station. Call me immediately if you hear from Josie."

"Okay. Ranger?"

He stopped for a second, looking at the fear in Lencha's eyes that echoed his own. "Find her. Please find her."

"I intend to."

As the truck roared into town, Caleb fervently hoped that he would find Josie. And he prayed even harder that she was still alive.

As JOSIE CAME THROUGH the back door, *Chula* leaped onto her jeans and crawled to her neck making chirping sounds. She stroked her with a shaky hand.

Lencha whirled around from the sink. "Josie, child." She held a hand to her chest. "Where have you been?"

"It's a long story. Where's Caleb?"

"Looking all over this town for you. The man's half out of his mind with worry and so am I. I'm getting too old for this."

"I'm sorry. I didn't mean to worry anyone. Please call Caleb and tell him that I'm back." She couldn't call him. She had to stop depending on Caleb and sort this out herself. But if she heard his voice…

The door flew open and Caleb charged in. Josie did the only thing she could. She ran into his arms.

He held her so tight she thought her ribs might crack, but she didn't mind.

He drew back. "Are you okay? Where have you been? What happened?"

Taking his hand, she led him to the table. As they took seats, Eric came through the door. "Josie, you okay?"

"Yes. I was just going to tell Caleb what happened." Eric looked worried, but she wasn't sure she could trust him. She really didn't know who to trust, except Caleb.

She told them about the dreams, Tracy and the fire, how she'd arrived at the cabin as if she were in a trance, unsure of how she got there.

"So you never saw who shot you?" Caleb asked.

"No. I was totally focused on getting Tracy out of the cabin. I never saw anyone else. That's my last memory of living in Beckett."

Caleb got up and went down the hall. In a minute he was back with a piece of paper. "I did a check of missing girls in this area last night. Tracy Williams was reported missing a week after you disappeared."

"Mae must have finally figured out something was very wrong when neither Tracy nor I called her back."

"That's why Dennis and I knew nothing about this girl," Eric said.

"Yes. But I did have a file," Josie replied. "I kept

it in my car because I didn't want anyone to see it until I'd had Tracy safely back with her mother. Wherever my car is, that's where the file is."

"Let's go over this again." Caleb resumed his seat. "Mae Williams said Tracy was involved with someone powerful."

Josie swallowed. "Yes. And Tracy had spent six months in jail for trying to extort money from someone. Mae feared Tracy had gotten in over her head and her life was in danger."

Someone knocked at the front door and Lencha let Dennis in. Josie told the story again.

Dennis wiped a forearm across his forehead. "We have to be careful how we handle this. Boone could be volatile when pressed into a corner and all our jobs could be at stake."

"You're missing the point," Caleb said, a slight edge to his voice. "Whoever killed Tracy also shot Josie."

Dennis shook his head. "This doesn't jell. Boone wouldn't get involved with a seventeen-year-old girl."

"Maybe he wasn't involved," Caleb pointed out. "Maybe Tracy had something on Boone and she was blackmailing him."

"Now that would fly. I'm sure there are a lot of crooked dealings in Boone's past. It's just not clear how a young girl would be privy to that."

"Me, neither," Eric put in.

Dennis took a long breath. "I'll be honest with you. I'm not questioning Boone. Someone else will have to do that." Dennis glanced at Caleb. "Probably you, Ranger."

"No problem," Caleb replied without hesitation. He'd gone toe-to-toe with Boone on more than one occasion and he wasn't looking forward to another. But Boone was going to admit the truth or one of them wasn't going to be left standing. "But I'm contacting the FBI so this investigation is official."

The unspoken accusation hung between the officers in the room.

Dennis finally nodded. "Probably best that way with Boone a possible suspect."

"Josie's life is at stake and I'm not taking any chances. And we'll need a good forensics team to go through the ashes to determine human remains."

"I agree," Eric said. "The FBI is much better equipped for that than we are. And I'll contact Mae Williams and have her in the office by this afternoon."

"I'll notify the FBI right now," Caleb said, glancing at his watch. "And we'll meet at the station at three."

"Good deal," Dennis said.

"We have to have a guard on Josie at all times." Caleb wanted to be clear on that one point.

"I'll get my shotgun." Lencha headed for her room. "No one's gettin' in this house."

"Thanks, Lencha," Caleb replied. "But I'm talking about a guard outside day and night."

"I'll see that it's done," Dennis assured him.

"That's going to be useless," Josie spoke up. "Because I won't be here. I'll be at the station helping with the questioning." She glanced at Dennis. "I want to be reinstated as an officer."

"Sure. No problem," Dennis replied. "I'll do it when you get to the office."

"Thank you. And for the record, I'll be the one questioning my grandfather."

"Josie?"

"Don't try to talk me out of it, Caleb. If my grandfather had me shot then he's going to admit that to my face."

"It's not a…"

Josie stood, her eyes as dark as he'd ever seen them. "I'll be at the station this afternoon. Now, I'd just like a hot bath." She turned and headed for the hall.

"Josie." Eric stopped her and walked to her side. "Has all your memory returned?"

"Yes." She smiled at Eric and Caleb felt a pain around his chest. "I remember us, but please don't pressure me. I'm so mixed-up right now."

"Don't worry. I'll be here for you."

Josie touched his cheek and walked on down the hall. Eric had a smile on his face. Caleb took a deep breath. This is what he wanted—for Josie to be happy— even if it meant his own heart was breaking.

JOSIE RAN A HOT BATH and sprinkled some of Lencha's special mixture in the water. Lavender drifted to her nostrils. Soothing, comforting lavender—that's what she needed. She sank into the water and tried to keep her mind a blank, but she couldn't do it. Too much had happened. Too many bad things. And all to her.

Unable to think about Boone, she tried to concentrate on something positive—her memory of Eric. Long ago, when she'd finally agreed to come to Beckett to visit, in hopes that Boone would stop his quest to have her father's body moved, she never planned to join the police department. Then she'd met Eric. Tall, blond and handsome, he reminded her a lot of her father. They hit it off from the start and before she knew it she was joining the force. Soon they were spending a lot of time together, on and off duty.

She'd had a serious relationship in college and dated a couple of cops in Corpus, but none of them made her think of weddings and babies. Eric did. After losing her parents, she wanted to be part of a family, have children. She could see them all with Eric's blue eyes. When he'd asked her to marry him, she'd happily agreed. Eric wanted to get married right away, but she couldn't until she resolved the situation with her grandfather. And you might say things were still the same. What did Boone have to do with Tracy? Until this situation was resolved, she couldn't even think about a future.

She stood, reached for a towel and stepped out. She'd loved Eric, but now when she thought of children, she saw them with big brown eyes. Caleb's eyes. Could she be in love with two men at the same time?

The door opened.

"Lencha!"

"What?" Lencha calmly closed the door behind her, unmoved by Josie's indignation. "I've seen you naked before. No big deal. We have the same equipment."

Josie rolled her eyes. "A little privacy would be nice."

"Then lock the door."

"The lock's broken."

"Oh. Right. I should fix that, but with just me here never saw the need." Lencha waved a bony hand. "Never mind. I need to put this cream on your back. We missed last night and we have to do it as soon as possible and while your skin is still warm."

Josie grabbed her robe and slipped into it. "Let's do it in the bedroom. There's more room."

"Fine, but hurry before your skin cools off."

Lencha was just looking out for her so Josie couldn't be angry. As she walked into her bedroom, she didn't hear voices. The men must have left, but she would be there at three to talk to Mae and Boone. She wasn't looking forward to seeing her grandfather again.

She stretched out on her stomach on the bed, letting the robe fall to her waist. Gathering her hair, she looped it over her shoulder. She hadn't thought much about her back lately. In the hospital she'd looked at it several times a day. The welts were raw and sore and they burned, some of them even bled. Sometimes she wondered how she survived the beatings. She shivered from the memory.

"Are you cold?" Lencha asked, kneeling on the floor.

"No. I was just remembering something painful."

"Mmm." Lencha's long fingers began to rub the cream into each scar, into each marred swath of flesh left by the rope and the board used by the cult leader. Lencha hummed while she worked and Josie relaxed. Her body went limp.

AFTER SEEING DENNIS and Eric off, Caleb hurried back into the house. He had to make sure Josie was okay after what she'd been through again, this morning. He stopped short in her doorway. Lencha was rubbing cream onto Josie's back again. As he stepped away, Lencha saw him.

"Ranger."

"I…I'll be in the kitchen." He'd never seen her back this close before. He'd seen the scars briefly the other night and when he'd danced with her sometimes he could feel them through her dress. When they were stranded after the wreck, he'd touched them, but now he could see them clearly. Some of the marks were wide and deep and he felt a little sick to his stomach at what had been done to her.

"Don't go." He heard Josie's voice and he stilled. "I want to talk to you."

"Now let that soak in good." Lencha pulled Josie's robe over her back. "If I could have gotten to these scars right away, I'd have had a better chance of making them disappear. Now there's a lot of scar tissue, but we'll keep working at it. In a month they won't be quite as bad."

"Thank you, Lencha." Josie rolled onto her back and scooted against the headboard, tying the belt of her robe tightly.

Lencha screwed the lid on the cream and pushed to her feet. "Better see what *Chula*'s into."

Caleb sat on the bed, his back against a post, his

eyes on her. God, she was beautiful. Her long dark hair and smooth olive skin seemed more dominant against the white robe. Eye-catching. Riveting. They were just words and could never describe her innate beauty. A beauty that he would remember the rest of his life.

"I didn't mean to just burst in." He tried to explain. "I don't want to make you feel uncomfortable."

She drew her knees up and pulled the robe down over them. "You never make me feel uncomfortable."

"But I know you're sensitive about the scars."

She rested her chin on her knees. "It seems like a lifetime ago when I went through that. Other times, it seems like yesterday."

For a moment her mind went back to the cult who'd found her on a street in Austin. They cleaned and doctored the wound on her head and she'd thought they would help her. They soon disillusioned her of that, calling her names that she'd never heard before. She was sure she wasn't as bad as they'd told her and in the days that followed she knew she was in a part of hell—a hell that she'd never heard about. They called their leader the prophet and he had six wives. He was looking for wife number seven and as she'd worked the fields and cooked, she'd noticed several young blond girls brought in for the purpose. When the girls wouldn't submit to the brainwashing, they'd kill them and burn their bodies. Josie had watched all this, cowering in a corner in a makeshift kitchen. She might not have known who she was, but she knew these people were evil.

Suddenly she knew, besides the obvious, why the fire frightened her so much. Her mind held the memory of Tracy and the fire. She trembled visibly.

"What is it?" Caleb asked immediately.

"I was remembering how the cult burned those girls' bodies in the fire."

"Don't, Josie," he pleaded, his voice soft and soothing.

"In my blank mind the fire frightened me for more than that reason. Tracy died the same way. I must have known that."

"Probably."

There was silence for a moment. Then she raised her eyes to his. "I have my memory back. Everything—even Eric. I wasn't sure I could trust him, but now I know that I can."

"That's good. Don't think about the bad stuff."

"But I'm still in limbo. I thought once my memory returned I would know who shot me. But I don't. It's turned into an even bigger puzzle than before. The shooter is still out there."

"Yeah." He studied the tip of his cowboy

boots. "Please don't scare me again like you did this morning."

"I scared myself. Dr. Oliver said I might have recall through dreams and she was right. When I woke up, I was standing in front of the ashes and I didn't have a clue where I was. Then in a blinding pain it all came back."

He leaned forward. "Do you want to talk about that day?"

"Yes."

"Try to remember as much as you can. Did you notice another car parked somewhere?"

She shook her head. "I just remember the flames and running to the window. That's when I saw her."

"How was she lying?"

"On her back. Her head was tilted to the side toward me and I could see her face clearly. She had blond hair."

"What else? Clothes? Did you notice her clothes?"

"Oh." Josie clasped her cheeks. "There was a blanket or something over her body and it was…was bloody. Yes. It was bloody."

He frowned. "Was the blood on Tracy? Or on the blanket?"

She closed her eyes. "The blanket was yellow, yes, a dirty yellow and it was soaked with blood."

"Was it blood or maybe just dirty?"

"It was blood, kind of a shiny maroon. It wasn't dirt."

"Was it near Tracy's face and neck?"

"No. In the center of the blanket."

"Anything else?"

She opened her eyes. "Her hair."

"What about her hair?"

"It was pushed back from her forehead and it looked wet."

Josie buried her face in her hands. "She looked so thrown away in that ratty deer cabin—thrown away like garbage. I can't believe my grandfather had anything to do with her murder. I just can't let myself believe that." She ran the palms of her hands over her face. "Because if I do that, I'd have to believe that he shot me or had someone else shoot me."

"Don't put yourself through this," he advised. "Wait until we have something more concrete."

She looked at him. "What kind of dealings could Boone have with Tracy?"

Caleb shrugged. "We could speculate all day, but only Boone can answer that."

"If he's in a mood to be cooperative."

"Yeah. It'll be like opening a bottle of aged wine. You have to do it very carefully and there's always a surprise in store. With the wine, it's usually delightful. With Boone, we'll have to wait and see."

Suddenly she threw her arms around his neck and hugged him. "You always make me feel so good."

He stroked her hair, willing himself not to let this get out of control. "You are happy about remembering Eric, aren't you?"

She drew back, her dark eyes as warm as any fire. "Yes, but I'm still struggling to connect the past with the present. 'Integrate' is what Dr. Oliver called it."

"It will happen. We just have to find the missing piece to this puzzle."

"I'm just so afraid we'll never find it and I'll never know and my life will be in limbo forever."

"Remember a ranger never stops investigating until the bad guys are caught."

She flashed a smile. "You're wonderful, Caleb McCain, and I don't know how I'm going to live without you." Her expression changed to one of sadness. "I'm trying to let go. I really am, but I may need to drink a warm glass of milk before bed for the rest of my life."

"Josie." He stood, putting distance between them because he knew her emotions were fragile and he couldn't take advantage of that.

"I'm being honest." Her eyes begged him to understand.

"I know." He reached out and touched her cheek. "We both know once this mess is sorted out your emotions will change. You and Eric will recapture what you once had."

"Yes." She leaned back against the bed. "Eric is very nice. I liked that about him from the start. Maybe that's why I felt such a connection to you. You and Eric have a lot of qualities in common."

"Maybe." He swallowed the lump in his throat, the truth like a wedge of ice in his chest. They both knew her dependency on him was ebbing. "I'm going to the police station for a while. I'll be back about two-thirty if you still insist on going."

"I do."

"Lencha is here with a shotgun. Wilbur Nash, an officer, is outside. Please don't let Lencha shoot Wilbur or anyone else."

"Did you try to take the gun from her?"

"Are you kidding?"

At her bubble of laughter, he walked out. He had to find the shooter and soon. His heart couldn't take much more.

CHAPTER FIFTEEN

THE MORNING PASSED quickly for Caleb. Mae was eager for news of her daughter and gladly agreed to a meeting. FBI agent Wesley Hawkins arrived at noon and they traveled out to the suspected crime scene. They didn't touch anything, leaving all the evidence intact for the forensic team. But Caleb did notice that the track also lead to the back of the cabin. A car could have easily been parked there and Josie would never have seen it.

When they reached the office, Eric had more information. The land and cabin belonged to Boone, as they all suspected. Wes gave Boone a call asking him politely to come in for questioning. From Wes's expression, Caleb knew he was receiving an earful. But the agent didn't back down, telling Boone if he didn't show, a team of law enforcement officers would drag him in.

Eric also had information on Mae and Tracy Williams. Tracy started running away from home after her father was killed in an accident at work.

Everything from drug possession to stealing to shoplifting and blackmail was on her rap sheet. Tracy's goal in life seemed to be to get as much money as fast as she could, any way she could. She lived with a guy named Tad Hoffman and his rap sheet was longer than Tracy's. Eric was still trying to locate him.

They'd run a check on Mae, a single mom working two jobs and struggling to raise three daughters. She was clean and all the information she'd given Josie checked out, too. Mae arrived early and Caleb left to pick up Josie, knowing she wasn't going to change her mind.

Josie took the oath in Dennis's office and she was officially back on the Beckett police force. Caleb took her to the room where Mae was waiting and let her handle the questioning, but he was listening carefully to every answer.

Josie stared at the woman in the room. In her forties, Mae was medium height, a little overweight with graying blond hair and a worried expression. She looked just like Josie thought she would.

"I'm Josie Marie Beckett," she introduced herself.

"Oh, my." Tears filled Mae's eyes. "You're alive. The nice ranger said you were, but for the last year I've worried and worried until I couldn't worry anymore. I just didn't know what had happened to you."

Josie pulled out a chair and sat across from her. She told her about the day she'd found Tracy and what had happened afterward.

"Oh my God!" It took Mae a moment for everything to sink in. She swallowed visibly. "So…so my daughter is dead?"

"I believe so. The FBI will confirm it in a few days after the forensic team gathers the evidence. I can't tell you how sorry I am."

Tears rolled down Mae's cheeks and she reached into her purse for a tissue. Dabbing at her eyes, she said, "I knew something bad had happened when neither one of you called me back. I finally called Frank and he said I needed to file a missing person's report in Beckett, but I explained I was afraid Tracy was somehow trying to extort money from Boone Beckett. I have two young daughters at home and if I filed a report in Beckett, I feared for their lives. Frank also knew of Boone's reputation and if Tracy had something on him then he might think that I was also in it with her. For my daughters, I couldn't take that risk. But I couldn't just do nothing so I had Frank file a missing person's report in Corpus, hoping that something would come of it. But as days turned into months I knew my daughter was likely lost to me forever."

Mae dabbed at her eyes again and Josie gave

her a minute. "Can you remember some of the things Tracy told you about the person she was meeting?"

"She was very excited and said she wasn't going to have to ask me for money again. All she had to do was name her price and it would be paid. She said that the person she was meeting was a little crazy, but one way or another she was getting her money. I tried to talk her out of it and begged her to come home. I begged until I was blue in the face, but she only laughed and said not when her gravy train was about to come in."

"You mentioned price. Do you have any idea what she'd meant?"

"No. Tracy hung out with a bad crowd. I cringe to think about what they were into."

Josie pushed a pen and pad across the table. "Would you write their names down, please?"

"Sure, but they're probably in jail or strung out somewhere." Mae took the paper and began to scribble names.

Josie crossed her hands on the table and braced herself for the answer to the next question. "Mae, did Tracy ever mention Boone by name?"

Mae looked up. "No. She said she couldn't let anything slip or the deal would be off and she wanted that money." Mae reached for her tissue again. "This is so different than the life my husband and I had planned for her. When Lloyd died, Tracy became someone I couldn't control." Mae hiccupped. "Your father was so nice and I'm sorry I got you involved in this."

Josie got up and hugged her, realizing how difficult this woman's life had been since her husband's death. She held no animosity toward Mae. "I'm fine now," she assured her. "We're just trying to find the person who did this."

"I hope you do, and soon."

"Thank you," Josie replied. "Would you please keep your cell phone with you at all times in case I need to ask you something?"

"Sure. And you'll let me know if my daughter is really…dead."

"Yes, of course. You'll be the first person I call. Again, Mrs. Williams, I'm very sorry."

As Mae left, Josie stared at Caleb. "What do you think?"

He was leaning against the doorjamb, his arms folded. He unfolded his arms and walked toward her. "I think Tracy was selling something."

"Me, too. But what?"

"She was into stealing so she might have come across something that she shouldn't have and she saw a way to make some money."

"Yeah, but—" Loud voices interrupted her and they shared a secret glance. "Boone has arrived."

Dennis stuck his head in. "Josie, you better come out here."

Josie and Caleb stopped short in the squad room. Lencha held her shotgun on Boone.

"I'm gonna blow you away like I should have done thirty years ago," Lencha hissed between clenched teeth. "You're a coward, Boone Beckett. A bigot coward. You hurt my Marie, but you're not hurting Josie, you yellow-livered snake in the grass."

"Lencha, I've put up with your nonsense out of respect for Izzy. He was a good man, loyal to Silver Spur, but my patience is wearing thin, you old bat."

Everyone stood motionless, except Josie. She walked over and took the shotgun out of Lencha's hands. "What are you doing?"

"He needs to die."

Josie shook her head. "I know you love me, but this is not a way to settle anything. Please go home."

Lencha raised her arms, said something in Spanish, spit in Boone's direction then stormed out.

Eric led Boone to a questioning room and Caleb introduced Wes as the FBI agent.

"Who the hell was that?" the agent asked.

"Someone I love," Josie answered shortly.

Wes held up his hands. "Okay. No more questions."

"I'm sorry," Josie apologized. "My family's a little out of the ordinary."

"No problem. Got a few of them in my family, too, and I love every one of them." He took a breath. "Who's questioning Mr. Beckett? He's not in a good mood."

"I'll handle my grandfather," Josie said.

Caleb caught her arm. "You don't have to. I can do it."

"He's right, Miss Beckett," Wes said. "It's best if someone else does the questioning."

"I'm doing it," she replied and walked out. She had to do this and no one was stopping her. This was between her and her grandfather and he was going to tell her the truth. But it crossed her mind that sometimes Boone's truth was different from anyone else's.

As she opened the door, Boone was tearing into Dennis. "Your job ain't worth squat now. Making me come down here like a common criminal. I own this town. I own you, you sorry bastard."

"In a good mood, huh, Boone?" Josie nodded to Dennis to leave and took the seat across from her grandfather.

"You keep that damn witch away from me."

Josie nodded. "Lencha's harmless."

"Yeah, right." Boone leaned back in his chair. "Took my damn cigar. Agent has allergies or something. I want my damn cigar!" He worked his mouth as if the cigar was in place. Evidently the cigar was Boone's comfort blanket—the only chink she'd ever noticed in his solid-steel armor.

"In a minute. I promise." She folded her hands on the table. "First, we're going to have a talk."

"Now listen, girlie. I don't know any Tracy Williams and I'm thinking of calling a lawyer." He removed his big Stetson and slammed it on the table.

"Do you want one?" Her eyes held his, knowing she had to give him that choice.

"Nah. I can take care of myself. Always could."

"Okay. Answer my questions and you can be out of here in no time."

His eyes narrowed. "And you might be gettin' too big for your britches."

Josie let that pass. "You own a deer cabin on County Road 249?"

"Yep. Burned down little over a year ago. Been meaning to have it cleaned up but never got around to it."

She kept her eyes leveled on him. "That night I found Lorna and Mason in…"

He groaned. "Not that again. You know, girlie, you can just keep beatin' that ol' horse, but once he's dead he's dead."

"That night I was angry at what they'd done to my father." She kept talking as if he hadn't spoken. "And all I wanted to do was get out of Beckett as fast as I could. I was throwing clothes in a suitcase when my cell rang. It was Tracy Williams. Her mother had called me a week earlier wanting to see if I could find her. Evidently Tracy was in Beckett to make a deal with a very powerful person and she was afraid for her life."

Josie paused, but Boone's bored expression didn't change. "Tracy told me where she was and she was frantic saying time was running out and begged me to hurry. Guess where she was hiding?"

Boone shrugged. "Haven't got a clue."

"On County Road 249 in your old deer cabin."

A shaggy eyebrow arched. "So that's it. This girl was found hiding on my property and I'm somehow involved." He frowned. "In what?"

Boone hadn't been told that Tracy was suspected dead. She decided to continue with the story, watching his expression and trying to judge if he was a very good actor or if he was telling the truth. With her grandfather, that wouldn't be easy.

"When I got to the cabin, it was in flames, but I could see Tracy lying on the couch. I didn't know if she was dead or alive and I had to get her out of there. The flames were fierce and hot and I ran to my car for my jacket to cover myself. I heard a loud sound and felt a piercing pain in my head, then there was darkness. I woke up on a street in Austin not knowing who I was or where I was."

She took a breath, determined to get through

this. "My head was hurting and I was so hungry. I started walking and a gang of boys stopped me and pushed and shoved me, laughing and taunting and trying to pull off my clothes. I screamed and screamed and fought back. No one came to help me, except these men in long brown robes. They quoted scripture and predicted hell and damnation for the boys and they ran off. When they realized I had no memory, they said they would give me a home and protect me. I got into the bed of an old truck and we left Austin and traveled to the farthest part of the Hill Country. To hell! You can't even imagine the torture they put me through. Because my skin and eye color were dark, I was beaten with a board or a rope until I was unconscious and during the day they worked me until my fingers bled. The horror and…"

"Stop." Boone briefly placed a hand over his eyes. "I don't want to hear anymore."

"But you need to hear it all." She leaned closer. "Do you understand why you're here?" She didn't give him a chance to answer. "The person who killed Tracy Williams also shot me. Tracy was meeting someone powerful in Beckett. There's only one person powerful in this town. *You.*"

"My God!" He paled. "You think I shot you!"

"I'm asking you to tell me the truth. I need the

truth, Boone." Her voice wavered and she hated herself for that weakness.

He reached across the table and took her hands and she didn't realize her fingers were clasped so tightly until he pried them apart. "Look at me, Josie. Look into my eyes—the same eyes as your father." She did as he asked. "I would never shoot you or hire anyone to shoot you. We got off on the wrong foot mainly due to my pride and pigheadedness, but I would never harm you in any way. You're all I have left of Brett. I know I'm crude and offensive and do a lot of bullshitting. Most of it's just talk. I would never hurt you, girl."

Ever since she'd met Boone she'd never known if he was telling the truth or not, but now she did. Her father's eyes looked back at her, clear and honest—eyes she'd trusted all of her life. As she trusted Boone now. He had nothing to do with Tracy's death or Josie's shooting.

He squeezed her hands. "Josie."

"I believe you." She returned the squeeze and dropped her hands to her lap. "But I had to be sure." She felt as if a gigantic weight had been lifted from her shoulders. She never realized how the thought of him shooting her had disturbed her. Ever since she'd met her grandfather, there had been a very fine line between love and hate. For the first time she knew where Boone's loyalties lay and maybe they could work on diminishing the line forever.

Her grandfather hadn't shot her. That filled her with joy for a moment, then reality returned. *Someone else had.*

"Who used the cabin?"

"Lots of people. It's not part of the Silver Spur. Henry Batson's wife died and all his kids had moved away. He was too old to ranch anymore and I bought the land from him so he could move closer to his daughter in Houston. Everyone in Beckett probably spent a weekend there hunting. It was well-known I let people hunt the property free. But in the last couple of years, the cabin has become so run-down that I don't think anyone used it. Then it burned to the ground and I was planning to have it bulldozed."

"Could you check with the vaqueros to see if they noticed anyone on the property?"

"Yep. Can do." He frowned. "So this Tracy girl is dead?"

"Yes. We believe she's dead. We're waiting for the FBI to confirm it."

Boone stood. "Think I'll go find my cigar and a stiff drink."

"Thank you," she said, also standing.

He eyed her for a moment. "Sorry I made you think that I would ever harm you."

"Maybe we can try for better communication."

"Maybe." He reached for his hat and walked out.

Caleb strolled in. "I guess we can cross Boone off the list."

"Yes." She sank into the chair. "You heard everything?"

"Mmm." He sat across from her. "I can see you believe him so I'm not even going to ask if you're sure."

Josie's mind was in a whirlwind. "The next most powerful person would be Mason, but I keep remembering what he told you—that he couldn't shoot me because I'm Brett's daughter."

"He wanted to for Lorna, so Ashley's paternity would never be revealed. But from his expression that day I could see that he couldn't. He couldn't fake that."

"So there's no need to talk to him?"

"At this time, I don't think so. Nothing in Tracy's life points to anyone in Beckett."

"This still doesn't make sense. What are we missing?" She tried to keep the despair out of her voice and failed.

"Josie…"

"Got something." Eric charged in. "Tad Hoffman's in a Corpus jail on drug-possession charges."

"Great." Caleb got to his feet. "This could be the break we're looking for. He might know who

Tracy was meeting in Beckett. I'll see if I can talk to him."

Josie reached for the list Mae had given her. "Eric and I will check out Tracy's friends. Maybe one of them remembers something."

The afternoon was busy as they tracked down several people. Caleb was waiting to talk to Tad. He was in court and an officer would call as soon as Tad was back in his cell. Josie contacted two of Tracy's friends and neither wanted to talk. With a little pressure all she got was that Tracy was coming into some money and acting strange. They said she stayed to herself a lot. The other guy on the list was in jail with Tad.

As Josie worked with Eric, a lot of good memories surfaced, memories of their relationship. Besides being handsome, he was a good police officer, dedicated and loyal. He was also patient and understanding, just as he was now. Not pressuring her because he cared about her. And she cared about him and *loved* him. Warm, fuzzy feelings filled her heart.

She glanced at Caleb, who was talking on the phone in Dennis's office. She loved him, too. But it was different. How, she wasn't sure. Then in a moment of clarity she realized she'd been holding on to Caleb because he was all she had. She needed him to get through each day. She needed that warm glass of milk because she was so afraid of the blankness of her mind and what it would reveal. With Caleb, she could handle it. But now she had her memory back and the fear wasn't so great. Once they found the shooter her fear would disappear completely and her attachment to Caleb would be gone.

Then she could concentrate on her future—with Eric.

When she'd started the journey back, she'd never imagined that two men would occupy her heart. But soon she'd be able to let Caleb go. She prayed they'd find the shooter and she could resume her life.

Without doubts. Without fear. Without Caleb.

BY FIVE O'CLOCK they still didn't have anything concrete. Caleb was trying to arrange a phone conversation with Tad, so he wouldn't have to travel to Corpus. Josie decided to call it a day, wanting to go home and talk to Lencha. There wasn't much else to do. It was all so frustrating. Everything hinged on a conversation with Tracy's boyfriend.

She walked into Dennis's office. Caleb hung up the phone. "No luck?"

"He's still not back in his cell. The lawyers are trying to work out a deal in court. The officer said it should be soon, but he said that an hour ago. If

I don't hear anything in the next hour, I'm heading for Corpus."

"Not much use me going with you," she said.

"No. They'll only let one of us see him."

She bit her lip. "You really think he might know something? No one else seems to."

"She lived with him so he knows more than the rest. Getting him to tell us could be a different story."

"I'm just so afraid we'll never find the truth." She couldn't stop the tremble that ran through her.

He stood and came around the desk. "The shooter is already nervous and soon we'll catch him. It's just a matter of time. I'm just hoping we can put this together before he tries again."

She knew he was right and he and Eric were doing all they could to catch this person. So she had to stay optimistic.

"I need to go home and speak with Lencha to make sure she's not planning some nefarious act for Boone. I'll wait for you."

"That's a good idea."

She glanced around the office. "Did Dennis leave?"

"Rhonda's been up with the baby and he's gone home so she can get some rest. There wasn't much he could do here with me commandeering his office. He said he'd be back in a couple of hours."

"With both of them in their forties, it has to be hard with a baby."

"Yeah. They're having to adjust their lifestyle, but it's clear they're both besotted with the little girl."

Josie tucked a wisp of hair behind her ear. "I'm glad they're happy. After losing one baby and having to give up another, they deserve some happiness. I remember we were planning to give Rhonda a baby shower,but…"

Caleb put an arm around her shoulder. "Go home and get some rest. I'll call you as soon as I hear from the Corpus police."

They walked out and Eric met them. "I'm going to Lencha's," she told him.

"I'll phone the guard," he replied and quickly dialed a number. As Eric hung up, he added, "I'll stop by later."

She smiled. "I'd like that." Everything was happening just as Dr. Oliver had told her. She was rediscovering her emotions for Eric. And she wasn't fighting it.

Caleb walked out with her. "Go straight to the house and don't leave without telling one of us."

"Yes, I…" Her voice stopped at the sound of thunder. But it wasn't a storm. The sky was clear and sunny. Soon the noise became clearer. The thunder of hooves. Horses. Caddo and about twenty vaqueros rode down Main Street. Each held a rifle.

"What the hell?" Caleb muttered.

The posse stopped and Caddo galloped forward. Today he rode the paint with a saddle and he raised the rifle high. "*Prima,* need help?"

Josie frowned at him. "Caddo, what are you doing?"

Caddo flashed a grin. "Orders. Big PaPa says protect *prima.*"

"Boone sent you?" She could hear the incredulity in her voice.

"*Sí.*"

Josie was stunned and very surprised that the Old West tactics warmed her through and through. But this was typical Boone. Her grandfather.

"Caddo, I don't think—"

"It's very good idea," Caleb broke in.

At her puzzled look, he added, "No one is going to try anything with these hombres guarding you, and frankly I like that."

Josie shrugged, not wanting to look a gift horse in the mouth. Her grandfather's heart was in the right place for a change. A squad car drove up and Josie walked toward it.

"I'll call you later," Caleb said.

She nodded and closed the door. All the way to Lencha's house the posse followed. People stopped and stared. Cars ran off the road and she was very glad when Lencha's house came into sight.

Caddo galloped to her when she got out, the horse dancing around until Caddo spoke harshly to him.

"No worry," he said. "Caddo keep you safe."

"Thank you," she replied and hurried into the house.

Caddo barked something in Spanish and the cowboys spread out around the house. Josie never felt so safe in her life.

CHAPTER SIXTEEN

CALEB WATCHED until the horses were out of sight. He went back into the station knowing Josie was safe—for now. He kept going over the whole scenario and something was missing because not one clue was bringing the principal players together. Something had to connect Tracy with a person in this town. He'd keep looking until he found it.

"Did I just see a groups of cowboys on horseback?" Eric asked, hanging up the phone.

"Yes. Boone's answer to protecting Josie."

Eric lifted a blond eyebrow. "Does Dennis know about this?"

Caleb glanced at his watch. "He hasn't returned yet. Must be having problems at home."

"Yeah. The baby's been fussy lately and not sleeping. Rhonda is completely worn-out."

"My brother has two kids. Being a parent is a full-time job." And Caleb knew that Jake and Elise loved every minute of it.

"Yeah." Eric picked up a pencil and twisted it. "Can I ask you a question?"

Caleb knew what was coming and for a second he started to say no. His involvement with Josie was none of Eric's business. But then, he had to admit that it was.

"Sure."

Eric studied the pencil. "You and Josie seem close." He glanced up. "What I'm wondering is how close."

Caleb met his gaze squarely. "I was taken with Josie since the first time I met her cowering in a hospital room. She was completely demoralized by what the cult had done to her, but they couldn't destroy her beauty or her spirit. Once I gained her trust, she began the long road to recovery. It was a struggle for a long time, but I was there for her and helped any way I could. Her personality started to emerge. She loves to dance and she's addicted to chocolate. Watching her is like glimpsing one of your South Texas sunsets—breathtaking with so many facets that you can never get enough." He paused. "Yes. I've fallen for Josie, but I know her life is here and not with me. I only want Josie to be happy."

"Thank you," Eric said simply, and Caleb could see the relief on his face. "And thank you for all you've done for Josie."

"You're welcome. Now let's hope that Tad has some info that will pull all this together so Josie can resume her life."

"I like the sound of that. Thanks for being so honest."

Caleb could do no less. His heart was telling him to fight for what he wanted, but his head was in control. In truth, though, it wasn't his decision. It was Josie's and he would never pressure her or cause her any more pain.

His pain was a different matter.

JOSIE PICKED UP the box of files in her room. She had to return them to the station. The piece of paper with Mae's phone number rested on top. How did it get in the box? She sat on the bed trying to figure that out. When she'd started searching for Tracy, she'd made a file with T.W. on it but she'd kept it in her car. She'd been working on the Wilkins file along with a couple of others and she'd left them on her desk, intending to work on them the next day. She'd called Mae that morning and evidently she'd left the number on top of the files. After her disappearance someone had evidently put the number in the Wilkins file, thinking that's where it went. Thank God it hadn't been thrown away.

Lencha walked in and Josie turned to her. Lencha

hadn't been in the house when she'd returned. Josie lifted an eyebrow. "Are you hiding from me?"

"Nope. Should I be?" Lencha was unflappable.

Josie kept staring at her, her expression demanding a straight answer.

"Okay. I lost it. When I heard Big Boone might have shot you, I couldn't think too clearly. I just wanted to hurt him."

"He had nothing to do with shooting me," Josie told her.

"Yeah, well…"

"He didn't, Lencha. Please believe me."

"Ah…he's still a *bastardo*."

"He's my grandfather."

"Ain't no way of getting around that one."

"No," Josie said and hugged her.

Lencha squeezed her tight. "I just got a call from Gloria Martinez. Her young daughter has gone into labor. It's her first and she's terrified."

Josie waved her away. "Go. Go deliver another baby and give it a kiss for me."

"Should be having your own babies," Lencha muttered.

Josie set the files on the dresser. "Right now I'm trying to get my life together."

"With two very handsome men," Lencha commented.

Josie whirled around. "Lencha!"

"And someone's going to get their heart broken."

Josie flopped onto the bed. "I know."

"Just as long as it's not you."

"I don't think I can avoid it," she admitted in a forlorn voice. "Two incredible men and I have to make a choice." She didn't know how she was going to do that. But she already knew Eric and their past was taking precedence.

Lencha patted her shoulder. "Your heart will lead you or we can do it with my tarot cards."

Josie smiled, well aware of Lencha's ability to attempt to foretell the future. Marie had always laughed at Lencha's predictions, not believing in the practices of her Mexican ancestors. Josie would keep away from them, too. Right or wrong, she'd make the decision on her own.

"Go deliver the baby," she said.

"Will you be okay?"

"Haven't you seen the armed cowboys outside?"

"Yes, and if they stomp up my garden there'll be hell to pay."

Her smile broadened. "They're scared of you and your evil doings and they wouldn't dare to do anything to upset you."

Lencha bobbed her head in agreement. "Good to have a reputation."

"Mmm."

Lencha kissed her cheek. "I'll let Caddo know I'm leaving."

"Bye."

Josie walked around the house thinking until her head began to hurt. She started to call the station, but Caleb would call if he had any news. Instead she made a ham sandwich cutting thick slices of Lencha's homemade bread. She was almost finished eating when she heard loud voices.

She hurried to the front door to see what was going on. Caddo and the vaqueros had a car surrounded. It was getting dark so she had to peer closer to see who it was. She yanked open the door.

"It's okay," she shouted to Caddo. Rhonda stood outside her car trembling, half-scared to death.

Josie ran to meet her. "I'm sorry. They're guarding me."

Rhonda held a hand to her chest. "I don't think I'll ever be the same again."

"Come into the house and I'll fix us something to drink."

Rhonda followed her. "Dennis told me what happened and I just wanted to visit for a bit. A neighbor is sitting with Jenny, who is finally asleep, and I needed to get out for a while."

They walked into the house and Josie closed the door, but not before she saw Caddo and the paint prancing up and down the front yard.

"I wish you'd brought the baby," Josie said, heading for the kitchen.

"She's been up all day and night. Dennis came home and finally got her to sleep. Jenny loves her daddy. I was just worn-out and got some sleep, too. When I woke up I needed some fresh air, and I didn't want to wake Jenny."

"I'm glad you came by. I left the station about five. Now I'm wishing I'd stayed because it's not much fun here by myself."

"Lencha's not home?"

"No. She's helping with a birth." Josie opened the refrigerator. "What would you like. Tea, fresh juice or coffee? Lencha doesn't allow soft drinks in her house. Says they're poison. I can brew some good herbal tea or…"

Josie looked up to see Rhonda pointing a gun at her. Her pulse skittered to a stop. "What…what are you doing?"

"I can't let you take my baby," Rhonda said in an unfamiliar voice. Her eyes were glazed over and filled with hatred.

Josie calmly closed the refrigerator, not sure what this was about, but keeping a close eye on the gun. Rhonda had had a nervous breakdown after the loss of her baby. It was very obvious that Rhonda was close to losing it now. Josie wasn't clear why the woman thought she would take her adopted child.

"I would never take your baby. You love Jenny and I would do nothing to change that." Josie said the words slowly and succinctly so Rhonda would understand.

"Why did you have to come back? Why?" Rhonda cried, the gun shaking slightly. "I couldn't believe it when Dennis told me, then I saw you in town with the ranger and knew I had to do something, to scare you so you'd go away again. I fired a gun through your window and that didn't work so while you and the ranger were at the station I took a sharp knife and punctured a tire on both sides. I heard Dennis talk about that one time, how a man had done that to kill his wife. That didn't work, either."

Josie heard the words, but they were too horrible to believe. She forced the words from her throat. "Did...did you shoot me?"

"I like you, Josie. I really do, but you're not taking my child."

Josie kept her eyes on the gun. "Did you shoot me?" Her voice was loud, demanding an answer.

"It was all done. I had the baby and was ready to leave when I saw you drive up."

"Oh my God!" Tracy Williams was pregnant! That's what Tracy was selling—a baby. Why had no one known that? Not even Mae. That explained all the blood.

"Tracy Williams sold you her baby?" Someone powerful—the police chief and his wife. Finally, something was making sense.

"Yes."

"But you went through an agency. It's a matter of record." Josie attempted to get the facts straight.

"Dennis forced me to give the first baby back. He said it was best to let the mother have her child. I hated him for that." She spat out the words. "He's never been there for me. Never!" Rhonda inhaled deeply. "But I kept the birth certificate. The agency kept calling and calling and finally I told them I'd destroyed it. I just wanted a baby, but I knew the agency wasn't ever going to give me one."

Rhonda had used the old birth certificate and no one had noticed. Josie took a deep breath, trying to stay focused. "How did you find Tracy Williams?"

"Dennis said I was being paranoid and irrational and I needed to see a therapist again. To get him off my back I agreed to go. I was sitting in the lobby of the doctor's building, angry that Dennis was forcing me to do this, when a pregnant girl sat down by me. We got to talking and I told her about the baby I had to give back. She said her boyfriend didn't want the kid she was carrying and for the right price she'd sell it to me. It was like a dream come true. For ten thousand dollars she'd give me the baby." Rhonda inched around the room, never letting go of the gun and never taking her eyes off Josie.

"I put the fear of God into her, telling her my husband was a powerful man in Beckett and if she reneged on the deal, he'd kill her. The silly bitch thought I was talking about Boone and I didn't disillusion her. But then she got greedy. She wanted fifty thousand." Rhonda heaved a breath. "I had to think fast because I wasn't losing that baby. I told her I'd pick her up in Corpus at a McDonalds and I did. I gave her special instructions not to tell anyone or the deal was off. I took her to the old deer cabin on Boone's property that no one ever uses and told her I had to go get the money from my husband. She was so gullible." Rhonda laughed, a spine-tingling sound that sent chills all over Josie's body.

"She actually thought I was going to pay her that much money. I kept stalling her, saying we had to take the money out of savings and that took time. But I was just waiting for her to go into labor."

"And she did, didn't she, Rhonda?" The whole scenario was falling into place.

"Yes. She called and said she'd changed her mind and was leaving. I hurried out there and she was in labor unable to walk out like she'd threatened. I delivered Jenny. Oh, she was so beautiful the moment she was born." Her voice grew dreamy. "To keep her, I knew I had to get rid of Tracy. Tracy saw how I loved the baby and she said just give her the money and the baby was mine. I wrapped the baby in a blanket and laid her on the floor, then I reached for the gun in my purse. Without a second thought, I pointed the gun at her and pulled the trigger. She didn't ask for any more money."

A senseless murder by a woman out of her mind with wanting a baby. Rage boiled deep inside Josie and she was desperately trying to hold on to her temper.

"I took the baby to the car and sprinkled gasoline on the back side of the cabin and lit it. As I was getting in my car, I heard another vehicle. I grabbed my gun and walked to the front of the house. I saw you getting a jacket out of your car and I knew what you were going to do. You were going to try and save Tracy. I couldn't let you. I raised the gun and fired again."

Oh my God! Josie felt the pain—the crippling, mindless pain.

CALEB PACED in Dennis's office, waiting for the call. He kept going over bits and pieces, trying to make them fit. Tracy had something to sell. What?

Her hair was wet and there was lots of blood. What did that say? He stopped as something occurred to him. Could Tracy have been pregnant?

That would make all the pieces fit. A baby. But who was she selling it to in Beckett?

The phone rang and he grabbed it before it even stopped ringing. "Ranger Caleb McCain."

"Ranger McCain, this is Lieutenant Will Sims. Sorry for the delay, but I have Tad Hoffman in my office now."

"Thank you, sir. This could help my case a lot."

"Just be prepared for some attitude. Hold on."

A rough-sounding voice came down the line. "Yeah."

"Mr. Hoffman, I'm a Texas Ranger, Caleb McCain, and I'd like to ask you some questions about Tracy Williams."

"That bitch. I get my hands on her and I'll wring her pretty damn neck."

Caleb thought about how to handle Tad. How to get answers quickly. "Are you aware that she had the baby?" Direct and to the point. He held his breath as he waited for Tad's response.

"Damn right. She was supposed to call me as soon as she got the money. But the bitch took the money and ran. Greedy whore."

There was a baby! Relief gushed through him. Now he had to find out who the buyer was.

"Mr. Hoffman, do you know who she sold the baby to?"

"Nah, some big secret. What the hell did I care? I just wanted the freaking money. Do you know where Tracy is, man?"

"We believe she's dead." Caleb answered. As the baby's father, he had a right to know.

"Ah, man, are you shucking me?"

"No. We believe whoever Tracy was meeting in Beckett took the baby and killed her."

"Ah, man." Tad seemed genuinely upset.

"Think, Mr. Hoffman. Who was Tracy communicating with in Beckett?"

"I don't know, man. I was so strung out most of time and I just wanted her to get rid of it."

Instinctively Caleb knew that was all the information Tad had. Drugs were the driving force in his life. When he sobered up completely, he might remember all that he'd lost. Might even make him go straight. Caleb could only hope.

"Thank you, Mr. Hoffman. I appreciate the cooperation."

"Does Tracy's mom know?"

"Yes."

"Ah, shit. She probably wants me dead."

"She's pretty upset right now," was all Caleb could say.

He hung up with a sneaking suspicion at the

back of his mind. Walking into the outer office, he found Eric. "Dennis still not here?"

"No, and I'm getting worried. He always checks in."

Wes walked in, waving some papers. "They found human remains, teeth and bone fragments beneath the ashes, but we have to wait to see if the DNA matches Tracy Williams."

Caleb told them about the baby.

"Dammit, how did that slip by us?" Eric slumped into his chair.

"Tad didn't want the baby and kept telling her to get rid of it. She knew her mother would throw a fit if she found out so Tracy kept it a secret. It became a deadly secret." The suspicion nagged at him. "Eric, go to Dennis's house and see if everything's okay."

"Sure," Eric agreed, but he looked puzzled.

"What's your feel on this?" Wes asked as Eric left.

"I keep thinking about the baby. I haven't met many people in this town with a baby about the age of Tracy's, except Dennis and Rhonda's."

"You're not thinking…"

"I don't like it, either, but I'm checking the dates against the courthouse records again. I only glanced at it briefly when I did the background check."

Caleb went to his laptop, knowing Josie was safe. They could have the name of the shooter within the hour.

THE RAGE INSIDE JOSIE reached a fever pitch and she had to hold herself in check. She had to know the whole story. She'd waited a long time to see the face of the person who'd sentenced her to hell. All she felt was an uncontrollable anger at what this deranged woman had done to her life.

She took a deep controlling breath. "Why did you take my body to Austin?"

"I tried to drag your body into the fire, but the flames were so hot I couldn't. Then there was your car. I didn't know what to do. Blood was oozing from your head and you seemed dead. I had to get rid of you and the car. No one was taking my baby again."

"So…" Josie prompted, having a desperate need to hear it all.

"The door was open on your vehicle so I dragged you inside. I couldn't leave my car there or people would know I'd been at the cabin. I ran to my car and drove it out to the highway and left it. I got the baby and her things and hurried back to your vehicle and started driving. I stopped at a motel somewhere and cleaned the baby and dressed her, then I fed her. She was so sweet and she seemed to know me. She was my baby, the one I'd been waiting for."

"You left me in the car?" She couldn't keep the horror out of her voice.

"Yes. I covered your body with a blanket I had

in my car. I phoned Dennis and told him the adoption agency called and they had another baby for us but the car had died on the highway close to where a fire was burning on County Road 249. I told him I caught a ride to Corpus to catch a bus to Dallas. He wanted to go with me, but I told him there wasn't time and I'd call as soon as I had any news. Then I started driving again. When I reached Austin, I found a rough-looking area and dumped your body in an alley. Not far away I took your things from the car, the license and tags and left it."

So simple yet so complicated. Her car had probably been stripped, and all evidence of Josie Marie Beckett had disappeared.

"I stayed in a motel and put your things in the trash. I caught a bus to Beckett the next day, but first I called Dennis to tell him the good news— I had the baby and was coming home. He was so excited and we were happy until…"

"Does Dennis know you shot me?"

"I told him earlier and he didn't see things my way. Pity, but it's done."

Josie had no idea what the woman was talking about, but clearly Dennis wasn't involved.

"We were happy, Josie. Why did you come back?"

Josie didn't answer, instead she asked, "Do you think you'll get away with this? You saw all the guards outside."

"I'll tell them you were so upset that you shot yourself and I couldn't stop you. They'll believe me."

"No. They won't. I'm not suicidal."

Rhonda shook her head. "Shut up. I think you're a ghost. You couldn't have survived that. You were dead. You should be dead."

At the callous words, the rage she'd been repressing suddenly exploded inside Josie and she wanted revenge as she'd never wanted it before. She wanted this demented woman to pay. She took a step closer to Rhonda. "Look me in the eye and pull the trigger. Go ahead. If you want me dead, you'll have to do it with me staring at you."

Rhonda waved the gun. "Stay back."

"Do you have any idea what it was like to wake up on that grimy street with no memory? Do you know what it was like to be held down and beaten until I passed out from the pain? Do you know what it was like to wash clothes on rocks until my fingers bled? Do you have any idea of the horrific pain you've caused me?"

"I had no choice. You would have told."

Josie stepped closer, feeling no fear. "Now I'm going to kill you. One way or the other you're going to die."

"Stay away," Rhonda shouted and tried to aim the gun.

Josie made a lunge for her and they tumbled backward. As they wrestled, Rhonda dropped the gun and it spun toward the cabinet. Rhonda kicked and scratched, but Josie was stronger, her anger driving her. The gun lay a few feet away and she snatched it, rolled away to her feet, the gun pointed at Rhonda.

It was the day of reckoning.

Rhonda Fry was going to die.

CHAPTER SEVENTEEN

CALEB CALLED the adoption agency, but he got the runaround. He asked to speak to the person in charge and soon Ms. Doris Quinten came on the line. She gave him the same spiel about confidentiality. He explained about the case he was working on.

"Please, Ms. Quinten, a young woman's life is at stake. All I need is a simple yes or no. Did the Frys adopt a baby from your agency?"

There was a long pause on the line. "Just a minute. I'll check the records, but I'm not promising anything."

Caleb waited, tapping his fingers on the desk.

Her voice came back on the line. "No, Ranger McCain, and that's all I can tell you."

"Thank you, Ms. Quentin. That helps a lot."

Caleb hung up, knowing he was close to solving this. Jenny hadn't come from the adoption agency. Could Jenny be Tracy's daughter? There was only one way to find that out—talk to Dennis and

Rhonda. He hurried for the door and stopped in his tracks.

Eric walked into the room pushing Jenny in a stroller. His face was deadly white.

"What happened?" Caleb asked.

Eric took a deep breath. "I...I knocked and knocked on Dennis's door, but there was no answer. His squad car was in the driveway so I knew he was home. I tried the door and it was unlocked. I could hear Jenny crying so I went in calling Dennis's name. I found him on the living room floor. He...he'd been shot. He's dead." Eric took another deep breath. "I grabbed the baby and came straight here. What the hell's going on?"

"Where's Rhonda?"

"I don't know. Her car wasn't there and..."

Caleb hit the door at a run and jumped into Caddo's truck. For Rhonda to shoot Dennis and leave the baby, she had to have something sinister in mind. He didn't slow down for stop signs or traffic. He had one goal—to get to Josie. The wheels ate up the dirt as he spun into Lencha's yard. He bailed out as the cowboys surrounded him, but he didn't pause in his sprint for the back door. It was locked and he kicked it in with his foot.

He charged in with his gun drawn and came to a complete stop. Josie held a gun on Rhonda.

"You're going to die, Rhonda," Josie said in a voice he didn't recognize. "You're going to know the pain and torture of having a bullet in your head. Pray that it's a quick death."

"Josie. It's Caleb. Give me the gun. You don't want to do this. Josie Belle."

She heard that voice, soothing and comforting— the voice that had been her solace for so long.

"Josie, give me the gun."

She'd heard it said that everyone had their breaking point and she had just reached hers. Because of this woman Josie had suffered unspeakable pain and she wanted revenge in the worst way.

"Josie, don't sink to her level. Give me the gun."

His voice reached the corners of her mind that were frozen in vengeance. Caleb was right. Shooting Rhonda wouldn't make her pain any less. It would only make her a criminal, too, and she didn't want justice that way. She turned and handed Caleb the gun.

Caleb took it, shoving his gun into his holster.

In a split second, Rhonda saw her chance and darted across the room and grabbed the knife Josie had used to cut the bread. She raised it in her hand and made a lunge for Josie, screeching, "You're not taking my baby!"

Caleb leaped for Rhonda at the same time that a gunshot echoed through the house. Caleb and

Rhonda fell backward to the floor. Both remained still.

"Caleb," Josie screamed, falling to her knees beside him. "Caleb."

Caleb shook his head and rolled away, blood covering his shirt. "Caleb." Her shaky hands caressed his face. "Are you okay?"

"Yeah." He rose to a sitting position and they both stared down at Rhonda with a bullet hole in her chest, the knife still gripped in her hand.

Caddo stood in the doorway with a rifle in his hand. He walked in and knelt on one knee to check Rhonda. "Dead," he said, and got to his feet.

"Damn, Caddo," Caleb said. "You almost shot me."

"Nah. No shoot ranger. Caddo's a good shot. Blood on ranger is from woman."

"Yeah," Caleb said. "Thanks."

Josie threw her arms around Caleb and held him tight. "It's over. It's finally over. Rhonda did everything for a baby. Tracy was pregnant."

"I finally figured that out."

"And she fired a shot through the window and stuck a knife in your tires."

"All for a baby."

"Yes." Josie quickly told him the whole story. Her voice quivered. "I really wanted to kill her. Your voice saved me. Just like in the hospital.

I'll never be able to repay you for all you've done for me."

"Just be happy, Josie Belle."

"I will." She saw Eric over Caleb's shoulder. Eric was her future. She knew that now. Everything Dr. Oliver had told her was true and she was so glad Caleb had been so honorable and not taken their relationship further. She would have been so torn about hurting him, but now she could accept her future with Eric without any guilty feelings. She could let Caleb go and they would part as friends—very good friends. She drew back and caught his hand and pulled him to his feet.

"Thank you," she said with a lump in her throat. Then she walked into Eric's waiting arms.

As Caleb watched them walk outside, he knew his heart had burst in his chest. But he would go on. He didn't have a choice.

Josie and Eric sat on the same bench she and Caleb had days earlier.

"Are you okay?" Eric stroked her hair.

"A little shaken up, but I'll be fine." The darkness wrapped around them and she rested her head on his shoulder. "I'm sorry it's taken me so long to remember us."

"God, Josie, don't worry about that."

She raised her head. "I want you to understand that Caleb was a big part of my life. He
made me feel safe and secure and I needed that.
I needed him."

"Were you in love with him?"

"I thought I was many times, but it was only
gratitude." She paused as the truth of that sunk in.
The truth was hell sometimes. She licked her lips.
"As I reconcile my past memories with the
present, please me patient with me. It will take a
while for me to fully let go of Caleb."

"I'll do whatever I can to make this easy for you."

"Thank you." She reached for his hand and he
clenched it tight.

"God, I'm glad you're back."

"Me, too." They stood and walked hand in hand
to the squad car. To their future.

WES ARRIVED and Rhonda's body was removed to
the morgue. Caleb changed his shirt and went
back to the station to finish paperwork. Josie and
Eric had disappeared and Caddo and the vaqueros
headed back to the Silver Spur.

All the loose ends had been tied up, except one—
Jenny. Raylene was keeping her occupied until they
heard from Child Protective Services. But they
needed someone to care for the child now.

Josie walked into the station, her eyes bright,

and she looked like a different person. And she was. Belle Doe was gone forever and so was her attachment to Caleb. He'd spent a whole year to accomplish one goal—to return Josie to her life. He just never realized that in doing so it would hurt so bad.

Josie suggested that they should give Mae the opportunity to care for her granddaughter and she happily agreed. CPS called and approved the arrangement and said they would contact Mae once she and the baby were back in Corpus.

Caleb called Beau to come and pick him up. It was the middle of the night and Beau said he was on his way, without one word of protest. That's what brothers were for and Caleb would need their support now. He could have waited until morning, but he had to leave Beckett as soon as he could. His heart couldn't sustain anything else. Josie was happy and safe—that's what he'd wanted. He kept reminding himself of that.

Mae arrived with her daughters and they were enthralled with the little girl. Caleb could see that Mae would do everything she could to give the child a good life, a better life than she was able to give Tracy.

Eric and Josie were talking to Mae, and Caleb quietly slipped out. That might be the coward in him, but he thought it was best that way. Beau would arrive soon and he had to get his things together. When he reached Lencha's, Caddo was repairing the broken door.

Lencha darted toward him. "Josie okay?"

"Yes. She's fine."

"Caddo stopped by the Martinez's to tell me what had happened and I made him come back and fix my door. Lawdy, what a mess."

"It's over now."

"Thank the Lord."

"My brother is picking me up so I'll just get my things together."

He walked into the house and threw his stuff into a bag, hoping Beau wouldn't be much longer. He wanted to go home.

In the kitchen, he set his bag on the table.

Lencha watched him, *Chula* on her shoulder. "Ranger, I know some *brujas* in Mexico who deal in love potions to attract the opposite sex. But I don't fool with that. Love comes from here." Lencha placed a hand on her breast. "No one can change that. When it's real, it's forever."

His gut tightened. "Lencha, I'll be fine."

"Got something to make you forget all your worries, though. Fix it right up."

"No, thanks." Caleb stopped her. "My brother will be here any minute." He walked over to Caddo, wanting to say something.

"Caddo…" Words failed him.

"Ranger, Caddo'll watch out for *prima*. No worry." Evidently Caddo could read minds, too.

"Thanks for the loan of your truck." He paused. "I hope you give the Becketts a chance." He wanted to tell him about family, love and patience, but he seemed to be emotionally spent.

As he was dredging up the right words, Caddo said, "Caddo'll handle the Becketts—his way."

Caleb just nodded, thinking that was probably best. Car lights turned into the driveway and Caleb grabbed his bag.

"Lencha, thanks." He gave her a hug and swung toward the door and stopped. Josie stood in the doorway.

"Were you leaving without saying goodbye?" she asked.

He stared into those beautiful dark eyes and couldn't lie. "Yes. We've already said goodbye." *Many times.* He kissed her cheek. "Have a good life, Josie Belle."

He breathed in her scent for a moment and hurried down the steps to the waiting car before he made a fool of himself.

JOSIE STARED AFTER HIM with tears streaming down her face. She wanted to run after him and what? She didn't know. It just wasn't easy to let go of someone she'd leaned on for so long. She loved Eric and soon Caleb would be a distant memory—a sweet, treasured memory. Wiping away tears, she took a deep breath.

"So you've chosen?" Lencha said from behind her.

"It wasn't a choice. This is my life," was all she could say.

"Then why the tears?"

She ran to her room and curled into a ball on her bed. Lencha came in and sat down. Josie flew into her arms and cried on her shoulder.

"Shh. Now, shh." Lencha patted her back.

But Josie couldn't stop the tears. They were cathartic, washing away all the pain, misery and heartache of the past year. It wasn't that she was crying about Caleb. She knew she didn't love him. Maybe she was crying because she didn't. Maybe she was crying because Dr. Oliver was right. Or maybe she was crying because some days a woman just needs to cry.

CALEB SLID INTO the passenger seat with a start. Eli was at the wheel, Beau sat in the back. Two brothers—that's what he needed now. Family.

He told them who had shot Josie and why and how it all had unraveled. It felt good to talk, to release some of the tension inside him, but the ache in his gut was still there.

"So Belle's getting back with her fiancé?" Eli asked.

"Yeah," Caleb replied. "He's a nice guy."

"How do you feel about that?" Beau asked from the backseat.

"They were in love and planning to get married. It's the right thing to do."

"You're a rotten liar." Beau obviously wasn't convinced.

"Let's talk about something else," Caleb suggested, wanting to put all this behind him.

"Yeah." Beau leaned forward between the two seats. "Let's talk about Eli and his pigheadedness. I called to tell him the mystery of Josie had been solved and you were ready to come home. He insisted on coming, then he insisted on driving, saying he doesn't trust anyone else's driving. How bullheaded is that?"

"You slept half the way, so stop complaining," Eli told him.

"What else could I do?"

Eli spared Beau a glance. "We can stop and duke this out if you want."

"Yeah. Like I have a snowball's chance in hell. You'd put my lights out in ten seconds. I'm not stupid."

"Remember that."

"You know you might need a lawyer one of these days."

Their nonsensical chatter went over Caleb's head. All he could see was Josie's face, her dark eyes and her sad expression. It would take time for her memory to fade. If ever.

"So all this was over a woman wanting a baby?"

He heard Eli's voice and brought his thoughts back to them. "Yes. After two miscarriages, a still-born baby and an adoption falling through, she was pretty much a loose canon."

"How sad."

"Yes. But now it's time to move on." Caleb sincerely hoped he could do that.

As Eli drove through the night, they talked about family, jobs, sports and anything that came to mind. They were brothers. They shared everything. Or almost.

At sunrise, they drove into Austin and dropped Caleb at his apartment. Eli and Beau both got out and Caleb knew they were both restraining themselves from pressuring him to go home to his parents or to stay with them. Instead they did the smart thing, gave him a bear hug and left.

"Come on, runt," Eli said to Beau. "I'll let you drive me home to my wife." Beau was six feet tall, but Eli still towered over him.

"You call me runt one more time and I might try to kick your ass."

Caleb could hear Eli laughing as the car door slammed.

He opened his door and went in. It seemed like a lifetime ago that he'd left here knowing he'd return a different person. His instincts were right. He was different in so many ways. But he couldn't think anymore. He was exhausted physically and mentally. Stripping out of his clothes, he fell into bed. Before sleep claimed him, he saw her face. How long before that stopped? A lifetime?

THE NEXT MORNING Caleb drove to Waco to visit his parents. The state of Texas had issued him another vehicle, but he went in his own truck. Today he was stronger and he just wanted to see his mom and Andrew. For a lot of years he took for granted the good life he'd been blessed with because it was tainted by memories of a father who hadn't wanted him. Meeting the Becketts brought all that into focus and made him realize what real family was all about—unconditional love. Love that Andrew had given him and Joe McCain never could.

As he drove to the garages, he saw Andrew's car was gone. It was Wednesday and he always met with the pastor of their church to go over songs the choir would sing for Sunday services. His mom and dad were both in the choir. Andrew would be back soon, but he'd have a chance to talk to his mom.

Sitting at the table drinking a cup of coffee, Althea talked to the dog at her feet. "Now, Bandy, I'm not giving you any more bacon." Bandy made a whining sound. "Oh, okay."

Reaching down with the bacon she saw Caleb and jumped up, wrapping her arms around him. "Caleb, are you okay? I was so worried after the wreck, but Beau assured me you were fine."

"I am, Mom."

She drew back and looked into his face. "And Belle?"

"Her name is Josie and she's fine, too. She's with her family and her fiancé."

She eyed him for a moment. "Sit. I'll fix you some breakfast. Anything you want."

He eased into a chair. "Bandy's looking good and fat." Bandy reared up on his thigh and Caleb patted him.

"Yes. He just needed some love."

"Mmm." *Don't we all.*

"What would you like to eat?"

"I'm not hungry. Coffee's fine."

Althea placed her hands on her hips. "You never turn down my cooking."

He tried to smile and failed. "I'd just rather talk."

"Sure." She poured a cup of coffee and brought it to him. Sitting in her chair, she scooted closer.

This time he did smile. Althea was his mother and she knew him inside and out and she was trying discreetly to offer comfort.

"Mom, I'm not sixteen with a broken heart."

"No. You're a grown man."

"Exactly and I can handle this. From the start I knew this day was coming. Josie is happy and that's what I wanted." He took a sip of coffee. "I don't want to talk about Josie. I want to talk about Joe McCain."

She drew back. "Why?"

"As a kid, I agonized over the fact that he wouldn't claim me, denied I was even his. I thought something was wrong with me and I caused your divorce."

"Oh, dear Caleb. That's not true."

"I know, but as a kid I was looking for something I already had—a loving father who wanted me and has been there for me every step of my life."

"Oh, yes, Andrew loves you with all his heart." She touched his arm. "But you've always known that. What's different now?"

"Me. Meeting the dysfunctional Beckett family made me see what exceptionally good parents I had. I let the stigma of my birth tarnish what I had, what I was given. And I know that hurt Andrew."

"He understood how you felt."

"How could he? I didn't. I couldn't understand what was so wrong with me that my own father didn't want me."

"Caleb, look at me."

Caleb stared into brown eyes so much like his own.

"It had nothing to do with you. It was me. Joe was an insanely jealous man and…"

"I know the story. Joe thought you were cheating on him with Andrew because you were in the choir together. When you became pregnant, Joe said it was Andrew's and you had several arguments where he would hit you." He swallowed. "The church helped you get out of that abusive situation and you left him, not knowing Joe had told Jake all his filthy lies. Jake wouldn't leave his father and I watched you grieve for many years for your eldest son."

"I'd made up my mind and I had to leave. I'd had one miscarriage from falling after Joe had hit me. I couldn't risk losing another. I had to protect you, but I lost another son in the process. I underestimated Joe and vindictiveness."

Caleb couldn't even imagine the kind of life his mother had had as Joe's wife. Her life was so different now, filled with love, laughter, compassion and kindness. All thanks to Andrew, his father.

"What I'm trying to tell you is that it doesn't matter anymore. Joe McCain doesn't matter. He's the one who lost so much by not knowing Beau, Eli or me. But I gained a real father and I want Andrew to know that, to know that I've put Joe McCain to rest forever."

"Oh, sweetheart, you've..." The sound of a door opening stopped her.

Caleb stood to greet his father.

Andrew hurried in, his eyes searching for Caleb. He grabbed him in a fierce grip. "Caleb, my son, you're home. We were so worried."

Caleb looked into this man's eyes and all he saw was love, love that had been there from as far back as Caleb could remember. A deep sadness pierced him for any pain he might have caused him.

"Hi, Dad." He smiled.

"Are you okay? We heard about the wreck." Andrew looked him over, searching for bruises or broken bones. But Caleb's injury was on the inside, his own personal pain and not something his parents needed to worry about.

"I'm fine, but I've been doing a lot of soul-searching and I want to apologize for all those times as a kid I couldn't get past the fact that Joe McCain didn't want me."

"Caleb, you were just a boy trying to find your way."

"Thank you for being so patient with me and thank you for being my father. I won't ever forget that again. You're my father in every way that counts."

"Son." Andrew hugged him and they stood father and son bound together by something stronger than blood. Love.

Althea wiped away a tear and joined the hug. "Now sit down," she ordered. "I'll make French toast and sausage."

"Great," Caleb said. "I'm hungry now."

A look passed between his mother and his dad and he knew they were worried about him. But he'd survive because he had this strong foundation of a family to lean on.

"If you have time, maybe we can get in a round of golf this morning," Andrew suggested.

"Sounds good."

"Eighteen holes?"

Caleb nodded. "Eighteen holes."

Over breakfast he told them what had happened in Beckett.

"Oh, how awful. Poor Belle…I mean Josie. I don't think I'll ever get used to that."

He knew the feeling.

"So Josie's happy now?"

"Yes, Mom, she's happy."

"I'll have to call Gertie and tell her. She keeps

asking about Belle. I mean Josie." Andrew corrected himself.

"We've met Ashley and she's quite charming, but so sad." Althea poured Caleb more coffee. "But she's the perfect companion for Gertie and they've been getting along very well."

"I thought they would," Caleb replied.

But she's not Josie Belle.

That was all Caleb could think.

CHAPTER EIGHTEEN

JOSIE'S LIFE SETTLED into a routine she remembered very well. There was something cathartic about routine. Something familiar. And she needed that.

She and Eric were building on their relationship, but they were taking it slow. She needed that, too. Boone had made Eric Chief of Police so he was busier than usual. Those times he was busy she spent on the Silver Spur riding with Caddo, visiting with Boone and actually having conversations with Lorna and Mason. Mostly they wanted her to talk to Ashley, which she did, and Ashley agreed to come home for a visit. Josie's life was falling into place.

Dennis's and Rhonda's bodies had been sent to Dallas for burial in a family plot. Josie still reeled from Rhonda's obsession to have a child. She'd done everything to make that happen—even murder. Murdering her husband and trying to murder a friend. Josie had to put that behind her and concentrate on the future.

The human teeth from the ashes had been identified as Tracy's, as they'd suspected, and the FBI released the remains to Mae. A memorial service was held to finally put Tracy to rest. She and Eric attended and spent some time with Mae and the girls. Jenny was blossoming in the care of her grandmother and aunts. Mae had been awarded full custody and Josie knew they were going to be fine. Jenny was where she should be—with her family.

And Josie was where she should be. At times she wondered about Caleb and hoped he was doing well.

She and Eric went to Corpus to go through her parents' things. Right after her parents' deaths, she couldn't do that. She needed all their stuff around her. The house sat on fifty acres. Her father had to have horses and Josie had sold them before she'd left for Beckett but now she had to do something about the house and the land. She couldn't quite bring herself to sell it yet, but she did give away all their clothes to Goodwill, saving a few cherished items, like the sweater her mother had knitted for Brett and Marie's wedding dress that she had also made.

Josie fingered the white silk and satin and thought she might get married in the dress. Eric wanted to set a date for September; now she wouldn't have to look for a gown. Sinking into a chair, she held the dress against her, almost able to see the smile on her mother's face.

Eric walked into the room.

"Shut your eyes," she shouted.

He immediately closed his eyes. "Why?"

She quickly placed the dress in the dark plastic and stored it in its box. "Because it's my mother's wedding dress and you can't see it."

"Why?" he asked again.

"Because I'm thinking of getting married in it and you can't see it before then."

His eyes popped open. "You're setting a date?"

She'd been hesitating, but she wanted all of her life back. "Yes." She smiled. "Let's look at a calendar. About the middle of September."

"You got it." He grabbed her and swung her around, kissing her deeply. "I know this has been hard for you."

She rested her head on his chest. It had—trying to live the life that was hers while a small part of her still struggled with the past and her feelings. Eric had been so patient and it was time to live her life to the fullest.

Now she had to tell Caleb. She owed him that.

She hadn't spoken to him since he'd left and they both knew it was best that way. Ashley had said that he'd come to dinner at Ms. Gertie's and that he looked very good. Caleb always looked good—a true Texan.

That night she wanted to call him, but at the last minute she chickened out. If she heard his voice, it would be too hard on her fragile emotions. Since she had his home e-mail address, she decided to e-mail him just a short note. She typed:

Dear Caleb,
Hope you're doing well. Just wanted you to know that Eric and I have set a date for the wedding in mid-September and I wanted to tell you myself. Wishing you all the best. Josie Belle

She wanted to say so much more, but she was sure he didn't want to hear another thank you. She quickly clicked Send and went in search of Eric.

CALEB WORKED UNTIL he was exhausted, but Josie's memory was still strong. He hated that he couldn't shake his broken heart. He knew from the start that he and Josie had no future. He wished his heart had gotten the message.

Grabbing a beer from the refrigerator, he headed for his computer to check his mail. His eyes froze on Josie Belle in the subject line and he immediately opened it. As he read, his already damaged heart crumbled into nothing. He didn't even think he was breathing.

She's getting married. His life just sank to some unexplained emotional depth of pure torture. What was wrong with him? He should be happy. He wanted her happy.

Clicking off the computer, he got up and ran his hands over his face, dredging up some honest emotions. He wanted Josie to be happy with *Caleb.* Oh, yeah. There it was. The knife in the gut—the knife of truth.

He'd been secretly hoping that Eric would turn out to be a scuzzbag. That truth didn't feel too good nor did he feel too good about himself. He took a long swig from the can, hoping the beer could erase her memory.

On his second can, the doorbell rang. Who the hell? He wasn't expecting anyone and he sure as hell didn't want to see anyone. The bell pealed again. Dammit. He stormed to the door and yanked it open.

His brothers stood there. All of them, Eli, Jake, Beau and even Tuck. Did they have a sensory antenna, or what? For weeks now they'd been showing up at the oddest times just when he needed a friend, a boost. But tonight he wanted to be alone.

"Hey, little brother," Beau said, holding up a six-pack, as did the others. "We brought beer."

"I don't…" His words trailed away as they walked into his living room. Beau carried the beer to the refrigerator.

"I'm really not in a mood for anything tonight," Caleb said.

"Why not?" Beau wanted to know, and Caleb wanted to smack him as he had when they were kids and Beau wouldn't take no for an answer.

"Beau, that's none of our business," Jake said.

"One beer, then we'll get out of your hair." Eli took a seat on the sofa and Beau passed around the beer. "Besides Elise, Ben and Katie are at our house and if I return this early, Caroline is going to give me one of those looks. She loves mothering Ben and Katie."

Jake plopped down by Eli. "You need to start thinking about having your own kids."

"Mmm." Eli took a swallow of beer. "Scares the hell out of me."

Everyone laughed, except Caleb. He wasn't in a laughing mood, but he knew there were few things in life that frightened Eli. He felt himself loosening up and he sat on the arm of Tuck's chair.

Beau brought Tuck a Coke. "Tuck's the designated driver tonight."

"Think I should have protested that." Tuck took the can.

"It was your turn," Eli pointed out.

"Are we getting so drunk we need a designated driver?" Caleb asked.

"Not me," Jake said. "I've got two kids and I gave that up when I became a father."

Eli slapped him on the back. "You just love reminding us of that."

"Hell, I'm the only one with kids. When are you guys going to do something about that?"

Beau shrugged. "Tuck and I are bona fide bachelors. Right?" Beau looked at Tuck for confirmation.

"Right." Tuck frowned at his drink.

"Yeah, right," Jake scoffed. "That would change in a heartbeat if your next-door neighbor, Macy, made the first move."

"And Tuck—" Eli got in on the friendly ribbing"—hasn't met the right woman. When he does, she's going to turn him inside out."

"Don't count on it," Tuck said.

Everyone knew Tuck had vowed never to marry or have children because he didn't know who he was. He was left as a baby at the Tucker's mailbox and they'd adopted him. Even though he had a happy childhood, he still wasn't passing down his genes.

As Caleb looked around the room, he saw a lot of scarred men, yet incredibly good men who'd managed to overcome their pasts.

"She's getting married." He hadn't even realized

he'd spoken aloud until the room became so quiet he could hear himself breathing.

They didn't have to ask who he was talking about because they all knew. Beau put an arm around his shoulder. "Sorry. I know that must hurt."

"Yeah," echoed around the room.

Caleb twisted the beer in his hand. "I told myself I just wanted her to be happy, but I was lying like hell. I was hoping Eric would turn out to be the biggest creep on the planet. But he's a nice guy and he'll make her happy. And no matter what I'm feeling now, I know she's been through hell and she deserves it." He sucked in a deep breath and tipped up the can. "Think I'll drink until I can't think or feel anymore, then I'll pick myself up and start living again." He stared down at the empty can. "I need another beer."

"We got plenty." Beau headed for the refrigerator.

"Hey, there's an Astros' game on tonight." Jake reached for the remote control.

Caleb made himself comfortable between Jake and Eli. "Thanks, guys."

"Any time, little brother," Beau said.

The game came on and Caleb leaned back his head thinking how lucky he was to have such supportive brothers and a friend like Tuck. Maybe by morning the pain wouldn't be so bad.

CALEB WOKE UP with a headache and, judging by the number of cans in the trash, he knew he'd had just a little too much to drink. He wasn't a drinker. He enjoyed a beer or two, a glass of wine, but nothing like the amount he'd consumed last night. But then, he supposed he had a good reason.

Josie Belle was getting married.

The thought caused his stomach to clench tight, but he'd had his drinking binge. Now he had to get on with his life.

By the time he had his coffee, showered and shaved, he was feeling better. He went to his computer to answer Josie.

Dear Josie Belle,
Glad to hear your life is back on track. Maybe all the pain you've endured will soon be a distant memory. May you and Eric have many years of happiness. Caleb

That was all he could write. He grabbed his hat and headed for work.

And a new future—without Josie Belle.

JOSIE DRESSED FOR DINNER at Silver Spur. Ashley was arriving at any minute and she and Eric were riding out with her to visit. It was the only way

Ashley would go and Josie thought it was time Ashley talked to her mother. She also thought it was time the Becketts started being a family or as close as they could get. She and Lorna would never be the best of friends, but at least now they tolerated each other.

She walked into the kitchen in a black slim-fitting dress.

Lencha turned from the sink, *Chula* chirping at her feet. "You're looking mighty pretty this evening."

"Thanks." Josie straightened her skirt. She was used to her uniform or jeans. "I hope everything goes well tonight."

Lencha's brows knotted together. "Why do you care? The old *bastardo*…"

Josie held up a hand, stopping her. "This feud with Boone has to end."

"Not until one of us is six feet under." At Lencha's tone, *Chula* scurried to the door.

Josie placed her hands on her hips. "Why do you hate him so much? Your husband, Izzy, worked on the Silver Spur all his life and when he couldn't work anymore, Boone gave him this piece of land and a house for all his hard work. And the taxes are paid until you die. Tell me why you still hate him so much?"

"My sweet Marie wasn't good enough for his

son." Lencha's gray eyes turned a frigid cold. "She was like my own daughter and when she left I vowed Boone would pay for her unhappiness."

"But, Lencha, in the end she was happy. She had twenty-seven years with the man she loved and Boone could do nothing about it."

Lencha lips compressed into a thin line.

"Yes, Boone is rude, abrasive, manipulative, controlling, offensive and I could go on. But he is my grandfather. You can't change that with all your curses and spells and Mama wouldn't want you to, either. Nor would she want you to live in bitterness."

"Best part of my day," Lencha said under her breath.

Josie suppressed a smile. "Mama's body is resting on Silver Spur, right next to Daddy's, the way it should be. Boone could have left Mama's body in Corpus, but even he couldn't do that. Their bodies are together just like their spirits are in heaven." She took a breath. "Please stop this vendetta. Mama would want you to."

Lencha nodded. "I'll give it some thought."

She kissed her cheek. "Thank you. That would make me happy."

"It doesn't reach your eyes."

"What?"

"For weeks you've been living this life you left

behind, but the joy that should be in your eyes isn't there."

"Lencha."

"When the ranger was here there was a natural light in your eyes that came from here." She placed a hand over her heart. "Just like when Marie looked at Brett."

Josie turned away. "I've got to go." She couldn't have this conversation. Lencha didn't understand. Caleb was her past, her time out of time, and she couldn't think about him. She just couldn't.

As she walked away she wondered why.

THE DINNER WENT WELL considering that Ashley insisted Caddo be there. And Caddo only spoke when prompted by Ashley. There was one tense moment when Boone confronted him.

"It's time to stop sleeping out on the prairie and live in that brick house Mason built for you. Time to live like a human being, a Beckett."

Caddo slowly laid his napkin in his plate and Mason rose to his feet, ready to defend Caddo as always. But Ashley beat them to it.

"Pa, I'm sure Caddo will take that into consideration and thank you for thinking of him."

Caddo flashed one of his grins and Mason remained standing, clearing his throat. "I have an announcement to make. Lorna and I are getting married."

Complete, total silence followed the statement.

Ashley was the first to speak. "Please don't do it because you feel it's something I want. It won't bring me home."

Lorna rose to stand by Mason. "We're getting married because we want to. We should have done it when my divorce was final. I can see that now."

"Hot damn. Here's to family." Boone raised his wineglass. "Never planned a family like this, but what the hell, you take what you're given." Then he added in his usual Boone fashion, "You kids better make me proud."

"Or we'll all be disinherited," Mason quipped, and they all laughed. They laughed as a family and they recognized that.

Ashley didn't talk to her parents alone, but Josie knew it was only a matter of time. Slowly but surely the Becketts were learning how to forgive and live together.

When Josie reached Lencha's, she wasn't sleepy so she turned on her computer. She saw Caleb's message immediately. Without thinking, her hand touched the screen.

I miss you.

No. She had to stop this. Maybe a part of her

was always going to need Caleb. Oh God, what was she going to do?

A COUPLE OF NIGHTS LATER Josie and Eric sat in Lencha's living room watching a movie. Lencha had been called out on a birth.

Eric played with her hair. "When are you going to move in with me?"

They'd talked about this several times and she still hadn't made up her mind. Instead of being positive about her life, she was having negative thoughts and she didn't understand what was going on with her.

She'd had a long conversation with Dr. Oliver and she explained that confusion was all part of the process of memory recall. She advised her to take it slow and to let everything happen naturally. In time, the confusion would leave and she'd be certain about her decisions, her life.

Eric kissed the side of her face. "We can look at houses if you want."

She rested her head against him. "I'm not sure." She had to be honest.

"Okay." He curled her hair around his finger. "Whenever you're ready."

It was July and she had on a sleeveless tank top. Eric's hand slid from her neck to her back and she instinctively pulled away.

Eric frowned. "You always do that."

"What?"

"Pull away when I touch your back. I know what you've been through and it won't bother me to see your scars."

"It's just…" She couldn't explain it to herself. Due to Lencha's herbal salves, the scars were much better, less noticeable. But something was holding her back.

Eric clicked off the TV. "What is it, Josie?"

"It's hard to explain."

"We haven't been intimate because you said you needed time and I've respected that. But it's been weeks and nothing has changed."

"I'm trying. I really am."

"You shouldn't have to try." He stood in an angry movement, then he took a deep breath. "We need to face some truths."

"What do you mean?"

"Have you ever allowed Caleb to touch your back?"

Her eyes flew to his and words stalled in her throat.

He ran a hand through his hair. "Whether you want to admit it or not, this is about Caleb."

"He brought me back from that black abyss of complete emotional despair. That's it."

"And for the past year he's been an anchor in your life."

"Yes." She brushed her hair away from her face.

He sat down beside her. "The truth is, Josie, that we're trying to recapture something that isn't there anymore. A year apart has changed both of us. You're different."

She chewed on the inside of her lip. "How?"

"We used to do silly things like walk in the rain. We even danced in the rain and we laughed and joked and enjoyed each other's company. Your eyes would light up when you saw me, but now, well…"

"I…" She wanted to explain, to give him a reason, but there wasn't one. Their lives were different now. He was different, too.

"Don't say you'll try again because that's not what I want."

She blinked back a tear. "You're right. I've been trying to accept my life, but it's not my life anymore. Through pain and suffering I've changed so much." She reached out and touched his face. "I do love you, though."

"But you're not in love with me anymore."

She bit down on her lip. "No. I'm sorry." It was a lightbulb moment. She'd read so much about PTSD that she'd allowed her real feelings to be overshadowed by her past. She wasn't making that inner connection with herself. Lencha saw it, but she didn't. It took Eric to show her that she shouldn't have to try to love someone. It should happen naturally. Maybe that's what Dr. Oliver had been trying to tell her.

Eric took her in his arms and held her. "Don't be. I'll survive."

"Thank you."

"Just decide what you want. That's what you have to do now."

Josie went to bed feeling lower than she had in a long time. She'd hurt Eric and she hadn't wanted to do that. But she was so mixed-up and she needed time alone to sort through what she was feeling, to establish that inner connection to her emotions.

She wouldn't allow herself to think about Caleb.

THE NEXT DAY SHE PACKED her things and said goodbye to Lencha and the Becketts. They all seemed to understand that she needed time alone and they knew she'd return to visit. But, like her parents, she had to leave Beckett to find true happiness.

She knew that now, and she said a tearful goodbye to Eric.

She drove to her parents' home in Corpus, her safe haven, the place she always went to solve her problems. Before Caleb. Although her parents weren't there, she felt a serenity and a calmness she needed to make decisions about her life, to find the real Joscelyn Marie Beckett.

At night she indulged herself with candy bars and warm milk and allowed herself to think about Caleb. Did he love her? What was real love? She'd thought that she'd loved Eric, thought it was the real thing. But time had changed her feelings. So if she gave it time these all-consuming feelings she had for Caleb would change, too. She just had to wait.

By the second week, she realized if she kept eating chocolate bars and drinking milk she was going to become a blimp. So she visited with old friends of her parents and friends from high school and college. She also stopped in at the police department where she'd worked and spent an evening catching up. Soon she'd have to find a job and the lieutenant said to just let him know when she was ready.

August turned into September and she hadn't made any real choices about her life. She cleaned the house and yard until she was exhausted, but the exhaustion didn't bring any peace or answers.

Brushing her long hair, she caught her reflection in the mirror. Her hand stilled and she looked at herself.

"Who are you?" she asked the woman in the mirror.

She'd thought she just had to regain her

memory and she'd know who she was. But she didn't. She was still a mismatched piece of furniture that didn't fit anywhere—not in Beckett, or the Silver Spur, or here.

Who was she?

Josie Belle. Josie Belle. Josie Belle.

The name floated through her head like a chord of music that drew attention. That's who she was—part Josie, part Belle. Because of what had happened beyond her control Belle would always be a part of her. That's who she was now. She suddenly realized why she felt so out of place. She wasn't the same person anymore. Eric had told her that. And now she knew it was true.

She was Josie Belle and Caleb was a big part of her. Still something held her back. Her old nemesis, fear—fear of him not loving her. She realized something else, too—she'd never been afraid to take risks. Why was she now? After much soul-searching she knew what she wanted. And she was going after it.

Josie Belle was going home.

CALEB ENTERED his apartment stretching his shoulders. He was dog-tired and he just wanted to go to bed and sleep for a solid eight hours. Most of the day he'd spent interrogating a murder suspect in a drug deal gone bad. That was the initial suspicion, but after further investigating it seemed the two men were involved with the same woman. Now they believed the shooting had nothing to do with the drugs. One man had figured out a way to get rid of the other. The woman had admitted that the shooter was in a jealous rage. Now they'd let a jury decide.

Caleb plopped down on the sofa and threw his hat into the chair across from him. Two men. One woman. Wasn't that familiar? But he held no ill will toward Eric. He'd wished them the best and he'd meant it. And he was moving on. He'd bumped into an old girlfriend at the dry cleaners who now lived in Austin. She'd just gone through a divorce and was very friendly. He might just give her a call.

But not tonight.

Probably never.

Removing his gun and his badge, he laid them on the end table. He reached to pull off his boots when the doorbell rang. Had to be his brothers. He wished they'd stop trying to cheer him up and stop worrying about him. Maybe it was time to tell them to back off and give him some space. He had to get that point across to his mom and dad, too. He was fine and he had to make them believe it.

He yanked open the door. "This…" The rest of the sentence fizzled into a puff of air. Josie stood there in dark slacks and a white sleeveless top that showed off her slim arms and heavenly, touchable skin. She was smiling—that smile that made him forget everything but her.

"Hi, Caleb."

"Josie." He looked past her for Eric and didn't see him.

"May I come in?"

"Oh, oh, sure." He stepped back, feeling a little dazed. What was she doing here? Maybe she was here to do some wedding shopping with Gertie. That's the last thing he needed—to talk about her wedding. "Eric not with you?"

"No. I'm alone."

"Visiting Gertie?" He was fishing for answers but he wasn't getting any.

"You could say that. I dropped my things at her house about an hour ago. I've been driving around trying to get up enough nerve to see you."

"Oh."

She licked her lips. "I just need that warm glass of milk in person."

"Oh."

"Eric and I broke up."

He shoved both hands through his hair, wondering if she was a mirage of his tired mind. "Excuse me?"

"We broke up. I tried to fit back into my old life,

but I've changed. I'm not in love with Eric any-more."

"You're not?"

She moved to within touching distance. "No. I'm not Josie Marie Beckett anymore, either. Took me a long time to realize that. I'm Josie Belle and she's in love with someone else."

He took a deep breath. "Josie, my heart is running about as fast as a Formula One racing car, so please put me out of my misery."

"I love you, Caleb McCain, probably from the first moment I heard your voice."

He grabbed her then and held her so tight he could feel her heart beating against his. "Oh, Josie Belle, tell me I'm not dreaming."

"You're not." She kissed his chin, his jaw and he took her lips in a sensual explosion of need.

The kiss eased the heartache and pain and went on as they explored and tasted each other in ways they'd been afraid to before. His hands traveled beneath her top and caressed her breasts, her skin until she moaned softly. He cupped her face, kissing her repeatedly. "I love you. I love you so much."

"Show me." She breathed raggedly, holding nothing back. This was natural, this was right. And she knew without a doubt that this was love. The real thing. The forever kind.

He swung her up into his arms, carried her into

the darkened room and laid her on the bed. She stood on her knees and stripped out of her blouse and bra. His hands ran freely over her skin, her nipples and the fire of need began to rage out of control. A need too long ignored. A need too long denied. Her hands quickly unfastened the buttons on his shirt and peeled it from his strong shoulders. Her lips tasted the heat of his skin and they hurriedly slipped out of their remaining clothes.

The boots took a while, but she didn't mind. Her lips explored the strong column of his neck and back. He turned and slid onto the bed beside her, holding her with hands that felt like velvet. He kissed and stroked every part of her and her hands were equally at work on him. Moans and sighs filled the room in a prelude to a crescendo that Josie needed as a woman. A woman loved by Caleb.

Their sweat-bathed bodies welded together, lips on lips, heart against heart as Caleb slid into her with a gentle thrust that throbbed, rocked and exploded into a wonderful spasm of pure delight that rippled through her whole body.

"I love you, Josie Belle," he cried a moment before he joined her in that incredible sensation of fulfillment.

Caleb had to take a couple of deep breaths before he could do anything but just feel. Sex had never been like this before, total, complete with a woman he loved. He was never going to be the same again. He would be better.

She ran her hand across his damp shoulder and he stared into her eyes. The bedroom light was off and he reached up to turn it on so he could see her fully. "You're more beautiful than I ever imagined."

She smiled that gorgeous smile. "So are you." Her hand trailed through the hair on his chest and lower. He caught her hand.

"I can't think when you do that."

"Do you need to think?"

He grinned. "Tell me what happened—quickly."

She sat up and told him everything that had happened since he'd left.

"I was trying too hard for something that should come naturally and Eric picked up on it. We had to admit the relationship wasn't working."

"I couldn't stop thinking about you, but I wanted you to be happy."

She looked into his eyes. "I am now that I've sorted out my feelings, past and present."

He gently pushed her long hair over her shoulder and his eyes went to the scars on her back. They weren't as pronounced as before.

"Lencha's salves are working."

"Yes, and I brought some with me and I promised her that I would use it daily. But my back is hard to reach. I'll need someone to help me." Her eyes sparkled.

"You found him. Where is it? I'll do it now."

"It's at Gertie's."

"Mmm. Guess this'll have to do for tonight." He lavished the scars with his tongue and lips. She had no problem with Caleb seeing or touching her scars. He was her soul mate—her other half.

She turned into his arms with a groan. "I can't talk when you do that."

"Let's don't talk or think."

"Deal."

She cupped his face. "I love you."

He smiled. "Keep saying that for about the next fifty or sixty years." Her lips met his and he vowed to love and protect her forever—just as it was meant to be.

EPILOGUE

JOSIE ADJUSTED THE PEARLS that had belonged to her mother around her neck—a gift from Brett. These days she knew exactly who she was. The doubts, fears and insecurities had completely vanished. She was a strong, resilient woman who could love and accept love. She'd been through hell and had found heaven.

I will always love you was being sung in the church as the guests waited for the bride to appear. She listened for a moment knowing she would love Caleb forever. They had the kind of love her parents had—deep and everlasting.

For a split second it crossed her mind that if Rhonda hadn't shot her, she would never have met Caleb. She shivered at the thought. Her life would have been so empty, but she didn't have to worry. Her life was now full and happy with a man she loved.

She'd found a job at an Austin police station and she and Caleb had bought a house not far out of

town, between his work and hers. After they
returned from their honeymoon, they'd start their
life together in their own home.

They had talked about where to have the wedding
and decided they'd have it in a small church outside
of Austin. Althea and Andrew didn't object to their
decision. They just wanted them to be happy.

The room was full of family and friends. Vin,
Caleb's aunt, Althea and Gertie sat on a sofa
talking. Lencha was fussing over Josie's cathe-
dral-length veil, making sure all the pearls were
sewn in place. A couple had come loose at Marie's
wedding. Lencha's hair was pinned up and she
wore a navy-blue suit, very different from the
Lencha she was accustomed to. Lencha wanted
this day to be perfect. Josie did, too.

The door opened and a pretty, strawberry
blonde came in. "Reverend Carpenter said you
have ten minutes."

"Thank you, Macy," Althea said, getting up from
the sofa. Caroline, Grace, Elise and Ashley were
making last-minute touch-ups to their face and hair.

"You look absolutely beautiful," Macy said to
Josie.

"Thank you."

Macy was helping Althea with a lot of the ar-
rangements, especially the rehearsal supper last
night, and Josie could see why Beau was waiting

patiently for her. Macy was sweet and energetic, but Josie sensed that Macy had a secret. It was probably just her cop instincts.

"Macy, would you please go over to the men's dressing room and tell the guys that the Reverend wants them at the front of the church."

"Yes, Althea."

"And, Macy," Elise called. "Would you please remind Jake that Ben needs to come over here. And it's about time for him to walk Aunt Vin down the aisle."

"Will do." Macy glanced at Josie. "Congratulations. You're getting one of the nicest guys around."

"I know. Thank you."

"Now it's time to put on your veil," Caroline said. Elise and Ashley brought it over and Grace helped to hold the long train.

As Caroline worked to pin it into Josie's hair, Katie walked up in her white dress. She was the flower girl and very proud of her duties. "I couldn't wear the dress I wore in Uncle Eli and Aunt Caroline's wedding. It's too small. I got big."

"Yes, you have," Josie said, remembering the wedding well. Katie was an absolute doll. "But you're still very pretty."

"You are, too," Katie said. "I like your dress."

"My mother wore this dress at her wedding. She actually made it."

"I helped sew all those baby pearls on it." Lencha joined the conversation. "Maria was a beautiful bride, just like Josie." Lencha grabbed a tissue out of her purse.

"I can't wait to get married. Mommy, will you make my dress?"

Elise appeared shocked. "Sweetie, that's a long, long, long time away and I might have to take up sewing lessons since I can barely sew on a button."

The women laughed.

The door suddenly flew open and Boone stood there puffing on a cigar. "C'mon, girlie, it's time to get you married. The ranger's chomping at the bit."

Gertie walked over and plucked the cigar out of his mouth and dropped it into a glass of water. "Have some manners, Boone. No smoking in here or anywhere else on the planet."

"You always were a bossy bitch, Gertie."

Gertie straightened her flamboyant hat of lace, flowers, feathers and chiffon. "And don't you forget it."

Boone just shook his head. "Mason's waiting to walk you down the aisle to your seat by Lorna." Gertie swept by him out the door. "Don't put his eye out with that damn hat. Women," he scoffed. "Never understood 'em. Never will."

"For women everywhere—" Ashley placed her

hands on her hips "—we'd appreciate it if you'd try a little harder."

"Good manners would be an improvement," Lencha muttered under her breath.

"Don't start, Lencha," Boone warned. "Caddo's waiting to walk you to your seat."

"I'm not saying another word. I'm going to be as quiet as a little mouse." As she moved past Boone, she quipped, "Just be careful I don't run up your leg."

Boone ignored her and Josie had to give everyone credit. They were trying to get along.

Boone clapped his hands. "C'mon, girls, its showtime."

Ashley began to pull the veil over Josie's face when Boone stopped her. "Wait." He walked over and kissed her cheek. He didn't say anything and Josie realized he couldn't speak. That had to be a first. She swallowed back emotions and stood.

Josie slipped her arm through her grandfather's.

Boone cleared his throat. "Wish Brett was here to give you away."

"Me, too." She squeezed his arm. "But you'll do."

Today was early December, the perfect time for a wedding. The perfect time to put all the pain behind them. Forgiveness did not come easily, but love did. In a little while she would become Josie Belle McCain and she would dance the night away in her husband's arms. She would never leave those arms again.

CALEB FIDDLED with his tie and still couldn't tie the damn thing. He was too nervous. Jake finally came to his rescue.

"I've never seen you so nervous." Jake tied it without a problem.

Before Caleb could respond, a knock sounded at the door. Beau went to answer it.

Macy walked in. "Reverend Carpenter wants you guys at the altar. Jake, Aunt Vin is waiting for you to walk her down the aisle and Elise is waiting for Ben. "

"Be right there," Jake replied.

"Caleb, it's almost time to walk your parents down the aisle, too."

"Thanks, Macy. I'll be right there."

Macy straightened Beau's tie. "You're looking mighty spiffy, Beau McCain. Save a dance for me."

"You bet."

When Macy walked out, Eli straightened Beau's tie and said in a high-pitched voice, "Mighty spiffy, Beau McCain."

"Don't start."

Caleb saw the look in Beau's eyes, they all did— that look of unrequited love. Eli gave him a hug.

"I don't know why I get paired with Grace at all these functions." Tuck broke the silence.

"Because you're such a nice guy," Eli told him.

"I like Grace," Beau said. "She has a sophistication and poise that makes a man wonder what she's like when she lets down her hair."

"It's like the sound of a chain saw cutting you into little bitty pieces," Tuck muttered.

Everyone laughed.

"Daddy, isn't it time to go?" Ben asked. He'd been sitting patiently staring at his reflection in his shiny new shoes.

"Yes, son, it's time to go," Jake answered.

"I'm gonna dance with all the pretty ladies tonight," Ben declared. "And I like Grace. She's pretty and she smells good."

"Yeah, she's pretty." Tuck got to his feet, relenting a little.

Caleb slapped him on the back. Tuck and Grace just never seemed to get along and Caleb never understood why. But he knew Tuck would be a perfect gentleman tonight because he was that kind of man.

"See you guys at the altar," Caleb said, hurrying out to meet his parents.

Althea brushed away a tear when she saw him.

"Mom, you said you weren't going to cry."

"I can't help it. I'm so happy for you."

"Me, too, son." Andrew hugged him.

Althea looped her arm through his and he walked his parents to their seats in the front row and he never felt more loved or wanted than he did at that moment.

He took his spot at the altar with his brothers. As best man, Beau was next to him. He heard the music and saw the bridesmaids as they came down the aisle, but nothing registered. He was waiting for one woman.

For a moment his attention was diverted as Ben and Katie strolled toward them. Katie was very carefully dropping rose petals. Then his throat closed up as he saw her on Boone's arm at the back of the church.

As "Here Comes the Bride" filled the church, Josie moved slowly down the aisle. She was the most beautiful sight he'd ever seen and he knew he'd remember this moment for the rest of his life. He'd thought she'd been lost to him forever. Now all he had to do was walk forward to accept this unbelievable gift he'd been given. Emotions swelled inside him and his knees buckled for a brief second.

Beau grabbed his arm. "You okay?"

He nodded. He was better than he'd been in a

very long time. He strolled forward with a smile on his face to meet his bride, the love of his life.

And nothing would ever get any better than this day.

* * * * *

Don't miss the next COUNT ON A COP *romance.* A Man of Honour *by Linda Barrett is available in November 2007!*

MILLS & BOON
*Super*ROMANCE

On sale 21st September 2007

A FAMILY RESEMBLANCE
by Margot Early

When Joe Knoll appears in town, claiming to be her
deceased husband's brother, Sabine is taken aback.
But how can she deny this man who brings such happiness
to her children – and to her?

FAMILY AT STAKE
by Molly O'Keefe

Mac Edward's twelve-year-old daughter has spun out of control,
and he's in danger of losing her. The only person who can
keep his family together is Rachel Filmore – the woman
who broke his heart…

OPEN SECRET
by Janice Kay Johnson

When Suzanne decides to search for her brother and sister,
whom she was separated from as a child, she cannot know how
dramatically her decision will change *all* their lives…

A TIME TO FORGIVE
by Darlene Gardner

Nine-year-old Jay Smith's Uncle Connor is her knight in
shining armour. But when sparks fly between Connor and
Jaye's teacher, Abby Reed, they uncover a stinging truth,
which they can only overcome together…

2 Books
and a surprise gift!

We would like to take this opportunity to thank you for reading this Mills & Boon® book by offering you the chance to take TWO more specially selected titles from the Superromance series absolutely FREE! We're also making this offer to introduce you to the benefits of the Mills & Boon® Reader Service™—

★ **FREE home delivery**
★ **FREE gifts and competitions**
★ **FREE monthly Newsletter**
★ **Exclusive Reader Service offers**
★ **Books available before they're in the shops**

Accepting these FREE books and gift places you under no obligation to buy, you may cancel at any time, even after receiving your free shipment. Simply complete your details below and return the entire page to the address below. You don't even need a stamp!

YES! Please send me 2 free Superromance books and a surprise gift. I understand that unless you hear from me, I will receive 4 superb new titles every month for just £3.69 each, postage and packing free. I am under no obligation to purchase any books and may cancel my subscription at any time. The free books and gift will be mine to keep in any case.

U7ZEF

Ms/Mrs/Miss/Mr ....Initials..............................
BLOCK CAPITALS PLEASE
Surname ....
Address...

....
....Postcode...

Send this whole page to:
UK: FREEPOST CN81, Croydon, CR9 3WZ